CHASING HEARTS

YAHRAH ST.JOHN

OLIVER HEBER BOOKS

PUBLISHER'S NOTE: This is a work of fiction. Names, characters,
places, and incidents either are the product of the author's
imagination or are used fictitiously. Any resemblance to actual
persons, living or dead, business establishments, events, or locales is
entirely coincidental.

COPYRIGHT © Yahrah St.John

Published by Oliver-Heber Books

0 9 8 7 6 5 4 3 2 1

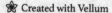 Created with Vellum

1

Bree Hart loved her job, but she hated that it kept her indoors forty-plus hours a week. Day in and day out, she sat behind a high-powered computer running simulations and manipulating geologic data to determine where petroleum reservoirs could be extracted. This was a big part of what she did as a petroleum geologist for her father's company, Hart Enterprises.

She'd worked at HE since graduating from The University of Texas in Austin with a graduate degree in petroleum engineering. Hart Enterprises depended on her ability to predict where to drill so they could make a great profit. Bree's handful of friends considered her work high stress and too intense, but she thrived on it.

Using her sixth sense along with high-tech machinery like seismic X-rays, on many occasions Bree had been able to determine where a drill should be placed to find oil deposits underground. Consequently, Hart Enterprises had made a killing. Some in the industry said Bree had the Midas touch and had put the African-American-owned HE on the international map, but she didn't think so. She did her homework. She studied the land, the earth, and its deposits.

Yet as much as she loved what she did, Bree wanted more. She'd wanted to be president of HE. Studying at her father's knee since she was old enough to ride a horse, Bree had always thought the presidency was the end game. But that all changed a year ago when her father, Duke Hart, made her cousin, Caleb Hart, HE's heir apparent. He was on track to become the company's president.

Bree loved Caleb. He was her rough-and-tumble cousin, the infamous bull rider who had a way with the ladies. After he met Addison Walker—a woman Bree had known from the debutante-ball circuit—Caleb fell madly in love and traded in his Wranglers for an office suit and tie at HE. Bree had never dreamed, however, that Caleb would push her out of a shot at her dream job.

But that's what had happened.

And it stung.

Real bad.

Caleb's rise to the presidency of Hart Enterprises was imminent. Duke Hart would be stepping down from the post next week. He was looking forward to spending more time outdoors. Running a billion-dollar operation did not compare to the high he experienced working with his horses and cattle. Bree had always wondered how he'd gotten into the oil business. He was a rancher to the core.

Ranching was a family business for the Harts. Bree's Aunt Madelyn and Uncle Isaac Hart ran Golden Oaks, a dude ranch in Tucson, Arizona, while her father had struck out on his own with his best friend, Elijah Williams, in Dallas. Now Duke Hart owned nearly four hundred acres of prime West Texas real estate.

Since the day Duke started drilling for oil, he hadn't looked back. Until Caleb. Now Bree would be forced to answer to Caleb instead of her father. Not that he was pushy or bossy. Bree just hated that Caleb had been given the keys to the kingdom and not her. It sat in her craw.

She knew she should get over it. Maybe Duke would change his mind?

~

"You're deluding yourself, baby girl," Abigail Hart told her daughter Bree when she stopped by for afternoon tea.

Because she was an early riser, Bree, as usual, had been in the office since six a.m. Today, she had left around three p.m.—not typical at all. No one said anything, however, because they knew she was a notorious workaholic. If a new drilling project was on tap, she'd put in sixty- to eighty-hour weeks—whatever it took to ensure a project's success. She was overdue to take off early.

"Why?" Bree asked, rising to her feet to pace the small parlor of her mother's three-bedroom home in Lakewood, about five miles northeast of downtown Dallas. Bree loved the wooded, hilly terrain and eclectic mix of old and new architectural styles here. "I know the oil business better than anyone. I have a degree in petroleum engineering. A degree, by the way, that I didn't even want, but Daddy made me go to school for."

"Your father is a stubborn man, Bree. You know

this because you're just like him. Once he's made up his mind, there's no going back."

Bree sighed.

Her mother patted the sofa she was sitting on. "Come. Sit. The tea is ready. It'll make you feel better."

"Is tea your cure-all for everything, Mama?" Bree inquired as she stared at her from the spot she'd just taken on the sofa.

In Bree's eyes, her mother was still the looker who'd caught the attention of a rascal like Duke Hart. Back in the day, her father was known for his reputation. According to Addison, Caleb's wife, Duke had even tangoed with Addison's mother, Lila, once. But it had been *Bree's* mother, Abigail, who stole Duke's heart and made him get down on one knee.

It had to be her mother's smooth walnut complexion and warm brown eyes. Or perhaps it was her petite figure—she was all of five feet. Maybe at a hulking six foot five, Duke enjoyed the idea of protecting Abigail. Whatever it was, he'd been enraptured with the genteel Philadelphia native who came from a respectful banking family.

Her mama had been equally swept away by the brash cowboy with a heart as wide as the state of Texas. Too bad Duke couldn't stop his womanizing ways. He'd lost Bree's mother because of an affair with a Las Vegas showgirl, which resulted in the woman becoming pregnant. Duke had dallied with her half-brother Trent's mama for all of five seconds, and Trent was the result. Except unlike her sister London's mother, Grace, Trent's mother, Adele, hadn't gone quietly into the night to lick her wounds.

She'd shown up at Bree's parents' door with Trent in tow demanding Duke do what was right. He did, but it cost him Bree's mama. Abigail quickly divorced

Duke after the revelation of the affair, but Bree suspected he retained a big place in her heart as her one true love and vice versa.

"A good cup of tea is a cure-all for heartache," her mother replied, interrupting Bree's trip down Duke's sordid memory lane. "What's on your mind, Bree? You were just deep in thought a moment ago."

Bree shrugged, tossing her shoulder-length dark-brown curls from side to side. "Just thinking how our family might have been different if Daddy hadn't messed up."

Abigail gave an unladylike snort. "No sense in going down that road, honey bun. It won't change anything. What's done is done. Your father and I have made our peace with it."

"Then why have you never remarried?"

"Perhaps I enjoy my solitude."

Bree raised a brow. "I think not. If you ask me, you never got over Daddy."

"Duke Hart is a hard man to get over." Abigail reached for her teacup, sipped, then added, "But he's moved on. I've seen him in the gossip columns. There's no shortage of socialites wanting him in their bed."

"Mama!" Bree was shocked by her mother's openness.

"What? I'm not blind. Your father is considered quite the catch in certain social circles. As are you."

"Me?"

Bree frowned. She wasn't on the market for a relationship. She had a full plate and no time to hold a man's hand or cater to his needs.

"Yes, you dear. Why do you persist in acting as if you don't need anyone?"

"Because I don't."

"So you don't need me, Jada, or London? Or what about your father? Or your cousin Caleb and the rest of the Harts?"

"That's different. They're family."

Abigail placed her teacup on the cocktail table in front of her and reached for Bree's fidgeting hands.

"Even though I never married again, I have always longed for the love Duke and I once shared, but I've never been able to find it again."

"That's because you haven't looked, Mama—"

Abigail cut her daughter off. "This isn't about me, Bree. It's about you and your refusal to let love in. I don't want you to look back with regrets that you didn't make time for love, for a family."

"There's plenty of time for that," Bree replied. "I'm only thirty-one. I can still have kids."

"Yeah well, I'd had you and Jada by the time I was your age."

"It was a different time back then."

"You're not getting any younger, Bree."

"Thanks a lot, Mama."

Abigail laughed. "Oh don't go getting in your feelings. You know I love you and I only want the best for you." She reached for Bree and pulled her into her bosom.

A smile returned to Bree's face as she basked in the glow of her mother's love. She raised her head from Abigail's chest. "Of course I know you do. And I adore you."

"Then heed my advice. I don't want you to miss out on a thing."

~

GRAYSON WELLS JUMPED out of the limousine before his driver could come around to open his door. He'd just arrived in Dallas after several long transatlantic flights from Dubai. He had returned to the States in response to his mother Julia Williams's urgent summons that he was needed at home.

Grayson tore through the front door of his ten-bedroom house in Preston Hollow and yelled for Sonya Rodriguez, his brother's caretaker.

"Hush, Grayson," she said as she came toward him with a frown. "I just got both Ms. Julia and Cameron off for a nap, and I won't have you waking them."

"Yes, ma'am," Grayson said with an apologetic smile.

But as soon as he was close enough, Sonya pulled him into a warm hug. "Oh, Sonya," he said as he squeezed the elderly Cuban woman. At five feet with a small frame and salt-and-pepper hair in a bun, some might think she wasn't a force to be reckoned with, but when Grayson was younger he'd feared her and with good reason. Those dark eyes of hers would train on him when he was up to no good, and he'd instantly stop whatever bad thing he was doing. "It is so good to see you," he said as they completed their embrace.

Sonya pulled away from him to size him up. "You as well, my boy. Let me have a look at you." She glanced down at his Italian loafers, then up to his designer jeans, button-down shirt, and the fashionable sunglasses he wore. She immediately took them off so she could stare into his eyes. "You're still the Grayson I know. Just fancied up a bit."

Grayson swiped the glasses from her small hands and pocketed them. "When you're hanging with a sheikh and the richest oilman on the planet, you have to dress the part."

"Does that also mean you've had to stay away so long from your family?"

Guilt instantly assailed Grayson. He had been gone on and off for the better part of the last decade, but it was how he'd made his fortune. Now he was back to claim what was rightfully his. "That was unavoidable," Grayson finally replied. "It was needed to give me the means to do what must be done."

"And does that mean getting even with Duke Hart?" a cold feminine voice said from above him.

Grayson glanced up and nearly recoiled at the sight of his once strong mother standing on the steps in a waffle robe with a silk scarf wrapped around her head. She looked so frail and small. It was like she had aged nearly a decade since the last time he'd seen her. She had to be no more than a buck o five at that. Is this what the cancer had done to her?

"Mother!" Grayson left Sonya's side. He rushed up the stairs to help his mother as she descended them to the foyer. "Should you be out of bed?"

"I heard your voice, and I just had to come down," Julia Williams said.

"And Cam?" he asked as he escorted her across the hall to the grand living room that faced the main doors of the house.

"I checked in on him. He's still napping," his mother replied. "He was so agitated knowing you were coming home that Sonya had to give him some medicine to calm him down."

"I'm sorry, Grayson," Sonya said. "He was just a bit hard to handle this morning."

"It's alright," Grayson commented. "You both have had a lot on your shoulders all these years with me gone."

"The doctors and money you've sent have helped greatly," his mother said.

"As money always does," Grayson stated. "But you needed me."

"And you're here now, son," Julia said as she patted his thigh. "Sonya, why don't you go bring us some of that sparkling cider you keep on hand for special occasions. We have to celebrate the return of our favorite son."

While Sonya left the room, Grayson turned to his mother. "Mother, why didn't you tell me how bad it was? Why did you let me stay away so long?"

"Because if you knew how bad it was here, it would have affected you. Affected your mind," Julia said. "And you needed all the skills you could to win. And guess what? Your gamble paid off."

Grayson nodded. Who knew his friendship with Arash bin Rashid Al Kadar, a sheikh he'd met while at a poker game, would turn into an endearing friendship that would last a decade? As sheikh of a small country of Kadar near Dubai, it was Arash who had invited him to come stay abroad and learn the oil business, but it was Grayson's timing for knowing when to up the stakes on a gamble that had paid off. Big.

In his mid-twenties, Grayson had become a millionaire nearly overnight after winning an opponent's oil field in a poker game. And after his first million, the second hadn't been far behind. Now the thirty-two-year-old had holdings in oil and media. But it had cost him.

Time with his family.

Time he would never get back.

"Yeah, but I should have been here with you and Cam," Grayson said. "Had I known your condition had deteriorated this rapidly, I would have come back much sooner."

"You're here now, and that's all that matters," Julia replied. "And you'll be here to take care of Cam if I can't."

"Don't talk like that, Mama."

"Grayson, you're a realist, and you and I both know the odds of me beating cancer for a second time—and lung cancer at that—are slim to none. You have to make your peace with this."

"I won't." Grayson jumped to his feet. "I'll get the best doctors. We'll find the best treatments to beat this." He refused to accept that he was powerless to help his mother. Not now. Not when he finally had the financial wherewithal to change her life.

"Grayson, don't you think that's what I've been doing—fighting. But eventually, you get tired. I've had to be strong for you boys for so long. When your father left . . ." Her voice trailed off.

"I know, Mama." Grayson didn't have to hear this story. He'd heard it hundreds of times. His father's departure from their lives when he was twelve had left Julia Williams a single mother of two boys, one of whom was a special-needs child. His brother, Cameron Williams, was autistic and had a limited IQ. He required constant care and couldn't be left alone for more than short periods of time.

It had been a lot for his mother to handle. And Lord knows, Grayson had done his best at twelve to be the man of the house, to pitch in when he could by doing the yardwork or helping with the bills while his mother worked two, sometimes three jobs to ensure they could pay Sonya, who'd been with Cameron since he was a toddler.

Thank God for Sonya. She'd stuck around even

after his father had departed and left his mother with a ton of debt. All they'd been able to offer Sonya, an immigrant from Cuba escaping an abusive marriage, was a roof over her head and food on the table. That had been enough for her, and she'd been by his family's side ever since. Grayson would always be grateful for her, and it's why he made sure she was well compensated now.

Eventually, with working jobs after high school, he and his mother had finally paid off the debtors, but it had taken years, including him foregoing college. But his mother, Cameron, and Sonya wouldn't have been able to make it if he'd struck out on his own and forgotten about them—and the only reason he had for the last decade was to become wealthier than sin.

Wealthy enough for payback.

"I'll make this right, Mama," Grayson said.

"I know you will. For years, you've been driven to bring Duke Hart to his knees. You even changed your name legally from Grayson Williams to Grayson Wells. So you must have a plan, yes?"

"I'm working on that," Grayson replied. And he had a prospect. He'd heard of a tract of land in Fort Worth that several oil companies, including Hart Enterprises, were vying for. The old man who'd owned it had passed away, and his children wanted no part of it except the money.

Grayson suspected he was on the right path to finding Duke's weakness. Once he did, he would exploit it.

~

BREE MADE it back home to the Hart ranch from her mother's house later that evening. She was heading upstairs to her room when her father's voice boomed all the way from downstairs. "Bree, is that you?"

She rolled her eyes. *Who else would it be?* She was the only one who lived at home. Jada had flown the coop a couple of years ago, while her sister London lived in New Orleans. "Yes?"

"C'mon over here," Duke Hart yelled. "Caleb and Addy are here."

Bree made a U-turn. She descended the stairs and breezed into the living room. She found her father sitting in his favorite easy chair. It was custom made to accommodate his large football-player frame. He looked comfortable in his usual ensemble of a cowboy hat accompanied by some faded Wrangler jeans with an enormous buckle, a plaid shirt, and well-worn cowboy boots.

Caleb and Addison were on the sofa. Her cousin Caleb was nearly as tall as her father with an athletic frame from years of bull riding. She greeted him with a smile and said, "Good evening."

She headed in Addison's direction and lowered herself to give her a hug. Addison was a little over four months pregnant, and her slender frame made her show a bit. "Hey, love," Bree said and kissed Addison on the cheek. "How are you feeling?"

Addison's doe-shaped eyes glanced at Caleb. "I'm starting to show, and I can't fit a thing. You'd think I'd be used to this after Ivy."

Caleb chuckled. "I keep telling her that she's the most beautiful woman I've ever seen."

"You have to say that," Addison responded, and the entire group chuckled.

"Where is little Ivy?" Bree inquired about Caleb and Addison's one-year-old daughter.

"With the nanny," Addison said. "She's been running a fever, so I chose to keep her at home."

"Too bad. I was going to give her lots of kisses," Bree replied.

"Drink, Bree?" Caleb stood up.

Bree shook her head. "None for me. It was a long day, and I'm going to retire for the night."

Her father glanced at his watch in disbelief. "It's seven o'clock."

"And?" Bree answered shortly.

The room fell silent while she and Duke stared each other down. Neither one was willing to give an inch. In the end, it was Bree who blinked first, but only long enough to bid everyone good night. She was nearly to the steps when Caleb stopped her at the foot of them.

"Caleb, can't this wait?"

"No, I was hoping you could meet with me tomorrow about a land deal we're interested in acquiring."

"Why? You know you don't have to keep doing this, Caleb."

"Doing what?"

"Acting like you value my opinion. Duke appointed you. You don't need my vote."

Caleb snorted, and a frown spread across his lips. "That's not what I'm doing. I'm well-aware that I don't *need* your approval, Bree, but I'd like to have it nonetheless. You could do a site visit and give me evaluation of its prospects. You're the best, and that's what I need."

Bree grinned despite herself. It was hard to stay cross with Caleb. It wasn't his fault that Duke had anointed him heir apparent. He'd just taken up the gauntlet as she would have. "Fine."

"How about we meet there tomorrow morning?"

Bree shook her head. "No. I'll go alone. I work better that way. Plus, I doubt you'd like to get those fancy clothes of yours dirty."

Caleb was wearing tailored dark slacks and a lavender dress shirt.

"C'mon, Bree," Caleb said softly. "You know as well as I do that I never minded getting dirty. I wouldn't have survived the bull-riding circuit if I did. These threads"—he motioned downward—"are just for appearances. I'm much more comfortable in a pair of my old Wranglers."

"It's good to see you haven't forgotten where you came from," Bree said, grasping the handrail. "We'll speak tomorrow."

Once she was in her room, Bree fell across her king-sized bed. This place, with its calming earth tones, was her sanctuary. As she relaxed, she began reflecting on her disappointments at work.

Before his appointment, Bree had always felt closer to Caleb than her cousins Noah and Rylee, a veterinarian and outdoors woman. It had always been Caleb who Bree had run to, and she hated the distance and tension that had arisen between them because of work politics, but she didn't know how to make it right. And she wondered if it ever would be.

2

Grayson returned to his office at Wells Oil in downtown Dallas with renewed vigor. He'd spent the last several months in the Middle East ensuring his pipeline was on track; he'd done what he'd set out to do. Now it was time he put his plan of revenge against Duke Hart into motion. His right-hand man, Levi Jackson, had been running the Wells Oil operation while he was abroad, and Grayson was leaving the office now to meet up with him for brunch to get caught up.

It was different being back in a suit and tie, though Grayson had ditched the tie somewhere around eleven a.m. He wasn't used to being so formal. In Dubai, he was usually dressed in jeans and a cotton tunic, so the slate-gray suit and white shirt with designer shoes he was wearing now signaled that he was stepping out of his comfort zone. He knew he had to dress the part.

"Grayson," Levi said, greeting him with a hug when he arrived at the restaurant.

"It's good to see you, Levi," Grayson said, shaking his hand and sitting down across from him.

"You as well."

A waitress came and offered coffee. Grayson nodded, and she began pouring. "Thank you," he said. He drank it black and took a sip.

"How's your mother and Cam?" Levi inquired. "I know it's been hard for you being away from them."

"Yes it was, but it had to be done."

Levi was one of the few people that Grayson confided in and who knew of Cameron's condition. It's not like he kept his brother a secret. Grayson loved Cameron. He just didn't want him in the public eye and under scrutiny. As Grayson's profile had risen over the years, so had the press's interest in his background.

How had a young man born so poor move up the ranks so fast to become one of the wealthiest oilmen in Dallas? They all wanted to know his story, but Grayson said very little about his past. To most, he was seen as a recluse. But when he did deign to go out, especially with a pretty lady on his arms, apparently it was newsworthy.

"But I'm back now. And you? How's the wife and kids?"

"Doing just fine," Levi said. "Mandy is a stay-at-home mom now. Found it was too hard trying to mother two kids and keep a day job."

"Sounds reasonable."

"But I doubt you're eager to talk about my missus since you're back in town," Levi said. "I assume you're back now for good?"

"You assume correctly."

"And your mission is still the same?"

"Yes it is. And I'm hoping you have some good news for me," Grayson said. "An angle. A way in?"

"I have a couple," Levi said. "The best being the one I sent you about a couple of days ago—the Johnson tract of land that borders the Hart ranch. Jack

Johnson had owned that tract forever. Been in the family for generations, but now that he's deceased, his children want nothing to do with it. They want to sell it even though it's rumored to house a wealth of oil underneath the soil."

"Why has no one cultivated it before?" Grayson asked.

"Because Jack's father was a rancher too and refused to sully the land by drilling on it, but now that Jack's dead . . ." Levi's voice trailed off.

"His family is willing to throw away their history, their legacy?" Grayson asked. Rage bubbled in his gut just thinking about how people could carelessly throw away their heritage. If he'd retained the land that would have been rightfully his father's, he would have made it a success. But Duke Hart had made sure that would never become a reality. "What's the other angle?"

Levi leaned back in his chair and regarded Grayson. "Well, this one works in conjunction with the land and is a much more personal aim at your adversary."

His eyes bore into Levi's. "Don't leave me in suspense. Out with it."

"It's rumored that Bree Hart, Duke's daughter, might be in the market to jump ship from Hart Enterprises."

Grayson was disgusted. "Another defector? What's wrong with people's morals and values?"

"Appears there's a beef between her and her old man. Bree wasn't too happy when Duke placed his nephew Caleb Hart first in line to become president of Hart Enterprises."

"And why would he do that? From what I've heard, the Hart girl is an excellent petroleum geologist. It's said that if there's oil to be found, *she* can find it." He'd never actually met Bree Hart, but her reputation preceded her.

"Damn right. And we would be lucky to steal her away from Hart Enterprises. It would be quite a blow to not only the company, but to Duke himself."

"Ah." Grayson rubbed his chin thoughtfully. "That's where the *personal* angle comes in. What better way to get back at Duke than to have one of his precious daughters working for the enemy?"

"She may need some convincing," Levi said. "Although she's upset with her father, from what I heard Bree is much like you and believes in family."

"Then I'll just have to convince her to see things my way, won't I?" And Grayson was sure he could. He was highly motivated.

He had years of pent-up anger that he'd directed at Duke Hart. It was a wonder he'd never confronted the man sooner, but Grayson had never been one to show his hand early. He studied his opponents, and Duke was a worthy one. Grayson was sure his daughter would be no different.

～

"You know this really isn't necessary," Bree said when Caleb insisted they drive together in his Ford Super Duty F-450 XL to the Johnson property that same day. It was now early afternoon. "You could have done this on your own. You don't need me."

"So you keep insisting," Caleb said, glancing at Bree. "But you and I both know Hart Enterprises wouldn't be where we are without you. Your input has been invaluable."

Bree glanced sideways at her cousin from the passenger seat. "You don't have to butter me up, Caleb. I'm here."

"Reluctantly. And it doesn't have to be that way, Bree. You and I can be a good team."

"There can only be one leader, Caleb," Bree said. Her father had taught her that: In life, there is one winner and one loser, plain as that. "We're most definitely not a team."

"I refuse to believe that we're always going to be at odds with each other, Bree. You're my little cousin, and I will always love you."

"Oh no you don't." She wagged a finger at him. "Don't go playing the family card, Caleb. That isn't what this is about."

"Then what is it about?"

"It's about fairness and equality," Bree stated vehemently, "none of which my father bothered to abide by when he chose you over me to run our family company. You know I love you, Caleb, and that's never going to change. But I *deserved* to at least be considered for the position. But no, the great Duke Hart felt I should play second fiddle, because I'm a woman."

"Bree—"

"Don't Bree me," Bree responded even though she knew her tirade sounded like sour grapes. "You know as well as I do that Daddy is sexist and totally old-fashioned. A woman's place is not at the top. She's to remain below the glass ceiling. Ha!" She laughed.

Caleb turned to her with a grin. "Do you feel better now that you got that out of your system? It must have been killing you holding that inside all this time."

Bree snapped her head. "Don't you dare make fun of me, Caleb Hart!"

His mouth curved into a devilish smile that Bree

suspected used to make all the ladies' hearts flutter in the bull-riding circuit. "You know I'm right," Caleb said.

Despite herself, Bree let out a loud chuckle. "Damn you."

"It's hard to stay mad at someone as lovable as me, isn't it?" Caleb said.

"Your arrogance is monumental."

"Yeah, well, someone had to ease the tension between us," Caleb replied, keeping his eyes on the road. "Listen, Bree. I know it's hard for you, and I don't discount your feelings. You have a right to your anger and to feel pushed aside. I just want there to be peace between us."

"I never wanted to feel this way, Caleb, but I kind of get how Trent feels," Bree said, and before Caleb could speak, she held up her hand. "Not that my baby brother isn't without his faults. It's just that as the year has gone by, the harder it's been to hold in my feelings. And it makes me wonder if I shouldn't leave and strike out on my own somewhere."

"Leave Hart Enterprises?" Caleb asked with a frown. "Is that what you really want?"

Bree shrugged. "I don't know. I'm just trying to figure out my place and where I fit in."

Their conversation eased into a comfortable silence for the rest of the trip in the truck until they made it to the Johnson estate a half-hour later.

It was blazing hot, but Bree didn't care. It was better to be outdoors and viewing the land than to be cooped up inside. She and Caleb had procured an invite onto the Johnson land and were walking the property. Bree had dressed for the occasion in faded blue jeans and a white button-down shirt. She'd added a blazer at the last minute because they would be meeting with Parker Johnson, the son of Jack Johnson.

He was rumored to be a tight-ass, and Bree felt it would be disrespectful if she didn't show a certain amount of professionalism. Not that it mattered. Parker was an asshole and had no qualms about selling off his family's heritage to the highest bidder.

She was glad when he'd chosen to stay inside his house and talk business with Caleb. That gave Bree a chance to make her way on foot around the land. She was touring the main house and garage when she saw the four-wheeler.

Bree glanced back up at the house. Caleb and Parker were knee deep in shop talk, and she wasn't about to go in there and ask for permission. Parker didn't care about his father's home, so why would he care if she borrowed his equipment to go for a ride? It would be much more fun than going to one of the remaining ranch hands and asking him to saddle a horse.

Bree pulled off her blazer, rolled up her shirt, and hopped on the back of the four-wheeler. She revved up the engine and was off.

As the wind coursed through her hair, she felt more alive than she'd felt in days. Of course, if Bree had her wish she would have never gone to college and become stuck in an office. She would have stayed and worked the land, but Duke had adamantly opposed that.

You will *get an education,* he'd railed, especially when he'd seen that she'd excelled at geography and sciences. *It'll come in handy, you'll see*, he'd said. And it had, for him. Her knowledge and skillset had helped make Hart Enterprises billions of dollars. Why couldn't he see that she was capable of so much more if given the opportunity?

When she came up on a ditch in the road, Bree turned off the vehicle, hopped off it, and grabbed her knapsack. She'd brought her soil kit on the off chance she could get her hands on a sample. Without an audience, she could really see if there was credence to Johnson's land having oil.

Bree wasted no time jumping down into the ditch, and when she did, mud splattered onto her white shirt. Oh well, she shrugged, she was used to being dirty. She pulled out her knapsack and began to get to work.

Nearly an hour later, the sun was high overhead and Bree was sweating her ass off and wishing she'd brought a hat or put on sunscreen. She was still in the ditch when she heard the roar of an engine above her. Bree looked up. She was sure it was probably Caleb and Parker coming to give her a talking-to about taking the four-wheeler without permission, but Bree wasn't going to apologize for it. She was doing her job and finding out the potential use for the land.

The engine turned off, and Bree saw a shadow move across the top of the ditch. With the sun shining down on her and without her sunglasses, which had fallen in the mud, she couldn't see who it was.

Bree placed her hand over her eyes to look up at the shadowy figure. Her heart stopped.

Standing high above her in a smart suit was the *most* attractive man she'd ever laid eyes on.

3

Grayson didn't know what to expect when he decided on the spur of the moment to come directly here after his meeting with Levi. He didn't have a formal invitation but wanted to do some digging of his own to make sure Jack Johnson's land was worth pursuing. What he hadn't counted on was finding a beautiful woman knee deep in the muck. Her riotous curls were tipped with mud and going in every which way.

He loved it.

He whipped off his sunglasses to get a better look. The woman had high, exotic cheekbones on a delicately carved face and a tempting mouth that looked like it was made to be kissed. Her skin was smooth and tawny and slightly burnished by the sun. From the looks of it, she couldn't be more than in her late twenties, early thirties. He wouldn't be robbing the cradle.

Was it the muddied white shirt, the curve-hugging jeans, or the big brown eyes staring up at him that instantly attracted Grayson? He answered his own question. *All*, he thought.

"Need a hand?" he asked, bending down so the distance between them wasn't so great.

She glared at him. "Does it look as if I need one?"

He smiled. He liked her fire. "No, I wouldn't say you do. You look quite at home down there in the mud."

She laughed. The sound of it was so rich and melodious that Grayson's groin tightened in response. Who *is* this creature?

"Are you going to just stand there watching me, or are you going to come down?" she asked.

Grayson looked down at his suit and expensive shoes. "I don't think I'm quite dressed to assist you in your endeavor."

"Ah, so you're one of them, are you?" Bree deftly gave him the once-over, from the top of his head to the shoes on his feet. "Looking to purchase the Johnson land?"

His skin prickled instantly. She knew more than he would have guessed for a ranch hand.

"Don't look so surprised," she said flippantly. "Some of us women actually have brains."

He watched in amazement as she climbed up the ditch. She had an athletic physique with B-cup sized breasts and a nice round behind. He swallowed, unable to turn away. He wanted to know more about her, maybe even ask her out on a date.

"Of course, I wouldn't think otherwise," he said.

She glared at him disbelievingly, tossed her knapsack over her shoulder, and strutted to the four-wheeler parked several feet away. Spellbound, he watched her generous behind sway with every step she took.

To his dismay, she swung her leg astride the vehicle and turned on the engine.

"Wait a sec." He rushed toward her, but before he could say another word, she'd already taken off and was clear across the field before he could get out, "I didn't get your name!"

As SHE TURNED off the engine in the garage, Bree released a long breath. She was used to riding four-wheelers on the ranch, so it wasn't the ride that had made her breathless. It was *him*.

The man who'd stood above her in the ditch was drop-dead sexy. Tall with massive shoulders, he'd been clad in a gray suit that fit his beautifully proportioned body to a tee. In just a few seconds, she'd taken all of him in. It was clear that he took very good care of himself. The outlines of his shoulders had strained against the confines of his fabric. What's more, there had been something about him.

Perhaps it had been his bald head? Or the sexy five o'clock shadow he'd been sporting or those bushy eyebrows? Or maybe it was that square jaw, which showed off his model-like features and warm-brown complexion? It had certainly given Bree pause, and she'd made no bones about staring at him. The man carried himself with an air of self-confidence. He certainly hadn't minded questioning her and why she was there.

"Bree!" Caleb called, startling her out of her trance.

Guiltily, Bree turned around and was met with Caleb's frown.

"Just what the hell did you think you were doing?"

Bree lifted her chin defiantly, undeterred by his tone. She was used to standing up for herself and now would be no different. "I was finding out if this place is worth our time and money."

"And?"

"That's yet to be determined," Bree said.

"Do you have any idea how irritated Parker was when you just ran off like that? We saw you from the bay window in the living room. He thought he'd have to send a rescue team out for you."

As if. "You know as well as I do that I'm quite capable of looking after myself."

Caleb sighed and circled his arms around her shoulders. "C'mon, let's tell our host that you've made it back safe and sound."

"Sure thing," Bree said but stared out over the open horizon. *Just who in the hell is that stranger?*

~

GRAYSON MADE it back home later that afternoon. He was too distracted to go back to the office after his encounter with the sexy woman in the mud.

Sonya and Cameron were in the kitchen making an early dinner when he arrived. The aroma of Cuban spices wafted through the air, and his stomach growled.

"Hey, guys," Grayson said, strolling into the kitchen.

"Grayson!" Cameron jumped off the barstool and rushed over to his brother's side, squeezing his middle. "I'm so glad you're home."

"I told you I was coming back," Grayson said, patting his shoulder.

Grayson had spent a good chunk of the morning with Cameron before making it into the office. His baby brother had been so excited to see him that he hadn't wanted to let him out of his sight. Only after Grayson had assured Cameron he wasn't going anywhere anytime soon had his brother allowed him to go to work.

Now Cameron nodded. "I know you said you were coming back, but you've been gone a long time. We missed him, didn't we, Sonya?"

"We sure did." Sonya winked at him as she stirred something in the pot. "Are you hungry, Grayson? I'm almost done with my famous arroz con pollo."

"I will be. Let me change, and I'll come back down." He headed toward the door but paused midstep. "And Mama? How's she doing?"

"Hanging in there, Grayson."

"Thanks, Sonya."

Grayson made his way up the stairs to the master suite, which housed a large bedroom with a custom-built king-sized bed that suited his six-foot-three frame. Adjacent was a walk-in closet with built-in shelves for his clothes and hat collection, along with a master bath complete with a Jacuzzi, rainfall shower, and double vanities. He'd never been much into tubs, but suspected when the time was right he would make good use of his Jacuzzi with the right woman.

For now, he'd settle for a cold shower to relieve the ache in his loins that had arisen after meeting the sexy woman with the corkscrew curls who'd escaped his grasp today.

As he undressed, Grayson pondered the thought. Initially, he'd believed she was a ranch hand, but her quick wit and knowledge of the sale told him he was off the mark. *So who is she?* He was dying to know, but he would have to put that question aside for now. He had more pressing business.

Levi had given him a good lead, and though he'd

gone to check out the land today, he was no more the wiser than he'd been before his visit. He needed a good geologist to tell him if the property was worth the price Parker Johnson was asking.

A geologist like Bree Hart, the woman Levi had told him about at their meeting earlier in the day.

Now that he was home and had a little time on his hands before dinner, he could do some digging and get a little more information about this esteemed geologist. After his shower, he wrapped a towel around his waist and padded to a nearby chair to find his Surface tablet. Powering it on, he quickly entered the name "Bree Hart" in the web browser. His breath hissed when he saw her picture.

It can't be.

Can it?

Bree Hart was the sexy woman in the ditch who'd given him an instant hard-on?

Pictures don't lie. She may have been a little dirty from the mud, but as he browsed her images online, it was definitely her. Grayson continued reading. When he was done, he was impressed with the woman. Not only was she accomplished in her field as a highly sought after petroleum geologist giving speeches and lectures, but she also didn't mind getting her hands dirty.

Today had proved that. She'd been in that ditch for the same reason: to see if the land held oil.

Grayson had to know the answer to that question, but Bree certainly wasn't going to give up the information willingly. He had to find a way in. Hadn't Levi said she wasn't too keen on her father these days? And if he wasn't mistaken, there had been a spark in Bree's eyes when they'd met and she had given him a long perusal. He was certain of it. He hadn't been the only one affected by their meeting. Now he just had to capitalize on that.

~

A FEW DAYS LATER, Bree was excited to be at a petroleum symposium. She was not only a speaker at the conference, but it would also allow her to search out job prospects. She didn't know when she planned to make her move, she just knew that the time had come for action. She refused to let her father take her for granted any longer. She was good at what she did, and it was just a matter of time before the right opportunity came along.

So today, much to her chagrin, she wore a sleeveless gray wraparound dress with a skinny belt and simple black blazer. Pumps adorned her feet along with a minimal amount of jewelry. She hated wearing heels, but she was determined to put her best foot forward.

She walked into the room full of confidence and was rewarded. Instantly, she was swarmed by several colleagues and industry leaders eager to speak with her. Bree had never understood why they made such a fuss about her abilities to predict oil. But she was in high demand for most of the morning, speaking with several business owners including a promising prospect who intrigued her with his request for alternative energy sources.

Finally, she was taking a break from lunch and heading to the dining room when someone caught her eye. His heated gaze across the corridor connected with hers, and heat prickled up Bree's spine. She hung back and watched the man from afar. He was talking to another man in what appeared to be an animated conversation, but periodically his focus would return to Bree. He *knew* she was there, waiting and watching him. The look he gave her was so galvanizing that a tremor tore through her.

There was something about the height and build of the man that was oddly familiar. And that's when it hit her. Earlier that week, she'd encountered that sexy stranger on Johnson's property.

And *this* man was him.

It had to be because he evoked the same reaction from Bree that she'd had during their first encounter. Her heart was thudding loudly and was unable to return to its natural rhythm.

Why was she so *aware* of him? What was it about this man that had her stomach tied in knots? Bree didn't care to find out. She spun around on her heel to make a beeline for the restaurant.

She was nearly to the hostess station when she felt someone behind her. When she turned around, he was there, but the hostess was already seating a couple in front of them.

"We meet again," he whispered in her ear.

Bree casually glanced back and feigned ignorance. "Do I know you?"

He laughed deep, warm, and rich, and Bree felt her insides curl. "You clean up nice, but then again you'd have to after the ditch I found you in last time."

Bree spun around, her light-brown skin turning red. "Well, I didn't realize I'd have an audience."

He grinned. "So you *do* remember me?"

She shrugged nonchalantly. She wasn't about to give anything away. "Now that you mention the ditch, I suppose I do."

The hostess returned. "How many?" She glanced

back and forth between Bree and the handsome stranger.

"Two," the man answered, and before Bree could respond, he lightly touched her back, ushering her inside the restaurant. *Who does he think he is?* It was awfully presumptuous of him to speak for her. She hadn't agreed to dine with him.

The hostess seated them next to the floor-to-ceiling window with a view of downtown Dallas. The stranger came behind her, scooting Bree's chair before taking the seat opposite her.

"I don't recall agreeing to lunch," Bree commented, shaking her napkin and placing it in her lap. "And furthermore, I don't even know your name."

"Then allow me to remedy both faux pas." He offered her his hand from across the table. "Grayson Wells. And I would be honored if you'd agree to have lunch with me, Bree Hart."

She frowned. "How do you know my name?"

The waiter came by and filled their water glasses before scuttling away.

"You're a successful geologist in a city all about the oil business," Grayson responded smoothly. "I'd think that would be obvious. Plus you're on the agenda." He inclined his head toward the flyer with her name and picture sprawled on it that was sitting atop her portfolio.

"And given your visit to the Johnson property, you're in the oil business I presume?" Bree inquired.

"You would assume correctly. And I just so happen to be in the market for a geologist for my company."

"Really?" Now *that* was a useful piece of information. Hadn't she come to the symposium for this very purpose? "Tell me more."

After the waiter came and took their lunch orders,

Grayson expounded on Wells Oil. Bree ordered a salad with grilled salmon while Grayson opted to go full hog with a T-bone steak complete with potatoes and a side of broccoli.

"You've achieved a great deal in a short amount of time. What accounts for your success?" Bree asked.

"Drive. Ambition. A desire to succeed at all costs."

"All qualities I can appreciate, but I'm not sure how I would fit in," Bree said.

"We're looking for someone with your valuable assets. Everyone in this town says you have the Midas touch."

Bree reached for her glass and took a liberal sip of water before setting it down. "They're mistaken."

"Have you or have you not successfully predicted oil for Hart Enterprises's last several fields?"

"I have, but—"

"No buts. Can't you take a compliment, woman?"

Bree couldn't resist smiling. She wasn't used to being spoken to in that way. "I can, but not if it's a load of hogwash."

"So you think I'm pulling your leg?" Grayson paused, then said, "We would love to hire you."

"You're not the first company to try to steal me away from my father," Bree quickly responded.

"But I'm the first man who has made you want to consider it."

Bree stared at Grayson. She suspected they were no longer talking about business, and that wouldn't do. She had a genuine interest in Wells Oil and could appreciate they needed someone to head up their geology division. They'd been around for seven years, but in this town they might as well be considered a start-up company. They needed someone like her at the helm.

Was she seriously considering this? Leaving her father?

Duke would have a cow if he knew she was even thinking of deserting him. He expected loyalty from everyone working for him.

"Bree, we should talk about this further," Grayson continued, "over dinner tonight."

"Dinner?"

"Yes. You could come over to my place. I promise you our family caretaker and friend makes a mean paella."

"I don't think that's a good idea."

"Why not? It's just a business discussion after all. We could talk more about the position, and you could share your goals and desires without an audience."

Bree glanced around, and they did indeed have several curious pairs of eyes staring at them. No doubt these patrons were wondering what Bree Hart was doing talking to the competition. But that wasn't why she didn't want to go to Grayson's. It was because her *desires* might go beyond the company to the man himself.

That signaled big trouble.

BREE WAS on edge for the rest of the day even after she'd given her lecture, which was well-received, and even now that she had returned home. As much as she'd enjoyed it, her mind kept wandering to Grayson's request to join him for dinner tonight. It all sounded innocent enough. They'd discuss his job offer over a meal without scrutiny, but Bree didn't think it was a wise move, not when she felt so heated around the man.

She thought she'd nearly combust if she stared too long into his dark eyes. Eyes that seemed to watch her as if capturing every movement.

She hadn't been this attracted to a man, since— well since Jacob Taylor. Jacob had been the only man Bree had ever truly loved. They'd met when he'd worked at the Hart ranch the spring of her junior year in high school. She'd been immediately enamored not just by his rugged looks, but how he cared for and treated the animals. At first, she came around the stables offering to help, then she was helping him muck out stalls. Then they were laughing and talking over a root beer since she was too young to drink. The next thing Bree knew, they were kissing. And kissing led to Bree's first sexual encounter. It had been amazing, and Jacob had stolen her heart.

They continued seeing each other in secret through the summer and into her senior year. That's until they got caught by the ranch foreman, who'd immediately gone to Duke. Bree would never forget the disappointment in her father's eyes. The way he'd looked at her with such scorn had nearly broken her heart. But she loved Jacob and wasn't about to give him up, no matter what Duke said.

But Duke had laid down the law. She wasn't going to end up some ranch hand's wife, laden with a bunch of babies and living hand to mouth. He fired Jacob and threatened that if he came within a hundred yards of Bree, he'd have him arrested for statutory rape. It had been a terrible time. Bree hated her father for taking away her first love. But Duke didn't care. He had big dreams for her while Bree would have much preferred to stay on the ranch with Duke, learning from the ground up. "I want better for you," Duke had shouted, "which is why you're going to college."

Bree had never been into school; that was her older sister London's thing. But Duke was immoveable on the topic and had forced her to get a higher education. She'd resented him for it, but surprisingly had found she had an understanding not only of the land but what it was made up of. So she'd stumbled into her career as a petroleum geologist.

But she'd never forgotten Jacob. She'd loved him, had given her virginity to him, and had always wondered what might have been if Duke hadn't interfered. Because he had though, Bree had shut down where relationships were concerned. She'd been afraid of getting hurt or having Duke run off the person she loved. So she'd focused on her studies, returning to Dallas from college in Austin to start at Hart Enterprises.

Since then, there had been no time for love and romance, much less sex. Bree couldn't recall the last time she'd been intimate with a man. *Has it really been that long?*

She was wondering what she was going to do when her baby sister, Jada, rang. Bree picked up her cellphone from her dresser and answered it.

"Bree."

"Hey, sis, what's up?"

"Well, we haven't talked in a spell." If Bree recalled, their last conversation was three days ago. "And I thought we could catch up. You know, fill me in on everything."

"Nothing much to tell, other than Caleb is really trying to make me feel included."

"That's good, isn't it? I know how upset you were, I mean, been, since Daddy announced Caleb's going to be the president."

"You're right. I am still hurt by his actions, but not

at Caleb, and I have to remember that. In the meantime, I'm considering my options."

"What does that mean?" Jada sounded intrigued.

Bree shrugged even though Jada couldn't see her. "Hart Enterprises isn't the only game in town."

"You would leave HE?" Jada inquired incredulously. "To go where? And with whom?"

"It's too soon to tell, but I've been invited to dinner tonight to discuss the possibilities."

Jada paused for several beats before asking, "Dinner? And would the invitation happen to have been extended by a man?"

"And if it were?"

"I would caution you to be careful about mixing business with pleasure," Jada warned. "Sounds like a recipe for disaster."

"I hear what you're saying, Jada, but this is a legitimate offer of employment and one I should give due credence to."

"You don't have to convince me, but perhaps you're trying to convince yourself. I mean, what's the deal, Bree?"

"He's charming, attractive, sexy, and smart." Bree stopped naming adjectives. She knew she was giving Jada too much ammunition to convince her to stay at Hart Enterprises.

"Wow, those are a lot of great attributes. I can see why you're apprehensive. A sexy, good-looking intelligent man wants to take you to dinner, and of course you want to turn him down."

"Well, we're actually not going out," Bree answered. "He invited me to dinner at his place."

"Oooh, the plot thickens," Jada murmured. "What else are you holding out on me?"

"Nothing. That's the God's honest truth."

"Dinner out is one thing, but dinner at his place is quite another. How do you know you can trust him? How do you know he won't make a move on you or isn't a serial killer or rapist?"

Bree instinctively knew she could trust Grayson despite having only seen him two times in her life. Something just told her that he was on the up and up with the job offer. After her lecture, she'd looked him up online on her cellphone and found he was indeed the president and CEO of Wells Oil. There hadn't been much else about him other than he'd been acquiring his wealth at a rapid pace and occasionally made time for the ladies. He'd only been linked with less than a handful of women over the years.

As for trusting him not to make a move? On that point, she wasn't so sure. Bree suspected that he'd felt the chemistry between them during lunch as much as she had. *Does that mean he'll try to make a play for me tonight?*

"Bree, are you listening to me?"

"Of course I am."

"And are you going to take my advice."

Probably not. "Sure I am."

"I don't believe you," Jada responded. "But please do me one favor."

"And what's that?"

"At least put some condoms in your purse."

"Jada Hart!"

Jada laughed heartily. "What? I'm just keeping it real with you."

"Yeah, well, keeping it real can go wrong sometimes." Bree chuckled. "But I will take it under advisement."

"You do that, and I can't wait to hear all the juicy

details because I know you're going to do the exact opposite of what I advised."

Seconds later, Jada was hanging up, making Bree feel terrible since she hadn't asked Jada how her news anchor job was going in San Francisco. *Next time*, she told herself. Meanwhile, she would need to shower and figure out what she was going to wear to dinner. Because Jada was right. She was definitely going.

4

Grayson poured himself a Scotch from the bar inside his study. He'd come home after the symposium and had been working ever since. Glancing outside as the sun began to set, he wondered if Bree Hart would show up for dinner. He'd told Sonya to expect a guest and that he'd like to dine alone with her. She'd assured him that she would see to his mother and Cameron's needs so he could have the night off. He didn't know what he'd do without her.

But of one thing he was certain.

Bree would come to him.

He sensed she liked adventure and a hint of danger. He'd dangled the carrot of a job on the stick, and he was sure she'd want to know more. He suspected she wasn't a woman who shied away from a challenge. She would come tonight, despite her reservations, just to show him that she was up for it. And he couldn't wait to see her.

An hour later, he'd showered and changed into jeans and a black V-neck T-shirt. He didn't mind wearing suits when the occasion required it, but he was most comfortable in jeans, which is usually what he wore overseas when he was in Dubai or in the desert with Arash. He missed his friend. Their friendship and business partnership abroad was one of the things Grayson cherished along with his family.

As Grayson studied himself in his bedroom mirror to ensure his T-shirt was tucked into his jeans just right, he reflected on the fact that he felt a duty and responsibility to avenge his father after the way Duke had swindled him. He intended to go about achieving vengeance through the normal channels and hit him in the pocketbook, where it would hurt. But Bree Hart was a wrinkle he hadn't planned on.

Would getting involved with Bree give Duke Hart the ultimate comeuppance?

A couple of hours later, the bell rang, but rather than Sonya answering the door, Grayson did. Bree greeted him with a friendly smile.

"Good evening," she said.

"Good evening," Grayson replied equally as formal. "Please come in."

"Thank you." She walked inside the foyer.

Grayson watched as Bree glanced around at the winding staircase and two-story atrium. While she did, he got a full look at her. She was dressed simply in jeans, a button-down plaid shirt, and cowboy boots. She wore a camel-colored leather jacket that looked as equally soft as the lady herself.

Throughout the symposium, he'd watched her interactions as she drifted from group to group. She had a natural ease about her that he found pleasant despite her last name. Knowing she was Duke's daughter had definitely added to his unabashed interest in her, but there was more. He wanted her. Wanted to kiss her. Touch her. He could easily imagine having Bree Hart ride him fast and hard in his bed.

"Nice place," she commented, interrupting his lascivious thoughts.

"Thanks," he replied. "C'mon," he said, inclining his head, "follow me." He didn't see his mother peeking over the banister watching them.

GRAYSON LED Bree down the long corridor past the formal living and dining room areas until they arrived at the large eat-in kitchen. He'd guessed that Bree wasn't the type who cared for formality and would appreciate the safety and comfort of the kitchen. Sonya had already done the liberty of heating up their supper. It was warming in the oven until Grayson took it out.

Bree glanced around, and he followed her eyes to the breakfast bar at the spacious counter and the large rectangular table in the nook facing the pool. The table had place settings for two and had several candles lit. Sonya had certainly set the mood for romance even though he'd warned her it was just a business dinner. At least for now.

"Where should I sit?"

"Anywhere you like," Grayson answered. "Care for a glass of wine?"

"Love one."

He busied himself uncorking the bottle of Cabernet Sauvignon that Sonya had left chilling in an ice bucket on the counter along with two wine glasses. The woman always thought of everything. He poured wine into the glasses and walked over to Bree at the bar and handed her one. He held his up in the air. "Cheers."

She raised her glass. "Cheers."

"I'm very glad you decided to join me for dinner tonight, Bree."

"Well, you did make the offer sound intriguing after mentioning we had the attention of the entire restaurant."

"I take it that much doesn't get lost in this town?" Grayson said. Although he'd set up Wells Oil seven years ago after he'd won his first oil well, he'd spent most of his time the last few years building up his business base abroad. So he was certainly out of the loop when it came to local gossip, though Levi had done his best to fill him in.

"Not much," Bree concurred, "despite this being a decent size city. All the major players know each other, so not much is lost. So—"

"So when you and I have lunch together—"

"There's talk."

"To your father?" Grayson inquired. It was imperative that Duke not get wind of his scheme.

"My father, Duke?" Bree shrugged. "He's not much into the oil business these days. He's content to let my cousin Caleb take the helm."

"Your cousin? Why not you? Or your siblings?"

Bree cocked her head and glared at him.

Have I struck a nerve? Grayson wondered. *Said too much? Given away that I've researched the Hart family?* He knew every sordid detail of Duke's past and his habit of loving and leaving women. First, there was a tryst with Bree's older sister London's mother back in the day. Then there was his decade-long marriage to Abigail Hart, Bree and Jada's mother, which ended because of his affair with his illegitimate son Trent's mama. Duke Hart certainly loved to play the field.

"And just how do you know I have siblings?"

Grayson shrugged. "Aren't the Harts fixtures in this town? It wouldn't be too hard to find out information."

She sipped her wine. "I suppose."

"Plus I prefer to know everything I can about the people I hire." He drank his wine and watched her over the rim of the glass as she digested that piece of information.

"Then you've heard or read the tall tales about my father, Duke?"

Grayson nodded. "He does have a reputation. Has it ever impacted you negatively?"

Bree put her drink down. "I know my father is no saint, but he owns up to his mistakes. He's always believed in being accountable for one's actions. It's one of the things I respect and admire about him."

Grayson didn't believe that for a second, otherwise the great Duke Hart would have fessed up about taking his father's land and using it to become one of the richest men in Dallas. But Grayson couldn't say that. He couldn't let on just how much he knew about Duke and his past. "Clearly you're very passionate about him."

"I am," Bree stated, lifting her chin to stare him in the eyes.

"Then why leave Hart Enterprises?"

"Now that's a story better told over dinner," Bree said. Rising to her feet, she walked over to the double-oven and opened the door. "What's for dinner?"

∾

BREE WAS happy that the conversation about her potential move from Hart Enterprises had been suspended. She just wanted to focus on the night ahead. She hadn't been sure of what to expect when she'd agreed to dinner at Grayson's home, but it most certainly wasn't a casual, laidback paella dinner with him doing the serving. She'd anticipated he'd have a chef and staff waiting on them hand and foot.

They'd moved from the breakfast bar to the cozy table in the large nook. Grayson brought over the casserole dish that had been warming in the oven along with a tossed salad from the refrigerator.

Dinner smelled divine, and Bree couldn't wait to dive in. She watched as Grayson refilled her wine glass, placed a healthy portion of paella on her plate, and left her to choose how much salad she wanted. He was a very interesting man. She'd thought he'd impress her with his wealth, but he hadn't.

Far from it. She liked that he'd dressed simply in relaxed jeans and a black T-shirt. The pairing showed off his physique well. He looked deliciously sexy, and Bree licked her lips. He glanced up at her and caught the action. Their eyes met across the table, and Bree glanced down. She tried not to focus on the heat coiling in the pit of her stomach. She'd come here about a job, nothing more. She would ignore the chemistry between them if it killed her.

Once Grayson had filled his own plate and sat back down, Bree reached for his hand. At the query in his eyes, she said, "Grace?"

He looked momentarily bewildered, so Bree did the honors. "Lord, we thank you for the food that's about to nourish our bodies and we thank the person who prepared it. In Jesus' name, amen!"

When she glanced up, she saw him staring. "Did your mama not teach you any manners?" she asked with a smile as she took a sip of her wine.

Grayson's eyes became flat and cold. "No, as a single mother of two boys, she was too busy working two jobs to keep a roof over our heads and food on the table."

Bree colored immediately. "I'm s-sorry. I didn't mean to be disrespectful."

His brows drew together in an agonized expression, but then he recovered. "Of course not. It's just you and I grew up very differently, Bree. You grew up in a life of luxury, while I . . ." He didn't complete his sentence. He reached for his fork and dug into his chicken dish.

Bree put down her glass. She knew how lucky she'd been raised as Duke's daughter, but times like these made her wonder if she was spoiled or ungrateful because her father had done so much to ensure their family's success. "And yet you have all this?" She spread her arms around. "That's quite a comeback. Care to tell me how you became so successful?"

"If you'll explain why you wish to leave Hart Enterprises."

"Touché."

He raised a brow. "Well, it's dinnertime."

Bree didn't answer immediately, choosing to taste some of the delicious dish that had been prepared. The flavors exploded in her mouth. "This is really good. Who made it?"

"Our housekeeper and family friend, Sonya." Grayson's eyes narrowed. "But don't try to avoid the subject, Bree."

She smiled. "I didn't plan on it. I'm a woman of my word." She sipped her wine again before continuing. "My father is stepping down from day-to-day operations at Hart Enterprises and instead will be focusing his attention on the Hart ranch. Ranching has been in our family business for years. My Aunt Madelyn and Uncle Isaac run a dude ranch in Arizona."

"If ranching is part of your family's heritage, how did he get into the oil business?"

"When the ranching business took a hit years ago, Daddy had to find alternatives to keep the ranch alive until business picked up, so he drilled on the land and voilà"—she flung her hand in the air—"he struck oil."

"That's quite a lucky coincidence, don't you think?" Grayson asked.

Bree frowned. "Not really. Dallas has been known to have substantial oil reserves underneath certain land such as the Johnson property you're interested in."

"Very true."

"Anyway, that was the start of Hart Enterprises, but deep down, ranching and horses have always been Daddy's first love."

"How does your cousin Caleb fit into the picture?"

"About six years ago, Caleb was injured in a bull-riding competition. We all thought he'd never walk again. I think it was then that he started thinking of his future. Consequently, my father was looking for a graceful way out. In the end, after rehabilitation, Caleb did walk again and my father felt Caleb—a *man* that is—would be better equipped to helm HE."

"Not you or one of his children?"

"London's a restaurateur, Jada's a news anchor of a morning show in San Francisco, and Trent, well . . . My dear half-brother is the screw-up of the family, so there was no way Daddy was putting him in charge."

"I notice you didn't mention yourself. Was that on purpose?"

Bree shrugged and started eating more of the delicious dinner before it got cold. She didn't like all the questions, though she knew he had a right to be curious why she'd leave her family business to join his.

"Are you going to answer me?"

Bree glanced up, and her eyes flashed fire at him. Grayson countered with a searing look of his own, but Bree couldn't take the heat. She looked away. She didn't like that with one glance this man could shift the conversation from business and back to whatever was going on between them.

There was an attraction there that Bree was doing her best to ignore, but Grayson made it awfully difficult when he looked at her like a cougar about to snap up its prey.

"My father thinks the oil business is too dirty for a woman to run, namely me."

"That's sexist and extremely short-sighted considering you run the head of his geology department and have been instrumental in the success of Hart Enterprises for the last decade."

Bree reached for her wine. Grayson was voicing her feelings and her anger with Duke for not seeing how much of an asset she was to the company. "I couldn't agree with you more, which is why I'm here tonight to hear out your proposal for me to jump ship and work at Wells Oil."

"Is that the only reason you're here?" Grayson wiped his mouth with his napkin. Then he clasped his hands as he searched her face with those amazing dark eyes that seemed to see right through her.

Bree was at a loss for words. Who was she kidding? Grayson was indeed reading her right, but she was set on fighting her feelings.

"What other reason could there be?" she answered as she lowered her eyes, her voice barely audible. She looked back up slowly.

Grayson scanned her face and held her gaze. Bree's heart thudded in her ears, and she could feel all the air in the room bottle in her lungs. Eventually, Grayson rose to his feet. "Why indeed? Perhaps I can tempt you with dessert?"

Bree watched him go over to the refrigerator and pull out a plate. "What is it?"

"Sonya makes the most decadent flan. It's Cameron's favorite." Grayson placed it on the breakfast bar.

"And who's Cameron?"

"My brother. He has special needs and lives with me along with my mother and his caregiver and our housekeeper, Sonya." Grayson removed two saucers and a cutting knife from the cupboard and drawer.

Bree glanced upward. "And where are they now?"

"They've retired upstairs for the evening to give us our privacy. We won't be disturbed if that's a concern for you," he said to her in a low-pitched voice.

"It-it's not," Bree said with a shaky voice. Actually, it was good to know that they were not alone. It would ensure Grayson would not make a move on her. "Your brother, Cameron, has he always required constant care?"

Grayson nodded as he cut her a slice of flan and placed it on a plate. Knowing his family was upstairs, Bree felt it was safe to join him at the bar. He slid the flan her way and began cutting himself a piece. "Thanks."

"To answer your question, yes, Cameron was diagnosed with autism. Although he can do for himself physically speaking, we couldn't allow him to live on his own, plus sometimes he gets easily agitated. He has no concept of bills or dealing with day-to-day stresses."

"It's commendable that you have him living here with you."

"Commendable?" Grayson frowned.

Bree grimaced because clearly she'd insulted him when she hadn't meant to.

"I shouldn't be commended for doing what's right," Grayson replied curtly. "He's my brother. It's no hardship. I would never, ever put him in one of those homes and forget about him."

"Of course not." Bree reached across the short distance and touched his arm, and an arc of electricity flashed between them. Bree felt it and so did Grayson, because his eyes darkened. There was a hunger in them that she hadn't seen before.

Desire.

Before Bree could protest, he was drawing her closer to him with pressure at the small of her back. She shivered, and her pulse quickened. He was making her feel hot all over. *What the hell is happening?*

She hadn't felt this way before. Ever.

Not even with Jacob, and he'd been very skilled in the bedroom. But this, this was different. She could feel something tangible coursing back and forth through herself and Grayson. She couldn't give in, because if she did, she was afraid of what might come next.

"Grayson!" The sound of a woman's voice from down the hall jolted Bree from Grayson's hands as if someone had thrown a bucket of cold water on her.

A late-middle-aged Hispanic woman entered the kitchen several moments later. "Grayson, Cameron is very agitated, and I need your help. I can't get him settled. I think he senses something is out of the ordinary."

Grayson patted the woman's arm as she neared him. "It's okay, Sonya. I'll handle it." He turned to Bree. "If you'll excuse me for a moment."

"Of course, take your time. As much as you need," Bree responded.

∼

GRAYSON WAS happy he'd been summoned upstairs. If Sonya's voice hadn't rung out, he would have been finally quenching his desire and kissing Bree full throttle. He'd wanted her from the moment they'd met, and downstairs when she'd touched him, he'd seen that she desired him as well. It was in her eyes.

But he couldn't ever forget that their relationship must be about business. He needed Bree to come aboard at Wells Oil so he could systematically destroy Hart Enterprises and get vengeance for Duke's wrong against his father. He shouldn't let his romantic interest distract him from his primary objective. But damn if that wasn't hard to do. Bree's beautiful face and body were everything he could ever want.

But he had to practice restraint, discipline. First, he had to ensure Cameron was alright and then convince Bree that Wells Oil was the best place for her.

When he arrived at Cameron's suite with Sonya, Cameron was very agitated and pacing the room. "Cam? What's wrong?" Grayson asked.

"Why, why can't we go downstairs?" Cam asked. "I want to go outside and sit by the pool."

"Of course you can." Grayson turned to Sonya with a question. "You're not a prisoner. I just had a guest, and Sonya was giving us some time alone."

"A guest, you mean a girl?" Cameron's brown eyes grew large with amusement.

A smile ruffled Grayson's mouth. Even Cameron could catch on to what he hadn't said. "Yes, it's a girl."

"Is she nice? Can I meet her?"

"I don't think that's a good idea," Sonya jumped in. "We should really let your brother and his guest enjoy their evening."

Cameron spun around to face his caregiver. "But I want to go outside, and I want to meet your girl!" He shot a look at Grayson.

Sonya looked at Grayson too. Clearly she was at her wit's end over Cameron's outburst.

"Alright," Grayson said. "You can meet her if you promise to be on your best behavior. Promise?"

Cameron came toward him and wrapped his arms around Grayson's middle. "Thank you, Gray."

"Grayson ...," Sonya began, but Grayson shook his head.

"It's alright, Sonya. C'mon," Grayson said when Cameron finally released him, "let's go meet my girl."

~

BREE'S HEART warmed the instant she laid eyes on Grayson with his brother. She was not only touched that he would allow him to meet her but by the way Grayson took care of him. She could see he cared about his brother deeply and that was an admirable trait. The more time she spent with Grayson Wells, the more she was starting to like him.

"Would you like to join us for dessert?" Bree asked Cameron when his eyes grew wide at the flan sitting on the counter. He was a slender young man, but equally as tall as Grayson, with whom he shared the same warm-brown coloring. He had a crewcut and brown eyes that matched his skin.

"Can I, Grayson? Can I?" Cameron looked up at his big brother.

"Of course. Pull up a stool, and I'll cut you a slice."

Bree watched Cameron scoot his stool next to hers
and eagerly await Grayson to cut the flan and slide
him a piece. He devoured it in less than five minutes
while Bree and Grayson continued to nibble on theirs.

Grayson made some coffee and he, Cameron, and
Bree sat at the kitchen table while Cameron finished
off more pie. Cameron apparently hadn't been in a
rush to leave his big brother's side, and Grayson hadn't
made him. Bree couldn't recall a more enjoyable
evening and told Grayson so when he walked her out
to her Audi nearly an hour later.

"Thank you so much for dinner and the dessert,"
Bree said once they'd made it to her car. "I had a good
time. And your brother, Cameron, is really quite
special."

"He is," Grayson responded. "I'm glad you can see
that." His eyes were clouded, and Bree couldn't read
what was going on behind them.

Bree nodded. "I could."

"We didn't get to finish our conversation and for
me to pitch to you why Wells Oil would be a good fit
for you."

"No, we didn't."

"I'd like to remedy that. How about lunch next
Thursday? I have to leave on a business trip over the
weekend but would love to talk with you more."

"I'll have to check my calendar, but I'm sure that'll
be fine." Bree unlocked the driver's side door and
turned to get in, but then she felt Grayson's presence
behind her. Bree slowly turned around to face him.
His face was mere inches from hers, and she thought
he might lower his head to kiss her when they heard
Sonya shout, "Grayson!" She was standing at the front
door. Obviously, he was needed right away. So instead

of kissing Bree, he opened her door wider and helped her inside. "Until then."

Bree nodded as he closed the door and spun on his heel to walk away. She was frozen and watched him disappear into the house. Talk about bad timing. *If Sonya hadn't interrupted us again, what would have happened?* Bree was both happy and disappointed. On the one hand, she knew mixing business with pleasure was a bad idea, but on the other hand, she was curious just what it would be like to be kissed by Grayson Wells. But fate had decided it wouldn't be tonight, and so Bree started her Audi and headed home.

5

Bree stared out the French doors as the morning light shone through the east side of the Hart ranch. It was her favorite view because she could watch the stable hands work the horses on their morning routine. She'd always had a love of animals. Maybe not as much as her cousin Rylee Hart, a veterinarian, but she could hold her own. Maybe that's why an affair with Jacob Taylor had appealed to her. He'd offered a simpler, gentler lifestyle than the one her father had planned for her.

Although dust and dirt ran through his veins, Duke Hart didn't want a man like Jacob for Bree. She suspected he would appreciate a man like Grayson Wells, a self-starter who'd grown a bet with a sheikh into a multimillion-dollar business and lived to tell the tale. Rumor had it that they were best friends or at least that's what the social blogs said.

But Bree didn't care about any of that. She never had. She'd always looked deeper inside a person to see what they were really made of. And last night, she'd seen who Grayson really was. He was not only a sharp-as-a-tack businessman, he was a brother and a son who cared about his family, and Bree respected him. More than that, she was attracted to the man. The chemistry between them had been obvious when she'd entered his mansion and had been palpable until the moment he'd walked her to her car.

She was thinking about just how fine Grayson looked in his faded relaxed jeans last night when her father walked into the sunroom. By this point, she had left the French doors and had sat down at the table in the center of the room.

At sixty, Duke barely looked a day over fifty because he got plenty of exercise working on the ranch. His smooth, brown skin looked freshly shaven.

"Morning." Bree didn't bother looking up from the newspaper she'd started skimming.

"Where were you last night?" her father asked as he sat at the head of the table. He helped himself to the carafe of coffee in the center of it and poured himself a mug.

Bree's eyes flickered upward. "Excuse me?"

"No excuses necessary. I asked you where you were," her father replied. "A decent young lady doesn't come in at all hours of the night. It's just not ladylike."

"And what would you know about that, Daddy?" Bree slammed her paper down on the table. It wasn't like she'd stayed out that late. She'd gotten in a little after ten. "As I recall, you were quite the rebel rouser in your youth."

"Don't sass me, Bree."

"I'm not trying to sass you, Daddy. I'm just saying it's the pot calling the kettle black."

He set his mug on the table with a thud and half of it spilled onto the tablecloth. He didn't bother cleaning it up. "Now you're trying to change the subject, and I won't have it."

"And I won't be twenty questioned like I'm an adolescent," Bree said, using the napkin in her lap to blot up the coffee. "I'm a grown-ass woman who can do what I want, when I want. And if you don't like it, I can move out and leave you alone in this mausoleum of a house, just like Mama, London, and Jada. And then where will you be?"

"Of all the . . ." Her father rose to his full height and towered over Bree. "How dare you talk to me like that!"

"I'll talk to you anyway I feel. It's not like you respect me. Why else would you choose Caleb over me to run Hart Enterprises? And now apparently you have a problem with my comings and goings? What is it that you want, Daddy? For me to live like a nun? Or maybe chained to my desk, never to have a life, a husband, a lover since you ran away the one man I ever loved? What exactly do you want for me?"

Her father stepped back and regarded her. He was as stunned as she was by her impassioned speech. Bree hadn't realized she'd been holding so much inside until now.

Duke whipped off his cowboy hat and flung it across the room. "Do all my children hate me?" His brown eyes focused intently on her. "First Trent, London, and now you. Have I really been such a bad father?"

Bree rolled her eyes upward as she leaned back in her chair to look at him. "Don't be so dramatic, Daddy. I'm telling you like it is. I'd think you can appreciate that."

"I do, but you packed an awful lot of accusations into that last punch. You care to talk about them?"

She shrugged. "Would it really matter? Will it change the outcome? Will you rescind your decision for Caleb to run HE?"

Her father remained silent.

"Or how about going to find Jacob and bring him back here to the ranch so I can have a slew of babies. How about that?"

Again, he was speechless.

"I didn't think so," Bree said. She pushed back her chair and stood. "I have to get to the office. I have a long day ahead." She started toward the doorway, but her father placed a hand on her arm.

"You know this conversation isn't over."

"Of course it is, Daddy."

Once she was in her Audi and on the way to Hart Enterprises, Bree let out a long sigh of relief. What had come over her? She'd never spoken that way to her father. But she'd also kept her feelings bottled up for far too long. She didn't know if he'd fully heard her, but now he knew that their relationship was a lot shakier than he'd ever dreamed.

GRAYSON MADE it to the office later than he'd intended that Friday morning. It had been a long night getting Cameron settled down after Bree's visit. Cameron couldn't stop talking about how much he liked her or how beautiful she was. And his brother wasn't wrong. What wasn't there to like about Bree Hart? She hadn't seemed to mind that Cameron had all but taken over the rest of their evening. Instead, she'd embraced having Cameron join them for dessert.

Grayson had to admit it was a helluva turn-on. He'd never met a woman so warm and generous. In fact, he'd never actually introduced a woman to Cameron. He'd kept most of his dates or conquests at arm's length, but Bree Hart wasn't one of those women.

She was smart, accomplished, warm, and giving. And he suspected if he wanted their relationship to develop any further, he would have to go deeper with her than he had with any woman before. He thought about that for a moment, and in the next instant decided that Bree could only be a means to an end despite his intense attraction to her. He sighed. Getting closer to Bree could get him valuable intel on Duke Hart—that's why he had pursued her in the first place, after all, he reasoned. With Bree's help, he could understand the man's strengths and weaknesses. Only then could he use them to his full advantage to destroy the man and all he had built.

LATER THAT MORNING, Levi strolled into Grayson's office and closed the door. "Hey, boss man. How goes your quest to bring down Hart Enterprises? Have you made any strides with Bree Hart?"

Grayson nodded. "We've shared a couple of meals together. Matter of fact, we have lunch scheduled for when I return from my trip."

"And what trip is that?"

"Just some personal business I need to take care of." It was actually a lead he'd gotten from a private investigator that may have located his father's former lawyer in San Antonio. If all leads were correct, he just might get some insight into how in the hell his father, Elijah Williams, had allowed Duke Hart to swindle him out of his land.

One way or another, he'd find out.

"Is everything alright?" Levi inquired. "Anything you need my help on?"

Grayson shook his head. "No, I've got it covered. I was just coming in to take a couple of files with me on the plane."

"You flying commercial?"

Grayson quirked a brow. "I meant jet." He couldn't recall the last time he'd flown on a commercial airline. After he'd made his first million, he'd made sure to find a reliable private airline company so he could fly in style.

"Of course you did."

"I'll see you when I get back. In the meantime, I need you to find me the hook to get Bree Hart to come work at Wells Oil."

"You mean her father's plans to hand the keys to the kingdom to her cousin aren't enough?"

"I want there to be no reason for Bree to turn me down," Grayson said. "I have big plans for her."

Bree was a fiery filly, and Grayson would need to have his wits about him when he convinced her that working for him was the right move.

THE NEXT WEEK, Bree was happy to wrap up her workday early on Tuesday so she could go home for a ride to blow off some steam. After changing clothes and packing a duffel bag with water, a flashlight, blankets, and some light snacks, she set off for the stables. However, when she arrived back at the Hart ranch just after four p.m., she found she was not alone. Addison was in the stables brushing down one of her horses.

"Addison, what are you doing here?"

Addison swung her long mane of jet-black hair in Bree's direction.

"Well hello to you too," Addison said. She turned back around to continue brushing the spotted coat of the American Quarter Horse that had already been saddled.

"I'm sorry if I sounded short," Bree said.

"You just hoped for some alone time?" Addison asked.

"How'd you know?"

"Because it's what you do when you've got something on your mind."

"And how would you know that?"

"I pay attention."

"And you? Should you even be riding while you're pregnant?"

"I'm pregnant, not disabled. The doctor said it was fine up until the third trimester. Plus like you, I like the air whipping through my hair."

"That's exactly what I need," Bree responded, taking the saddle off the hook. She walked over to her Palomino and opened the stall. Her horse immediately lifted her head to greet her.

"How's my Coco?" she cooed as she rubbed the mare's back. "Miss me?"

The mare snorted as if she intuitively understood Bree's question. Bree reached into her pocket for a treat, which the horse immediately took out of her hand.

"Rough day?" Addison asked.

Bree shook her head. "Just a lot on my mind."

Addison hooked her foot in the stirrup and swung herself over the horse. "Then let's hope a nice long gallop will clear it up."

"I'm with you." Bree wasted no time saddling up her mare and hopping on her back.

Soon she and Addison were galloping across the horizon on the hundreds of acres that made up the Hart ranch. Bree didn't mind the company because Addison was quiet as if she too were lost in her own thoughts. Bree was unsure what to do. Should she consider Grayson's offer to come work for Wells Oil? It would certainly be a challenge. She'd probably worked at Hart Enterprises for too long, and maybe it was time for her to work for another company to see what she was really made of. It hadn't taken long for her to climb the ranks at HE, partly because she was family but also because everyone claimed she had the gift for smelling oil.

Bree knew it was less about a gift than it was equal parts luck that she'd been so successful. But would she have the same trajectory at Wells Oil? Was it worth the upheaval to her family, because Bree knew her father wouldn't take it too kindly that she was working for the competition.

Of course, it didn't sit well with her to be dishonest. She believed in straight talking. Always had. And always would. It was one of the traits she'd inherited from her old man, and one that had served her well. Despite the fact he'd appointed Caleb as the soon-to-be CEO, Bree knew it would kill her old man if she left the company, *his company*. But she'd have to tell him the truth.

Eventually Bree and Addison stopped for a break near a retention pond. Bree pulled out a blanket from her duffel bag and laid it across the grass.

She sat down cross-legged, and Addison joined her, stretching out her long legs. Bree pulled out her canteen and took a long swig of water. Addison did the same while Bree searched her bag for her snack. She pulled out some jerky and began munching. She offered some to Addison, but she shook her head no.

"Care to tell me what's on your mind?" Addison asked.

Bree glanced out over the horizon and seconds ticked by before she finally said, "I've been offered an intriguing proposition, one that would take me away from the family business and potentially move me to one of its competitors."

Addison nodded. "Ah, if anyone can understand wanting to break free from underneath your father's thumb, it's me."

"That's right," Bree said. "You used to work for Walker Trucking." Addison's father, Benjamin Walker, owned an oil tanker operation in Dallas that included transporting oil for several oil companies except Duke Hart's. Bree recalled there was some bad blood between Benjamin and her father. Duke had been a ladies' man back then and had nearly stolen Addison's mother, Lila, away from Benjamin, which Benjamin had never forgotten.

"Yeah, I did. Because he wouldn't allow me to be a geologist mucking in the dirt while Duke pretty much made it a requirement for you. I got stuck majoring in marketing and finance at Texas A & M University."

Bree rolled her eyes. "You didn't do too bad for yourself, Addison. You've got a great job at Hayes & Hayes."

"That was only after Caleb's accident paralyzed him and he broke up with me. I'd worked for Walker Trucking with my father's COO for a number of years before I branched out on my own and went to Paris after our breakup. It was a twist of fate that I landed that gig with Hayes & Hayes and came back to the States."

"That's because you and my cousin were meant to be together."

Addison nodded her agreement. "Even though I'd met Raphael, I don't think I ever fell out of love with Caleb."

"You see," Bree said, pointing her finger, "that's the kind of love I want. The kind of love that transcends time."

Addison leaned back on her forearms and regarded her. "Who knew you had such a romantic streak in you, Bree?"

"Just because I'm a tomboy and don't mind getting my hands dirty doesn't mean I don't want love and passion. I just haven't found the right man."

"But you have *now*?"

"Wh-what do you mean?"

"I'm just picking up on a vibe. Have you met someone? Is that what has you so on edge . . . and had us galloping for an hour?"

"Yes. No. I don't know. Maybe," Bree finally said. "It's too soon to say. I just know that, that it felt different when I was with him. Like, well like I couldn't catch my breath. And I thought I'd felt that way before with Jacob, but that was just puppy love compared to this."

"And that scares you?"

"I don't know if it scares me so much as I've been down that road before and had my heart trampled on, so I'm not too excited for a repeat. I'm used to keeping things casual in my relationships."

"But this man makes you want more?"

"More than I should because he could be my boss."

"Wait a second. The man that has your heart aflutter and you short of breath could become your boss?"

Bree nodded. "Should I choose to accept his offer?"

"Oh this is complicated," Addison said, rubbing her belly, deep in thought.

"Any advice you care to give me?"

"Be careful, Bree. Your sixth sense is on to something and being cautious wouldn't be such a bad thing."

Was Addison right? Should she be cautious as she had been for nearly the last decade, trudging through life and living day to day for work and family? Or maybe, just maybe, she should be the risk-taker she'd been in her youth before Duke had squashed her dreams and take Grayson up on both of his offers.

The job offer.

And the unspoken offer of becoming his lover.

Both were on the table.

The question was, what was she going to do about them?

6

Grayson sipped Scotch on his private jet as it made its way back to Dallas on Tuesday afternoon. His trip to San Antonio hadn't been as successful as he'd hoped. He'd thought speaking to the lawyer who'd helped Duke swindle his father out of his money would have given him more insight, but it hadn't.

In fact, the man had been anything other than cooperative despite Grayson's towering presence and threat to prosecute if he found any wrongdoing. The man had pretty much told Grayson to take his best shot. Had Duke paid him off so handsomely that he felt no guilt for what he'd done to his father?

Apparently not.

The lawyer had turned nasty, telling Grayson what a loser his father was—how he'd been a perpetual gambler and something of a ladies' man. He recounted that Grayson's father could often be found hitting the underground gambling establishments with a different woman on his arm every night. He and Duke shared womanizing ways. Why hadn't his mother told him any of this? Had she known what her husband had been up to and turned a blind eye?

Abigail Hart sure hadn't turned her head when Duke had cheated on her. She'd dropped him like a hot potato, but his mother had stayed with his father, Elijah Williams. Why?

All these questions coursed through Grayson's mind and muddled his brain along with the Scotch. All this time, he'd thought he was doing the righteous thing, the honorable thing avenging his father's company, but had he gotten it wrong? Was his father nothing but a drunk, gambler, and adulterer? But even so, that didn't give Duke the right to cheat him.

Reaching for the airplane phone, Grayson dialed his friend Arash. Grayson would trust Arash with his life and knew he would be a sounding board. Unfortunately, Abdul, Arash's personal assistant, advised Grayson that his boss was in a closed-door meeting and would have to call him back.

Grayson slammed the phone down back in its cradle and sucked in a deep breath. He really wanted to vent to someone, and Arash was the only person who would understand. He threw back the remaining Scotch in the tumbler, leaned in the reclining chair, and closed his eyes.

His mind wandered to Bree with a mass of curls tumbling to her shoulders and an impressive behind that he wouldn't mind curving his hands around. He hadn't been able to stop thinking about Bree since he'd spent time with her at his house.

He wanted her.

Even though he reminded himself that he shouldn't. Becoming romantically involved with her was a bad idea and would complicate an already sticky situation. But it wouldn't be the first time Grayson had crossed lines or traveled in ethical gray areas. He wouldn't have been able to amass the small fortune he'd made in the last decade if he hadn't been willing to take risks. But he'd always played fair, even if it meant the other man didn't come out ahead.

Had it been the same with Duke? Is that why my father ended up with nothing?

It was doubtful. There was always a choice. And if the two men had been as close as everyone said they were, Duke wouldn't have been able to swindle his best friend. Grayson certainly couldn't imagine treating Arash that way and being able to sleep at night. No, Grayson had to get justice for his father, for his family, for the life that had been taken from him, Cameron, and their mother. All is fair in love and war.

"Mr. Wells," the pilot's voice came across the speaker, "We're about to land soon. You'll want to put your seat upright and buckle up."

Grayson sat up and adjusted his chair. He needed to stay strictly business with Bree.

～

BREE WASN'T surprised when she received a call from Grayson the next evening confirming their lunch date for Thursday. She'd been eagerly anticipating it. She'd successfully wrestled the urge to cancel. She was no coward and whatever was going on between her and Grayson, she had to see it through.

That's why on the appointed day, she arrived at his office dressed for a business meeting. She wore a V-neck cream dress, which stopped just above her knee, a simple black blazer, and sandals. Her hair was in a loose updo with a few tendrils to frame her face, and she wore a bit of makeup. She hardly wore any to begin with, but she was putting her best foot forward with a light dusting of bronze powder, mascara, blush, and lipstick.

So she was surprised by the slight scowl that greeted her when she was led into Grayson's office. Had she made a mistake coming here? Flummoxed, Bree spun around to leave, but before she could make it to the door, Grayson caught up to her in several long strides and shut it.

Bree stepped backward, and her gaze flickered up to connect with his obsidian-colored eyes. "Grayson?"

"You look different," he stated matter-of-factly.

Bree's face tensed. "Is that a problem? Is this or is this not a business meeting? I believe there is an offer on the table that we're here to discuss, or did I get it wrong?"

She knew she hadn't, but she had to set boundaries. She wasn't going to rush headlong into bed with him despite the fact he was staring at her like she was his next gourmet meal.

He stood straight to his full six foot three inches. "Yes, we are, but I admit I was hoping for the easygoing woman I spent the evening with last week. This, this beautiful creature in front of me I admit has me thrown."

"If that's your backwards way of playing me a compliment, I accept, I think," Bree said, one corner of her mouth pulling into a slight smile.

"You know it is," he murmured.

Bree's heart fluttered. He knew just the thing to say to cause her heart to go arrhythmical. Despite the prickles going up her skin, Bree returned her focus to the business at hand. "The job?"

"Ah yes, please." Grayson motioned her to a nearby round table that faced the view of the Dallas skyline. He helped Bree into her seat before taking his own. "I have an offer for you, and I'm hoping it might seal the deal."

"Oh really, and what's that?"

"In addition to running the geology department, Wells Oil is starting some new alternative initiatives. I thought that might be one way to tempt you to come and work for me."

"And the other?"

"A seat on the board. Your voice will be heard along with mine on major decisions affecting the company. You'd have a seat at the table, something you don't have at Hart Enterprises."

Bree sat back in her chair. Grayson's offer was nothing short of amazing. She'd never had a place at the table. It had been one of her biggest beefs with her father. He was willing to allow her to play around in the dirt for him, but not give her a voice to affect change. Grayson was doing that. What's more, this offer was being extended to her on the day Caleb was officially becoming president of HE. Talk about poetic justice.

Bree smiled broadly. "You certainly came prepared to play ball."

"I play to win," Grayson said.

Bree was sure he did. Wells Oil had sprung up out of nowhere and exploded into the oil scene in Dallas, a full-fledged player. It was said it was because of his global—or should Bree say "Middle Eastern" influences—that he'd become so successful.

"I'm sure that's really important to rich moguls like yourself," Bree replied, "but there are other considerations."

"What more could you want, Bree?" Grayson asked. "Being a board member comes with all the privileges that entails, including giving your opinion and expertise on business deals in the company. It's what you said was lacking at HE, yet I sense hesitancy on your part. Am I wrong?"

"You're not."

"Then what is it?" His eyes devoured hers from across the table.

A tightness clutched Bree's chest. She couldn't tell him what it was.

∽

GRAYSON MOVED his chair closer to Bree's to test the waters. When she didn't push away, he knew he had to press her harder to work for him. If he couldn't get his pound of flesh from Duke, at least for now, he would do so with Bree. Of course, it would be no hardship to spend time with her. The reality, however, of having flesh-and-blood Bree in his presence was causing riotous sensations to course through him. When she'd walked through his office door, he'd nearly lost his mind.

Gone was the rough and tumble cowgirl or tomboy he'd encountered on several occasions, and in her place was a professional woman who'd come to negotiate terms. The cream dress clung to her generously petite curves and called out to everything male in him. He was summoning all his strength to remain focused on business and the goal of bringing Duke Hart down.

And that's why he decided to exploit the physical attraction between himself and Bree to seal this deal, even though it made him feel a little dirty doing so.

He reached across the table and touched her hand. The arcing spark that coursed through him forced his eyes upward and they connected with hers. His eyes remained glued on her and what he saw reflected in those depths told him she was just as aware of him. There was a hunger lurking in her eyes just like he felt in his gut. He watched the rapid rise and fall of her breasts and could see her inner struggle to push her feelings down.

"Bree," he said her name again in something akin to a caress. "There's not another offer like this out there. To get on the board of a rising oil company in its infancy stages, you must see what an opportunity this is." He squeezed her delicate hand in his as if willing her to acquiesce to him. "You *must* come work for me."

BREE'S BODY heat rose at Grayson's words. *For God's sake, what's wrong with me?* She was burning up from just one touch from this man. All her thoughts were short-circuiting, and she couldn't think straight. She could feel a fine sheen of sweat on her forehead and trickling between her breasts.

Quickly, she rose to her feet and moved away toward the window and the view. Grayson was right. His offer of overseeing Wells Oil's alternative energy initiatives was right up her alley, but the addition of a seat on the board was quite another.

She felt his large hands on her shoulders and stiffened.

"What more can I offer you?" He was silent for several seconds and then said, "Stock options. I'm willing to offer you a healthy stock package if you'll sign on the dotted line. Today."

Bree turned around quickly. "Today? I thought I'd have time to think this over."

"You've had a week since we last met to think

about coming to work with me, have you not?" He touched her again. This time his thumb traced downward to her chin, coaxing her face upward to meet his gaze.

"You mean work *for* you?"

Grayson grinned. "I don't run a dictatorship, Bree. I value my team's thoughts and opinions as I would yours. We would be working together, *closely*." He'd added the last word for effect, and that's what Bree was afraid of.

The way he was touching her now made her tremble with barely there contact. She averted her gaze and stared at her sandals. She couldn't take all this sexual energy. It was *too* much.

"Look at me, Bree."

His request was more of a command than a plea that Bree felt she had no choice but to obey. She let her gaze travel upward, and his black irises sucked her in. He was so darn good-looking, and the power he seemed to have over her was undeniable.

He stroked her cheek. "God, you're beautiful," he muttered.

The instant the words were out there, it was like he'd broken the spell and tossed a bucket of cold water over her. Bree moved away. If she agreed to his offer, there would be a working relationship, nothing more. She couldn't, mustn't let herself get caught up in the romanticism of all that *this* man had to offer.

Bree extended her hand toward Grayson. "You have yourself a deal. When do I start?"

～

GRAYSON STARED at the door after Bree left and allowed a smile to spread across his lips. He'd succeeded in getting her to acquiesce and come work with him. She hadn't been an easy sell, even though he'd thrown everything in his arsenal at her, including, of course, tapping into the heat between them. There was no doubt that they found each other attractive. But Bree seemed intent on forcing her feelings down and keeping their relationship at arm's length. He'd seen it when he'd caressed her and she'd pulled away from him.

Grayson wasn't offended.

Bree was right to keep him at a distance. After all, he planned on hurting her father. He was determined not to hurt her too.

7

After her meeting with Grayson, Bree made a decision on her way into the Hart Enterprises office later that afternoon.

She had to move off the ranch.

As much as she hated the idea and would miss the wide-open space, the fresh air, her horses, and all the great people who worked there, she needed her privacy. More than that, if she didn't move out, Duke would be in her business wanting to know who she was working for and why. He'd try to pressure her to come back to HE, but she wasn't going to.

She'd made up her mind, thanks to Grayson's incredible offer. The salary he'd put on the table was outrageous but deserved in her opinion, and the stock options and running his alternative energy initiative program were certainly conversation starters. But it was the seat on the board that had appealed to her most.

And he'd known that it would.

He'd shown a ruthlessness in his single-minded purpose to ensure she worked for him. Bree could see why Grayson had amassed a small fortune in such a short time. He wasn't afraid to take risks and go all out for something he wanted. And today, Bree had gotten the distinct notion that was her.

He'd ensured she would not walk out of his office without signing on the dotted line. And she'd done just that and gotten so much more than she ever hoped for or would ever have at Hart Enterprises.

As she walked toward Caleb's office, Bree took a minute to stare at the Hart Enterprises logo, HE. A bit of nostalgia tore through her. She'd always thought that *she* would run the company with Duke one day, but alas that was not to be and she couldn't cry over spilt milk.

Bree stopped by Caleb's assistant's Millie's desk. "Is he in there?" she asked, pointing to the door.

"Yes, go right on in," Millie said as she buzzed Caleb on the intercom.

Caleb rose to meet Bree, buttoning his suit jacket. The newly minted president of Hart Enterprises looked at home behind her father's massive oak desk. It appeared out of place in this era of sleek, modern office furniture and décor, but Caleb seemed content not to change anything.

"Hey, cuz." He walked over to Bree and pulled her into a hug. "Not that I'm not happy to see you, but what are you doing here?"

"Can't I drop by to say hello?" There was no way she was going to congratulate him on officially becoming president today, however, and Caleb knew that.

"Of course," Caleb said warmly. "It's always good to see you, but it's a pleasant surprise. Come." He led her to a nearby couch. "Sit, and let's catch up."

Bree allowed him to lead her even though a social visit was far from her mind. She didn't relish sharing her news. She loved Caleb, but she had to do what was in her best interest as he'd done when he'd accepted the presidency of HE.

"I'm sorry to stop by unannounced," Bree began, "but this couldn't wait."

"Oh yeah." Caleb sat back lazily, crossing one leg over the other. "What's going on?"

There was no use in beating around the bush. Bree just had to spill it. She reached inside her satchel purse and pulled out an envelope. She handed it to Caleb.

"What's this?"

"My resignation." After her meeting with Grayson, she'd gone home and typed it up.

"What?" Caleb sat upright. "What do you mean?"

"I think it's pretty clear. I'm quitting. I've accepted a position with another firm."

"Why? And with who?"

Bree sighed. "You know why, Caleb."

Caleb shut his eyes tight for a moment, then he opened them and stood. "You don't have to do this, Bree. There's room enough for the both of us here at HE. I thought after we talked we were on the same page."

"We are. I've come to accept Daddy's decision, but as I've said before, that doesn't mean I have to like it."

Caleb rubbed his head, messing up his neat crew-cut. "And I suppose there's no talking you out of this?"

Bree shook her head. "The decision is made, and I signed a contract."

"With who?" he repeated.

"Does it really matter?"

"Of course it does. Is it with one of our competitors? McMann perhaps?"

"No."

"Are you going to tell me who you're going to work for?"

"I will," Bree said, "just not right now. I need to let it all sink in."

"You're being awfully cryptic."

Bree knew she was, but the less Caleb or, in this case, her father knew, the better. Otherwise, he'd try to interfere. She knew her father would waste no time finding out what company she was going to. She wasn't going to make it easy for him. And if she told Caleb, he'd go running to blab everything. No, she had to play this closer to the vest.

"Very well. I accept your letter of resignation and wish you all the best, Bree. I know you'll do great things wherever you go." Caleb offered her his hand. She rose to her feet and shook his hand in return.

"Thank you, Caleb."

"You're welcome," he said, and then he pulled her into his embrace. "But I can't say the same for how Duke will respond once he finds out."

"Oh I know," Bree said. Her father was going to blow his stack, but she was prepared to take his wrath because she was moving out and on with her life and away from his influence.

BREE WAS fearful of how her father would respond to her work and personal news, so she'd asked her mother to dinner with the two of them. Abigail Hart hadn't wanted to attend, but Bree had pleaded that she needed someone on her side. She'd been right on all fronts.

Duke vacillated between anger, shock, and surprise when she finally spilt her news during dessert.

"What the hell do you mean you're leaving Hart Enterprises?" her father roared. "You've been working at the company since you've been out of college. It's where you belong. It's a family business."

"It hasn't felt like a family business since you announced Caleb would become president, and now that he is—"

"Caleb *is* family."

"Of course he is, Daddy. Just not immediate family, but that's besides the point. I told you how I felt a long time ago, and you discounted my feelings, my wishes, my dreams. No more."

"So you retaliate by leaving the company?" he snapped. "That's childish."

"Duke," Abigail chided him, "you don't have to talk down to Bree."

"I'm not, Abigail," he replied, his voice softening as it always did whenever her mother was around. That's why Bree had brought her in as a reinforcement.

"Of course he would think that, Mama," Bree said, glancing at her, "because Daddy can only see his side of things." She turned to Duke. "You've never been willing to listen to other people's opinions. Well, my opinion counts!" Bree's voice rose even though she had been determined not to get into a shouting match.

"You're acting out the same as Trent, and I won't tolerate it," Duke said.

"Tolerate it?" Bree huffed. "I'm not a child that you can order around anymore and send off to college because I'm dating someone you disapprove of. I'm a grown woman capable of making my own decisions."

"Did you know about this, Abigail?" Duke asked, turning to her. His tone was clearly accusatory, but Abigail didn't rise to the bait.

"Of course not, Duke. But you know as well as I do

that Bree hasn't been happy for some time. Her decision to leave shouldn't come as a shock to you. Instead, you should be happy that she's found a place where she fits in."

"She fits at HE," Duke stated firmly.

"This isn't up for discussion, Daddy. I was merely informing you of my decision out of courtesy, but since you insist on treating me like a child, you might as well know that I'm moving out too."

"What?!"

"I'm well past the age of living with one's parents. I've found my own place." She'd just found it that afternoon. After she'd left Caleb's office, she'd immediately called a realtor friend from her debutante days and told her about her situation.

Emma had been only too willing to help Bree. Since Bree wasn't ready to purchase, Emma had shown her a fabulous two-bedroom apartment that was not far from Wells Oil. Add that it came with a resort-style rooftop pool, twenty-four-hour fitness center, and a Starbucks bar, and Bree didn't give herself anytime to rethink her actions. She signed the lease on the spot.

Of course, she didn't have any furniture, but Emma sent her a text with a well-known Dallas interior designer who could assist her in finding her style. And Bree was all set. Everything couldn't be coming together more perfectly, until now.

Duke fumed at the head of the table. "So you're not only leaving HE, you're leaving the ranch? Do you want a new family as well?"

"That's not fair, Duke," Abigail said, stepping in. "Your other children either live on their own, like London and Trent, or moved out a long time ago, like Jada. Isn't Bree entitled to the same consideration?"

Duke stared across the table at Bree for several long moments, and she wondered if he was going to answer her mother. "Of course she is," he said softly. "It's just that . . ." He didn't finish his sentence, and he looked down.

"It's just that what?" Abigail pressed him to continue.

When he lifted his eyes, Bree was shocked to find they had turned misty. "It's just that Bree's always been different," he said. "Not that she's not your daughter, but she's always been the most like me. And it's been just the two of us for so long. I, I guess it's hard to see her go."

Bree was touched and a bit stunned. She'd never heard her father say anything even remotely this revealing.

Abigail reached across the table and patted his hand. Her father covered his large one over hers. A look passed back and forth between her parents, one Bree couldn't read. She was just thankful her mother had agreed to come, otherwise Duke would have been unmanageable.

"I'll be back," Bree said, interrupting the moment, "to visit, that is. Coco would miss me too much."

"You and that damn horse!" Duke said. "Ever since you laid eyes on her, you've been inseparable."

"Then you know you'll see me often."

He nodded.

"Alright, well I'm going to go upstairs to pack," Bree said. She was getting a distinct vibe that her parents wanted some privacy.

Abigail glanced up when Bree rose as if remembering she was still in the room. "I'll be up to say goodbye before I leave."

Bree nodded and headed for the door. When she

turned to look behind her, she noticed her parents were still holding hands.

~

GRAYSON FINALLY REACHED Arash later that evening. His friend had left him several messages, but he'd been preoccupied with work and Bree.

"My friend," Arash said on the other end, "it's good to finally speak to you. You've been a hard man to catch up with since you returned to the States."

"I'm sorry, Arash. I've had some business to attend to."

"You mean the business of exacting vengeance against those who stole from your father, I presume?" Arash said.

"The very same."

"And how's that going?"

Grayson's mind wandered to a petite woman with corkscrew ringlets hitting her shoulders. "I've made some strides."

"And you're sure you want to do this?" Arash asked. "Because once you go down this path, there's no turning back."

"Yes of course. Do you doubt I can do it?"

"Of course not, Grayson. Once you've put your mind to something, you're single-minded in your focus to achieve it. I just hope it will give you the peace you desire."

Grayson didn't know if it would give him peace, but it would certainly teach Duke Hart a lesson and make him think twice before he swindled another person. "Don't worry, Arash. I have things under control."

"Excellent. Then you won't mind me coming for a

visit in a few weeks? I have some business to attend to in Dallas."

"Of course not. I look forward to having my old friend here and showing you the town."

"Consider the matter settled," Arash said. "We'll speak soon."

Seconds later, the phone was dead. Grayson didn't take offense to Arash's straightforward manner. He appreciated it.

He might not get the peace he craved, Grayson thought, but he would get what he desired, even if he couldn't touch her. He wouldn't get romantic with Bree Hart, but he was determined to get to know her all the same.

8

The next two weeks went by very quickly for Bree as she got her Hart Enterprises staff up-to-date on current projects and decorated her apartment. All this left little time for Bree to get nervous about starting work at Wells Oil. Surprisingly, Duke hadn't interfered. Bree suspected her mother was behind him backing off and giving her the breathing room she needed. So when the day finally came for her to start her new job, Bree wasn't the least bit apprehensive.

As she was putting away her personal belongings in her office, which just so happened to be on the same floor as Grayson's—though on the opposite side, thank the Lord—a knock rattled her door.

Bree glanced up and was surprised to see Grayson standing in her doorway sporting a rather large grin. She'd have thought he'd be too busy to be bothered to remember her. But he was clearly pleased with himself for something.

"Good morning," he said and walked into her office without an invitation.

"Good morning," Bree said as she placed several family photos behind her on a back shelf. "You're looking very happy this morning."

"Of course I am," Grayson said. "I've landed one of the most sought-after geologists to work at Wells Oil, and I stole her away from one of the largest companies in town."

"Don't pat yourself on the back too much," Bree replied.

"I know talent when I see it," Grayson said. He reached behind his back and pulled out a bamboo plant. "Welcome to Wells Oil."

Bree accepted the gift. "Thank you. This is a lovely gesture and a fabulous choice."

"When I saw it, I thought of you."

So he'd been *thinking* about her? Bree had certainly been thinking about him since their last encounter when his mere touch had caused her to nearly melt. She'd been happy for the reprieve of two weeks to get her equilibrium on an even keel. It had helped her focus on working for the man and to not think of the two of them in bed together.

"Again, thank you," she said.

"You're welcome. Now why don't you put all that down and allow me to give you a tour."

Bree raised a brow. "Do you give every new employee a tour?"

"Only ones I like," Grayson said cheekily.

She couldn't resist curving her lips. "Alright." Bree laid down the books she'd been about to put on her desk. There would plenty of time to make her office her own. "Let's go."

Over the next thirty minutes, Grayson showed her around and Bree had to admit she was impressed with the operation. Although not as large as HE, it was certainly on its way to competing with the big dogs. When the tour was over, Grayson returned her to her office, and she stood awkwardly in the doorway. "Well, thank you. That was intriguing," Bree said.

"I'm glad you think so," Grayson responded. "We still have a long way to go, but I'm positive with talent like you leading the way with me, we'll do great things."

"Thanks for the compliment. Now let me get to work." Bree turned to go, but Grayson's next words stopped her.

"I'll see you at noon."

"Excuse me?" Bree asked, pivoting on her heel.

"I'd like to take you out for lunch on your first day."

"No need. I've already arranged for lunch with my team in the geology department. Another time?"

His eyes were unreadable, but he said, "Yes, of course."

Seconds later, he was gone and Bree closed the door to her office and leaned against it. She took several deep breaths. She hadn't arranged lunch with her team because she hadn't had the chance. But she wasn't about to get caught up in Grayson's web, and certainly not on her first day. She had to keep her distance and make sure their relationship stayed professional.

It was the only way she could ensure she would be successful in this new position as well as keep her sanity.

~

GRAYSON WASN'T HAPPY. He didn't like being thwarted. He'd been thinking about Bree for weeks, and now that she was finally at Wells Oil, he'd planned on making inroads in the relationship department. He knew he couldn't have her physically—and that it would be wrong, considering she worked for him—but he wanted to get to know her better on a platonic level. But she wasn't having any of it.

And that continued to be the case for the remainder of the week. Whenever he stopped by her office, she was either on the phone or in a meeting or just not there. He'd resorted to other measures to find out what she was up to and had learned her schedule from her assistant. If he had to play dirty, then that's what he would do. Bree was in his crosshairs, and there was no way she was getting away.

ON FRIDAY, nearly a week after she'd been an employee of Wells Oil, Grayson learned she would be at one of his oil sites for testing. He hadn't been out there in months and knowing that Bree would be there afforded him just the opportunity he needed to spend time with her.

When he arrived, Bree was busy with her team, so Grayson busied himself with touring the plant and speaking with the head foreman. Soon, Grayson was immersed in the plant and learning more of the practices, so he didn't see Bree join him until he sensed her presence.

He glanced up to find her peering at him in the pit.

"Grayson."

"Bree." He finished his conversation and then climbed the ladder to join her on dry land.

"What are you doing here?"

"It is my company, is it not?"

Bree chuckled. "Yes, it is. I'm sorry. I'm just surprised to see you. Do you always make it a habit of stopping by the plant?"

"If my schedule permits."

She eyed him suspiciously but didn't say anything further. "Well excuse me. I'll be heading out then." She turned and began walking swiftly away from him.

Grayson had to jog to catch up with her. "Are you all done for the day?"

"Yes, I have what I need."

"Join me for a drink?"

"I don't think so." Bree continued toward the door.

Grayson wasn't going to be deterred this time and followed her to her Audi parked outside. Standing at her driver's door, she spun around and faced him. "Grayson, what are you doing?"

"Unsuccessfully trying to get to know my new employee. I'd like you to join me, and this time I'm not taking no for an answer."

Bree shifted on one foot. "I don't think this is a good idea."

"Duly noted. Now follow me to Stirr. They make a mean cocktail, and you'll love it. C'mon, I don't bite."

He could see her mind racing. She wanted to refuse him again, but instead she acquiesced. "Alright, fine. But I can't stay long."

As he hopped in his Bentley, Grayson was glad Bree had finally given in because he certainly wasn't about to give up. He was determined to break through the wall she held around her.

～

BREE FOLLOWED GRAYSON TO STIRR, a restaurant and bar known for its delicious cocktails. She'd thought he'd want to take her to some pretentious martini bar, which wasn't her style at all. Instead he went casual with a neighborhood joint.

They found seats on the rooftop on one of the unoccupied sofas, and a waitress immediately came to take their order. Grayson ordered a Jack Daniel's and Coke while Bree opted for a beer.

Grayson shot her a quizzical look.

"I grew up on a ranch surrounded by cowboys," Bree said, curling her legs underneath her on the couch as she faced Grayson. "This is their drink of choice."

"A woman comfortable in a man's world. I like it," Grayson said, eyeing her.

"Hasn't always been easy. Growing up on the ranch had its challenges, especially with a father like Duke."

"He was hard on you?"

"I was a tomboy and wanted to be just like him when he'd rather I'd be like Jada and be a debutante. I never envisioned myself in a genteel Southern lifestyle as someone's wife."

"So you don't want to get married?"

"I do. *One day.* Just not now. There's just more I want to achieve before I settle down to be someone's wife and mother."

The waitress came with their drinks and set them on the cocktail table.

"And you?" Bree inquired, taking a swig of her beer. "Do you want to get married?"

"No, I don't think it's in the cards for me." Grayson's voice was sure and firm.

"Why not?"

"With taking care of mother, Cameron, and running my business, I'm not sure I'd have time to adequately devote to being a good husband."

"So you're celibate?" The words flew out of Bree's

mouth before she could retract them. Grayson would be able to see exactly where her mind was going. He had that effect on her.

He smiled, and Bree's stomach flipped at the sexy grin spreading over his lips. "No, I'm not celibate. I find time to enjoy the opposite sex. Like I'm doing now."

Bree laughed nervously, and her eyes flickered to the bottom of her beer bottle. "I don't count. I'm your employee."

When she glanced up, his eyes seared hers and Bree swallowed. "Yes, you are. But you're a woman—a beautiful woman." The moment Grayson said that, he knew he was losing control. He knew he should stay professional, but he felt a strong vibe of interest from Bree too. To hell with it, he was going to go with the flow.

"Grayson . . ."

He shrugged. "What? I can't comment that I find you attractive? I'd be blind not to."

She blushed, and Bree could feel her cheeks turning scarlet, but all she said was, "Thank you."

Sensing her unease with the conversation's direction, Grayson began discussing business. Bree started to relax. She was in her element, and they chatted animatedly about the alternative energy project and Grayson's hopes for the geology department.

When the sun began to set and Bree's stomach began growling, Grayson convinced her to stay for a bite to eat. They retired into the restaurant for dinner and eventually dessert.

Nearly three hours later, Bree realized how much she'd enjoyed Grayson's company just as she had when they'd shared dinner at his mansion. If she didn't stop herself, this could quickly become habit forming. Eventually after coffee, Grayson walked her back to her Audi. They stopped at the driver's side to say their goodbyes.

"Tonight was fun," Bree said awkwardly, turning around to face him.

"So we can see each other again?" Grayson asked, leaning forward. His actions forced Bree backward into the door of her vehicle. He had her caged in, and she wasn't fighting it. He was so close she could smell the musky aroma of his cologne. She liked it, but then her professional switch turned on and she denied what she was feeling. "Grayson, don't."

"Don't what?"

"Act like we're attracted to each other."

His lips lightly grazed her ear as he whispered, "I think tonight showed that we are. And I suspect that's why you've been hiding from me all week."

She frowned. "I haven't been hiding." Though that was a bold-faced lie—it was exactly what she'd been doing. Because of *this*, *this* heat between them. "I'm just trying not to confuse things."

"I'm not confused. I know what I want. And I want you."

"I need to go." She turned, reaching for the driver's door handle, but Grayson pressed himself against her backside and she could feel exactly what she was doing to him.

He was hard.

For her.

Because of her.

Her breathing hitched, and that's when Grayson went in for the kill.

~

LONGING TO TOUCH HER, Grayson spun Bree around in his arms.

Finally.

Trying to tamp down his attraction to Bree hadn't worked. For weeks, she had been all he could think about. And now she was right in front of him. He was holding her tight. She swallowed, and that made him watch her beautiful elongated neck. Made him want to put his mouth where her pulse beat. But instead, he kissed her on the lips.

They had begged to be kissed. Kissed by him. And he was happy to oblige. He grasped her face, lowered his head, and took her mouth again. His lips brushed softly across hers, letting Bree get used to the idea before settling on them more firmly. She was hesitant at first, but when he swept his tongue over her lips seeking entry, she released a long-held sigh and then Grayson deepened the kiss. He knew exactly what Bree needed and began licking and stroking her with his tongue.

He lifted his head long enough to say, "Kiss me back, Bree. You know you want to."

Several seconds later, she wrapped her arms around his neck and Grayson gleefully slid his hands down her backside and clutched her behind. Then he captured her mouth with his in a ravenous kiss. His tongue stroked deep and fast inside her while his hands moved lower to leisurely knead her breasts through her thin shirt. When he tugged on one of her nipples with his fingers, she moaned softly and he left her lips to nuzzle his nose in her hair before trailing a path of hot, wet kisses down her neck.

He liked it when she turned her neck slightly, giving him better access. He curled his arms even tighter around her middle and pressed his erection into her. She gasped at the contact and rocked against him. He could feel her arousal and his vibrating through them both. That would be Grayson's undoing. He had to stop before things got out of hand.

His breath was ragged as he slowly released her.

She looked up at him questioningly with passion-glazed eyes. Grayson thought twice about ending their frenzied encounter, but they were outside a restaurant —not the ideal place to take their relationship to the next level. Because when that day came, Grayson would lay Bree naked across his bed and take his time properly tasting and worshipping her body from head to toe.

BREE WAS UNRAVELED. How had she let Grayson kiss her, much less fondle her out in the open where anyone could see them? She'd been out of control just now letting him have his way. But hadn't she known, intrinsically, that it would be that way with him if they were alone together again?

She'd felt it that night at his mansion, but they'd been disturbed by Sonya. Otherwise, Bree had always suspected that Grayson would have kissed her, and she would have let him. Enjoyed it even as she had now. As Bree faced Grayson outside her car, she licked her lips remembering the feel and taste of his mouth on hers. His kisses had given her a glimpse of how Grayson would be as a lover. His hands had been a torment, gliding up and down her feverish body. At one point, she'd heard a low whimper escape her lips as pressure built inside her as he pressed his bulging manhood between her thighs. If he hadn't stopped, she might have begged him to take her right there on the spot.

What is wrong with me?

She looked up into Grayson's swirling dark eyes.

"That shouldn't have happened," she said quietly.

"It was inevitable," he answered.

She was chagrined by his flippant response. "Is this the reason you asked me out?"

He looked down, and after a few seconds, he peered into her eyes. "There's been a chemistry between us, Bree, ever since I caught you in that ditch. And you and I both know it."

"I know no such thing." But he was right, there had been a spark between them at that first meeting and their subsequent meetings. "And besides, it doesn't matter."

"Care to elaborate?"

"I work for you," she began, but then corrected herself, "*with* you. And it isn't a good idea mixing business and pleasure."

"I beg to differ," Grayson stated. By this point, he no longer cared a lick about keeping the professional and personal separate. He was really into Bree. He wanted her no matter what. His deeply set eyes were focused on her. "There could be a great amount of pleasure derived from our mixing the two together."

Bree shifted uncomfortably from foot to foot. Grayson was trying to confuse her, muddy the waters. "I came to Wells Oil to prove to myself and my father that I'm a force to be reckoned with, not become your next plaything."

"First off, you're not my plaything. Do you think I would have hired you at the outrageous sum that I did and offer you a stake in my company and a seat on the board just to have you in my bed? C'mon, Bree. I'm not that hard up."

Bree flushed hotly. "I-I . . ." There were no words. She didn't have a comeback for that one because Grayson Wells was not only a wealthy man, but an attractive one. Despite his travels, there would be any number of females willing to throw themselves at him. She just happened not to be one of them. "Listen, you're right," she began. "I'm sure you can have your pick of women willing to be your lover. I just can't be one of them. You hired me to do a job, and you need to let me do it."

Bree didn't wait for Grayson's response. Instead, she hopped in her Audi, revved up the engine, and roared out of the parking lot as quickly as she could.

She didn't look behind her to see Grayson staring at her dust.

~

"Is EVERYTHING ALRIGHT?" Grayson's mother asked him the next morning when they sat together for breakfast. He'd had a miserable night and hadn't gotten much sleep. It was now well after eight a.m.

"Yes, everything's fine." Grayson sipped his coffee. "Why do you ask?"

"You seem antsy," she replied. "And not yourself." Julia paused, then said, "It's the Hart girl, isn't it? You have a thing for her."

"Mother."

"What?" She drew up her shoulders. "I know I'm right. I saw you with her when you invited her to the house for dinner."

"Why didn't you come down? I would have introduced you."

"I don't need to meet the daughter of Duke Hart. I assume she's just a means to an end to get back at Duke."

Grayson stared at his mother. "Not necessarily. I like her."

"What the hell is that supposed to mean? You're supposed to be getting payback for your father, Grayson, not sidling up and getting cozy with Duke's daughter. You mustn't lose your focus."

"I haven't," he said tightly.

"Then you're fooling yourself. You're enamored with that girl, and she could be a snake just like her father. I mean, how much do you really know about her?"

All he needed to know, Grayson thought, but he wasn't about to get into that now. He rose to his feet. "I have to get to the office. I know it's Saturday, but I have some loose ends I need to attend to."

"Will you promise me to keep your distance from the Hart girl?"

Grayson stared at her. That was a promise he would never be able to keep. He wanted Bree Hart, and he intended to have her. But he'd never lied to his mother outright, so he said, "Tell Cam I'll see him later tonight, alright?" And with a wave, he walked swiftly out of the kitchen.

Once in his car, Grayson sighed in relief. What his mother didn't know wouldn't hurt her. Besides, it wasn't up to her who Grayson did or didn't spend time with.

It was just a matter of time before he and Bree would finally quench the hunger that had been building inside them.

9

The next couple of weeks breezed by for Bree. She was enjoying her new position at Wells Oil. It was the first time in a long time she'd truly felt valued for what she brought to the table. And speaking of tables, today she was attending her first Wells Oil board meeting. There wasn't much to discuss, but the alternative energy project Grayson wanted her to head came up under New Business at the Monday meeting.

During her presentation on the subject, Bree made a case to the board for why oil wasn't the only sustainable source of energy they could utilize. Afterward, Grayson asked her to stick around after everyone left. Now it was just the two of them in the boardroom. Grayson wasn't giving up trying to spend time with her. And for Bree's part, she noticed that he wore his suit like a second skin. It showed the breadth and width of his shoulders and chest. His arms and torso bulged with power, letting every woman know that there was a beautiful body underneath that could do wicked things to a girl. Bree blinked several times as she realized Grayson was speaking to her. "What was that?"

He gave her a sexy grin. "I asked you what you thought of the meeting."

"I enjoyed it." She liked sitting at the big boys' table and not being told she didn't have a place or voice like she did at HE.

"Good. I'm glad." Grayson eyed her.

Bree hated it when he looked at her like that. His eyes blazed with desire, and he was definitely taking off her black pencil skirt and pale pink silk shirt with his gaze. Or maybe he was thinking back to the kiss they'd shared a couple of weeks ago. Since then, she'd done her best to keep their relationship professional, but Grayson wasn't making it easy.

And now here they were alone again. Didn't he understand that she was doing her darndest to forget that kiss and how it had felt being in his arms?

"I was hoping you could join me and my friend Arash for dinner tonight. I don't often to get see him, but he'll be here on business and I was hoping to introduce you."

"You mean Sheikh Arash bin Rashid Al Kadar?"

"The same."

"You want me to come to dinner? With you? With both of you?"

"Yes, I believe I said that already," he said with a smile in his voice.

Bree had heard the rumors that Grayson was friends with a sheikh, but to be invited to dinner with the two of them was more than she would have thought possible. She'd never met a real live sheikh. This was a request she could get on board with. Dinner wouldn't just be between her and Grayson, but with Arash as well. "Of course. Count me in."

~

LATER, at home, Bree was a nervous wreck. She didn't have a thing to wear to dinner with a sheikh, so she called her sister Jada, who answered on the third ring.

"Well if it isn't Miss Independent," Jada said on the other end of the phone.

"Hello to you too, sis," Bree said. "What's with the attitude?"

"Maybe it's because I'm the last to learn that you've not only left HE, but you've moved out of the ranch too. What the heck?"

"Listen, I'm sorry, Jada. Everything just happened so quickly."

"And you couldn't text me or London for that matter? I had to hear it from Daddy of all people. And trust me, he is not happy about it. He feels like you've betrayed him by leaving the company, but most of all the ranch."

"I know," Bree replied, "and I'm sorry about that. But I couldn't stay there forever. Hell, you left years ago. Why don't I get a pass? Am I supposed to live there until I'm a shriveled up old maid?"

"Of course not. It's just that, that Daddy's terribly lonely without you. And you guys always had a rhythm, a harmony."

"Not anymore, Jada. We haven't in a while."

"After Caleb joined HE?"

"Yes, maybe before then when Daddy ran off Jacob."

"Are you still harping over that fool?" Jada huffed. "He wasn't meant for you. Otherwise he wouldn't have let Daddy run him off."

Bree released a long sigh. "I know that, alright? But it doesn't mean I've forgotten. Besides I'm enjoying the single life, and it's why I have a hot date tonight with two men."

"What?" Jada sounded perplexed. "You're not doing some kind of freaky threesome to show your independence, are you?"

Bree roared with laughter. "Of course not. I'm going out with my boss, and his best friend is a sheikh."

"Wow! That does sound impressive. What about that black keyhole knit dress you bought a few months back?"

"Oh yeah." Bree headed straight for her closet to pull out the dress. She held it up to the light as she balanced the phone in her other hand. She'd only worn it the one time when she and Jada had painted the town. The dress was tasteful but also flattering to her figure. "What would I do without you?"

"You certainly better not find out," Jada said. "Anyway, wait a second. Is the job you accepted with the same man you had dinner with at his place?"

Damn. Bree was hoping Jada would have a short-term memory.

"Well? I'm waiting."

Several seconds ticked by and Bree debated fibbing, but in the end told the truth.

"Yes."

"The evening that I told you to bring condoms?"

"I brought no such thing," Bree said with a rush.

"Humph. I'd suggest you bring them tonight," Jada said. "It's clear your *boss* is still very much interested in you, and you would do well to be prepared. Sheikh or no sheikh."

"I have to go, Jada. I have to get ready for my date. We'll talk soon." Bree quickly hung up with her baby sister before the conversation could take a more embarrassing turn.

A FEW HOURS LATER, Bree was ready when a car arrived to pick her up to take her to the highly anticipated dinner; but she was disappointed to find the car empty when she slid inside the backseat. She'd been so sure that Grayson would fetch her himself since he seemed determined to spend time with her. It was why she'd added a touch of her favorite perfume at her pulse points, taken more time with her unruly shoulder-length curls until they hung in ringlets, and donned the flattering keyhole knit dress.

Maybe Grayson was tiring of chasing after her and had decided to look elsewhere. Tonight could simply be as he'd suggested: a chance for her to meet a friend and important ally of Wells Oil. So why did she feel a swarm of butterflies in the pit of her stomach?

GRAYSON WAS FRUSTRATED by the turn the evening had taken. His intention had been to pick up Bree from her new apartment. He'd learned that she'd moved out of the Hart ranch and was forging on her own. He wondered if he had something to do with Bree's newfound independence. Or perhaps that was wishful thinking?

Nonetheless, he'd meant to fetch her so he could spend some quality alone time with her in the car. Unfortunately, Cameron had been out of sorts tonight and acting out. Sonya was having a hard time settling him down, so Grayson had stayed longer to calm him. Cameron hadn't been happy to hear that Grayson was going out and leaving him again.

After Grayson's return, Cameron had been attached to him at the hip and didn't like it when

Grayson went out. Cameron's fears were justified. Grayson *had* stayed away too long, and now Cameron was afraid each time he left that he wouldn't come back. Grayson would have to show Cameron rather than tell him that he wasn't going anywhere until Cameron felt secure again.

Consequently, Grayson was now driving himself in his Bentley and would be late to dinner with Bree and Arash. Arash would be on time, as usual, and Grayson was sure he would charm Bree. Grayson's stomach knotted at the thought of leaving his friend alone with *his* woman. Because Bree was certainly his, and he wasn't the sort of man who shared. But he also wasn't blind. With the sheikh thing going for him, women flocked to Arash. He just hoped Bree wasn't one of them.

BREE ARRIVED AT THE RESTAURANT, and the driver helped her out of the car. "Thank you," she said. When she tried to tip him, he shook his head and told her Mr. Wells had already taken care of him.

Of course he would, Bree mused. Grayson thought of everything except coming to pick her up himself. She tried not to be disappointed by his absence, but she was.

When she walked inside the restaurant, the maître d' greeted her by name. "Ms. Hart, I presume?"

"Uh-yes." She gave a firm nod. How did he know who she was?

"Mr. Wells sends his apologies that he wasn't here to greet you personally as a family matter required his attention. But he asked that I show you to your table.

His guest, Sheikh Arash bin Rashid Al Kadar, has already arrived."

A family matter? Bree hoped everything was okay and that no harm had come to anyone. "Thank you. I'd appreciate that."

She followed behind the maître d', and he led her to a table where an attractive Middle Eastern man sat with two hulking men standing only a few feet behind him. He stood when she approached and greeted her with a dazzling smile.

Arash was a good-looking man. Jet-black hair reached his shoulders. He had a dark-tan complexion, sculpted jaw and cheekbones, and he wore an impeccable three-piece suit that fit his athletic physique. She was sure he broke a lot of hearts.

"You must be Bree," Arash said, coming toward her with an outstretched hand. He covered both of hers with his and brought her right hand to his lips and kissed it. "It's a pleasure."

Everyone seemed to know who she was. Exactly what had Grayson told them? "A pleasure to meet you as well, Sheikh Arash bin Rashid Al Kadar." Bree had done her research to make sure she knew how to greet him and curtsey toward him.

"Please don't," he said, motioning her to stand. "That really isn't necessary. Please have a seat." He pulled out a chair for her, and Bree sat down.

"Thank you, Your Highness."

"Call me Arash."

Bree smiled. "Arash it is." She glanced up and found him staring at her. This made Bree wonder if she had lipstick on her teeth or something.

"Forgive my rudeness," he said, offering her a sudden, arresting smile. "It's just that you're just as beautiful as Grayson mentioned."

"Did he?" Bree flushed, wondering what else Grayson had said about her.

Moments later, the maître d' came over with a bottle of expensive wine. Arash tasted it first before the maître d' poured them each a glass. Arash held up his drink, and as if reading her mind, he added, "Grayson's said nothing but good things. He spoke very highly of you and the work you're doing for him at Wells Oil."

Bree was comfortable discussing her work. "The position is very rewarding."

"More than it was at your family's company?"

"Yes," Bree stated, looking Arash in the eye. "My opinions were not always valued, and I suspect if they'd come from a man they would've been accepted."

"I understand your plight," Arash said. "I too am trying to change my country's view of women's rights, but that's hard to do after centuries of one way of thinking."

"My father is very much stuck in the Middle Ages."

Arash chuckled at that. "I like you, Bree. You're direct. I can see why Grayson is so infatuated."

"Don't like her too much, my friend," a deep masculine voice said from behind them.

Bree's breath hitched in her throat, but she was frozen and unable to turn around. Arash rose to greet his friend. Grayson was finally here and according to Arash, was infatuated with her? *He must be mistaken, right?*

She could see them out of the corner of her eye and waited with bated breath for the men to finish their embrace. After they took their seats, it wasn't Arash who caught her attention anymore. It was Grayson.

"Bree," he said as he extended his large hand across the table to cover hers, "forgive my tardiness. It was unavoidable."

Bree was afraid to look at him, but she sensed Grayson's urging her to do so and when her brown eyes connected with his, she had to force herself to keep breathing. His eyes were fixed on hers, so she drank him in. He looked delicious in a gray suit with a purple tie. It suited him.

"Grayson." She swallowed the lump in her throat.

"Ahem." Arash coughed several times, reminding Bree and Grayson that they were not alone.

Grayson turned to his friend. "Have you ordered?"

"Only a bottle of their finest," Arash responded with a grin. "Bree and I were just enjoying it when you arrived."

"And flirting with Bree, no doubt," Grayson said with a laugh as a waiter appeared and filled Grayson's glass with the wine that had been chilling in the bucket.

"Are you jealous?" Bree asked, finding her voice to engage him. He'd momentarily flustered her with his good looks and searing gazes, but she could hold her own with two attractive and successful men.

Grayson cocked his head and regarded her. "If I were?"

"I would say you shouldn't be. We are only employer and employee after all."

Grayson growled something underneath his breath, and Arash looked amused at their exchange. Was it that obvious that Grayson and Bree wanted to jump each other's bones? Bree was doing her best to remain professional.

"Something tells me there's more going on here than meets the eye," Arash said, "but I'm afraid it will have to wait for another evening. I'd love to hear what's going on with Wells Oil."

Bree was happy with the conversation during their four-course meal. She learned how Grayson had won his first oil well during a high-stakes poker game in Dubai with Arash. Even more, she enjoyed hearing their stories about their adventures.

"Grayson was getting me, a royal, into much trouble," Arash said during dessert and coffee. "Imagine how upset my father, a traditionalist, was that I was nearly kicked out of grad school due to excessive partying with this one." He inclined his head toward Grayson.

Grayson chuckled and pointed to his friend. "It wasn't that bad." He turned to Bree, and added, "He's exaggerating."

"Oh I doubt that," Bree said. "I suspect both of you were a handful."

Arash and Grayson looked at each other and said, "Yeah, we were."

"And now Grayson's come back home to do right by his family and take care of them. It's honorable."

Bree glanced at Grayson and their eyes connected. "Yes, it is."

"Bree met Cameron," Grayson added.

Arash's eyes widened as he stared at his friend. "Did she?"

Bree glanced back and forth between the two men. There was definitely a conversation going on even though neither man spoke. Was it unusual that she had met his brother? "Yes, I did, and he's a wonderful young man. I liked him a lot."

"And he liked you as well," Grayson said.

"What's not to like," Arash said, giving Bree a conspiratorial wink. It had its desired effect.

"Watch it, Arash!" Grayson said with a forced grin that in no way hid that he didn't care for Arash flirting with her.

Bree ignored him. "So how long are you staying in town, Arash?"

"For about a week or so. I'm here to conclude some business, and then I'll be heading back to my country."

"I would love to visit it one day and see your culture for myself in its natural habitat. Sounds very interesting."

"And I would love to host you"—he glanced at Grayson—"*both* someday soon. Now if you'll forgive me, I really must retire for the evening. I have an early meeting tomorrow."

"Of course." Bree stood, and Arash once again took her hand and kissed it.

"Bree, it was a pleasure spending the evening with you. You're delightful." He turned to Grayson, and the two men shook hands.

"Excuse me for a moment," Grayson said and walked out with Arash.

Time away from Grayson gave Bree a chance to reflect on the evening. It had gone rather smoothly in her opinion, but there were times when she'd caught Grayson staring at her. There was no mistaking the lust in his eyes, and it caused a coil of desire to surge through her. She'd never felt this aware of herself or her sexuality before, but Grayson was making her feel sexier than she'd ever thought possible.

When he returned several minutes later, he leaned forward and whispered in her ear, "Are you ready to get out of here?"

Bree nodded but didn't dare turn around for fear of what she might find. She didn't have to wait long.

Grayson made his intentions known when he walked her through the restaurant and to the valet outside. "I'll be driving you home."

"Alright." But hadn't she wanted time alone with him earlier and been disappointed when he hadn't been inside the car? Of course, now that the moment had arrived, she was more nervous than she'd anticipated.

It took the valet a few minutes to return with Grayson's car. When he did, Grayson helped Bree inside. His touch sent a flurry of emotions straight through her. She had to get a hold of herself. He was just driving her home for Christ's sake, nothing more.

Or was it?

Any attempt at small talk was tossed aside as sexual tension frissoned through the air between them. Bree was a ball of nerves by the time Grayson pulled up outside her apartment building.

She forced herself to turn around and look at him. She wished she hadn't. Before she could stop him, he reached over, unbuckled her seatbelt, and pulled her toward him. His lips came down firmly on hers in a determined kiss that raided her mouth and senses, leaving little doubt of his intent. Searing heat surged though Bree's veins and lodged low in her abdomen.

She felt Grayson's hands seeking her breasts through her knit dress. She knew she shouldn't let him touch her but didn't push him away. Instead his fingers trailed possessively down the swell of one of her breasts until they reached her aching nipple. His thumb teased it until it hardened for him. She hated that her body was so treacherous. It was wrong to get involved with Grayson, but she had no self-control around this man.

He lifted his head long enough to say, "Ask me up, Bree."

"I-I don't think this is a good idea."

"Christ, Bree. Do you have any idea what you're doing to me?" Grayson growled and to prove his point, he grasped her hand and placed it over his erection that strained in his pants. "I need to be inside you."

Oh God! Had she done that to him? Bree opened her eyes, and Grayson's sought hers in the dark. Denying him would be denying herself what she'd wanted and been craving for weeks. But she had to. "I'm going up alone."

"There's going to come a time, Bree, that there will be no escaping what's happening here between us. And when that time comes, I will make you mine. You can count on that."

And that was a promise Bree was sure he'd keep.

10

B ree couldn't escape Grayson at the office that week. Everywhere she went, he always seemed to materialize despite her attempts to avoid him. At least she was having success avoiding calls from her sisters, Jada and London. They had been wanting to know what happened with Duke, Hart Enterprises, and why she'd moved from the ranch. Bree wasn't about to defend her decisions to anyone, however, so for now she wouldn't be answering their calls.

Through all this, Bree couldn't get Grayson off her mind. He wasn't backing down from their attraction to each other. He had stopped by with coffee for her one morning before work. Their conversation had been brief, but it had been clear to Bree that he was merely giving her a reprieve.

The next week, he invited her team out to lunch. Bree had been sure it was a ploy to spend time with her, but Grayson barely said a few words and had sat on the opposite end of the table. Later, she'd found out that he periodically took departments of Wells Oil out for lunch. His employees loved it because it made him seem more approachable.

In the middle of that week, Bree needed to leave a

message with Grayson's assistant, Rosalie, about her thoughts on the alternative energy project. As Bree stood at the assistant's desk, Rosalie was on the phone and looked alarmed when she placed the receiver back in the cradle. Bree had to ask, "Are you alright?"

"No, not really." Rosalie bit her lip, and Bree could see her trembling.

"I-I can't reach Mr. Wells, and it's urgent."

"What's going on?" Bree hadn't known he wasn't in the office. "Is there anything I can do to help?"

"I doubt it," Rosalie responded, wringing her hands. "It's about his brother, but I can't reach Mr. Wells and I have strict orders that any call in regards to Cameron should be dispatched to him immediately."

"Who called?" On high alert, Bree stepped in.

"I really shouldn't betray a confidence."

"I'm aware of Cameron's condition."

Rosalie sighed. "He's gone missing, and his care-taker is out of her mind with worry."

Bree patted the woman's hand. "It's okay, Rosalie. I'll go to the house and see if I can be of assistance."

"You'd do that?" Rosalie seemed surprised by the offer.

"Of course." She'd only met Cameron one time, but she felt a special friendship with him and perhaps she could help out Sonya. "If Mr. Wells should call, tell him what's happened, but let him know I'm on my way."

"Certainly, Ms. Hart."

Bree quickly departed, rushing to her office to grab her purse. She wasted no time getting to her car and speeding down the expressway to get to the Wells mansion in Preston Hollow. It took her longer than she would have liked due to rush hour traffic, but at least she'd arrived and could try to help. But first she pulled out her cowboy boots from her trunk, replacing her heels.

As soon as she pressed the doorbell, the door immediately swung open. The disappointment on Sonya's face was evident. "Oh, I was hoping you were Grayson."

"I'm sorry I'm not," Bree responded. "I tried to reach him as well, but his phone keeps going to voicemail. But when I heard about Cameron, I just knew I had to help."

"Please come in." Sonya motioned Bree into the foyer.

Bree glanced up and saw an older woman at the top of the stairs. "Who's that?"

"Cameron's mother, and she hasn't been feeling well since her chemo treatments yesterday. She's unable to help me search the grounds. I'm just so worried, Ms. Hart. It's going to be dark soon, and Cameron hates the dark."

Bree patted the woman's hand to calm her frayed nerves. "Well, I'm here now, and two pairs of eyes are better than one, right?"

Sonya nodded.

"So why don't you tell me where you've looked, and we'll divide and conquer."

"But you're not dressed to go traipsing around."

Bree glanced down at her wool skirt and sweater.

Sonya immediately told her that she had searched most of the house but hadn't gotten to the stables, pool, and guesthouse.

"Alright, why don't you do another sweep of the main house and I'll search the rest of the grounds. Sound good?"

The two women separated and Bree headed for

the door, but she couldn't resist glancing at the top of the stairs. Grayson and Cameron's mother had disappeared, but why hadn't she come down to introduce herself? Bree shrugged. She didn't have any time to wonder. As Sonya had stated, it would be getting dark soon, so she had to get started. It was critical they find Cameron.

GRAYSON SIGHED as he got in the back of the car and turned on his phone. It was late and he'd stayed at an off-site business meeting much longer than he would have liked, but he'd been in intense negotiations and didn't want to step away for fear he wouldn't get to sign on the dotted line.

He was basking in his latest victory when his phone began beeping as voicemail after voicemail and texts began coming in earnest. He scanned the texts. There were some from Rosalie, Sonya, and finally Bree. All of them said that Cameron had gone missing.

"Dammit!" Grayson swore. "Todd!" he called out to his driver. "I need you to put a move on it. I need to get home as soon as possible."

Then he was dialing Sonya's number. When she answered, he listened. She was a wreck over the fact that she'd let something like this happen. He knew that she prided herself on the care she took of his brother. He tried to reassure her. "Sonya, there's nothing you could have done. Cam's been a handful lately. I don't know what's going on with him, but we'll figure it out. Don't blame yourself. You've been nothing but a steady, constant presence in his life."

"Thank you, Grayson. I appreciate you saying so.

It's just I've searched everywhere in the house and come up empty. I'm hoping Ms. Hart will find him outside."

Grayson was shocked that Bree had involved herself. "Did Ms. Hart explain how she found out?" He listened and learned that Bree had heard about Cameron's disappearance from his assistant. And instead of leaving it to Sonya or Grayson, she'd stepped in herself. He was not only grateful for the help, but he respected the hell out of her for helping when he couldn't. She could easily have turned her back and said it wasn't her problem.

He was quickly liking Bree Hart more and more each day.

~

IT HAD BEEN NEARLY an hour and the sun was starting to set. Bree had yet to find Cameron. She searched the pool and guesthouse and came up empty. Then she decided to hit the stables. They'd always been her favorite place. Perhaps it was the same for Cameron.

She got her answer when she found him curled up and sound asleep on the floor of a mare's stall next to her baby foal.

Bree lowered herself into the hay, uncaring that she was wearing a skirt. "Cameron," she said. She roused the young man by lightly touching his shoulder.

He woke with a start and looked at her warily. Blinking several times, he brought her into focus from the haze of sleep. "Bree?" he whispered.

"Yes, you remember me?"

He nodded enthusiastically. "You're Grayson's girlfriend."

Bree considered correcting him, but thought better of it. She didn't want to upset him. "Yes, I am."

"He likes you," Cameron said. "His eyes get big when he looks at you."

Bree smiled. "Do they?" She hadn't noticed. "What are you doing here all by yourself?"

Cameron frowned. "Miss Sonya wouldn't let me see the new foal. Told me I'd be in the way, and I wanted to see."

He leaned over and patted the soft skin of the foal, who'd curled up alongside him. "Do you like horses, Bree?"

"I love them, so I can understand wanting to see one being born. But you really should have told Miss Sonya where you were going. Maybe she would have liked to come with you."

Cameron frowned. "I suppose."

"She was really worried about you. And so was I."

"You were?" Cameron's voice rose when he spoke. "But you haven't been back in weeks. I-I thought maybe you didn't want to come back because I was here, because Gray has to take care of me."

Bree patted his knee. She felt terrible that he felt it was because of his illness when that was far from the reason. "That's not why, Cameron. I've just been really busy. I'm actually working with your brother at his company."

"Do you like your job?"

"I do."

"Does this mean that you'll come visit us a lot more now?"

"I'd like to know the answer to that question as well." Grayson's voice interrupted their conversation.

Bree's gaze tore from Cameron, and she glanced up to find Grayson looking down on them from the stall doorway. How long had he been standing there? And why did he have to look so handsome in a trench coat and two-piece suit?

"Grayson."

"Bree." He offered her his hand and Bree took it, allowing him to lift her to her feet. She brushed off the needles of hay from her skirt while Grayson helped Cameron up.

"Cameron, you know we're going to have to talk about your behavior today," Grayson said sternly.

Cameron was appropriately ashamed and lowered his head, but then he glanced at Bree and she gave him a tentative smile. So he looked up at Grayson. "Can we do it later? Bree's here, and I want her to stay." Cameron came over and linked his arms with Bree's.

Bree noticed that Grayson couldn't resist smiling at the action.

"We can talk later. It's time for dinner anyway." Grayson glanced at Bree. "Is it too much to ask you to stay for dinner?"

"Of course she's going to stay. She's your girl-friend," Cameron answered for her, and before Bree could say another word, Cameron led her out of the stables.

～

GRAYSON WASN'T SURPRISED to learn that Bree had found Cameron. His brother was as taken with the woman as he was. Not many women would insinuate themselves into a delicate family matter involving an autistic sibling, but Bree wasn't just any woman.

She'd shown more depth and character than he'd ever seen in in any other woman, and it was a helluva turn-on. And this time, it had nothing to do with how beautiful she was or her curvy figure, though she did look scrumptious in that snug-fitting wool skirt and sweater. She made the outfit look sexy, whereas it might have looked ho-hum on another woman.

He watched her from across the table as she interacted animatedly with Cameron and Sonya. Bless her heart, he'd never seen the older woman so relieved as she'd been when the three of them walked through the door. Sonya had tried hugging Cameron, but he'd pulled away and told her he couldn't breathe. When she began to scold him, Grayson had stopped her and told her there'd be time later to discuss his punishment. In the interim, for tonight, they were going to be thankful he was safe and sound.

Grayson removed his jacket and threw it over the back of his chair. His mother chose that moment to make her appearance. She was wearing a lounge set, and a scarf covered her head. Grayson hated to see her so ravaged by cancer, but he was determined to do all he could until she went into remission. He would accept no other alternative but a full recovery. "Mother," Grayson said. He rose and walked toward her. "How are you feeling?" he asked as he helped her into a seat.

"Better, now that Cameron is here." Julia offered a half-hearted smile. Then she gazed in Bree's direction. "And you are?"

Bree smiled at her from across the table. "Bree Hart, ma'am. It's a pleasure to meet you." She extended a hand, which Julia shook begrudgingly. *Did Bree notice Mother's reluctance?* Grayson wondered. If she did, she was too polite to mention it.

"Bree is an employee of Wells Oil," Grayson said.

"And Grayson's girlfriend," Cameron said quietly.

Grayson saw a blush creep up Bree's light-brown cheeks. "Cameron," Grayson said in a chastising tone.

"What?" Cameron said, looking back and forth between the two of them.

"It's okay, Cameron," Bree said, patting his arm affectionately. His brother hadn't left her side since they'd come in. Grayson had never seen Cameron take to someone so quickly like he had Bree. "Grayson and I are friends as well as colleagues."

Julia's eyebrows rose as if she didn't believe a word Bree had said, but she didn't utter another thing. And so the evening continued with Cameron as lively as he'd ever been. When dessert ended, Sonya recommended that he retire, but Cameron wasn't having it. "I want Bree."

Bree's eyes lit up with joy, and Grayson could swear he saw tears in them. "You go on up with Miss Sonya, and I promise we'll spend some more time together when I'm here again. How does that sound?"

"Alright, Bree." Cameron leaned over and gave her a quick hug and then rushed out of the room with Sonya right behind him.

Grayson and his mother were in shock. Cameron didn't particularly like to be touched. It was a product of his condition, so for him to hug Bree was huge. Not to mention Bree had said she'd visit again. Grayson hoped she didn't just mean to see his brother.

"I'm going to retire," Julia said as she rose to her feet.

"Do you need my help?" Grayson asked, blotting his lips with his napkin as he stood.

"No, no." She patted his shoulder, urging him to sit back down. "You have guests and important business. I'll leave you to get on with it."

After she left, Grayson leaned back in his chair and glanced at Bree. "What a night, huh?"

"You're telling me."

"Listen, Bree," Grayson said, sitting upright again, "I don't know how to thank you for stepping in and finding Cameron."

She shrugged and reached for her coffee mug. "It was nothing really."

Their eyes met, and he held her gaze. "You and I both know it's not nothing. You were, I mean, *are* incredible." He stood again, and this time he wasn't going to be stopped. He walked straight toward Bree and pulled her to her feet and into his arms.

"Grayson—" She didn't get out another word because his face was inches away, and then his mouth found her lips. He kissed her softly and gently, but as Bree's body began melding into his, his kisses became desperate and hot. He parted her lips and took her mouth with his tongue.

Grayson was hungry for Bree, and he knew she was hungry for him. So why act like they didn't want each other? He was tired of pretending.

He wanted her now.

He wanted to learn all the textures and tastes of her mouth. Explore the secret places on her body that would bring her the most pleasure. Feast on her until she cried out his name.

Bree wound her arms up around his neck, and that was all Grayson needed. He lifted her up and carried her out of the room and upstairs to his bedroom.

WHEN BREE OPENED HER EYES, she was aware that her surroundings had changed from the well-appointed dining room to a space with soaring ceilings and dark-colored walls—a masculine room.

Grayson's room.

He laid her across the bed, covering her body with his as he kissed her again, hard and fierce. Bree had no choice but to hold on to him for dear life. Grayson was doing wicked things with his tongue in her mouth. She could feel her skin heating up at his kiss and his touch. His hands were roving down her body, awakening her and evoking a passion that had lain dormant for too long. But Grayson . . . she'd let him *do* anything, *have* anything, including her.

She was his for the taking, and he knew it.

Grayson lifted his head and upper body to look upon her. "Bree." His eyes were dark with desire. "I want you. Say you want me too."

She nodded.

"I need to hear you say it," he urged.

"I want you, Grayson." And to show him, she reached for his tie, loosened it, then slid it over his head and tossed it aside. Then she began unbuttoning the tailored shirt he'd been wearing underneath his suit. He helped her by shrugging out of the shirt.

When Bree saw his naked torso, she couldn't resist touching him. Her hands reveled in the hard steel of his chest, and she wanted to taste him. She lowered her head and licked one of his nipples. He released a long sigh, and Bree took it to mean she was on the right track, so she skimmed and teased the nipple with gentle flicks of her tongue before gliding over to pay respect to his other nipple.

"Bree." Grayson lifted her head to look at her. "I think it's me who should be paying homage to you."

"In time," she countered. "I'm having too much fun." She bent her head again and teased a trail from his nipples to his flat stomach and lower abdomen until she came to his pants. She unbuckled the belt first, then undid his zipper. In one final action, she lowered his pants and his briefs mid-thigh, and his erection sprang free.

He was big.

Bree couldn't resist a smile and licked her lips even as she wondered how she was going to fit him inside her; but there would be time for doubt later. Right now, she wanted to taste him, so she pushed him backward and Grayson fell onto the bed. Bree sidled up next to him, and he lifted his hips so she could rid him of the pants and have unfettered access to *all* of him.

Grayson didn't seem to mind that she was taking control. In fact, he seemed to relish it as he lay back against the pillows and watched her undress. He shouldn't be the only one naked. He grinned as she stripteased in front of him, first lifting her sweater over her head and throwing it in the heap with his clothes, followed by her skirt, bra, and panties. When she was as naked as he, she crawled on top of him and straddled him.

"Bree, you're killing me," Grayson said when she took hold of his shaft.

"I know." She smiled wickedly. "Lie back and enjoy it." She lowered her head and devoured his crown.

SWEET JESUS, Grayson thought as he thrashed his head on the pillow. He hadn't expected Bree to take over in the bedroom. He'd been intent on being the one to *do* anything and everything *to* her, but instead she was the one in control. He suspected that it was a turn-on for her to be leading their first sexual encounter. And he didn't mind giving up control, *for now*.

But turnabout would be fair play. And real soon.

The shoe . . . He couldn't finish the thought because a low moan escaped his lips.

"Ah . . ."

Bree was on her knees pumping him with her fist and bobbing her head up and down on his shaft. Grayson held her head as she began sucking, licking, and stroking him with equal pressure. When Bree increased the tempo and cupped his balls, he twisted and writhed, pushing her away.

He wouldn't let her get the better of him.

When he came, he would be inside her. "That's enough," he said, hauling her upward and onto the pillows. He stretched out over her and peered into her brown eyes. Soon she was underneath him, her lips looking soft and delicious, so he took them, thrusting his tongue into the sweetness she offered. When he finally lifted his head, he admired her lovely body.

Her breasts were beautiful, and he couldn't help the litany of praise that poured from his lips as he kneaded one breast in his palm.

"God, you're stunning," he whispered. "So absolutely perfect." He pinched her nipple, rolling it around between his thumb and forefinger. Then he captured the bud in his mouth. Bree writhed. Grayson knew exactly where to skim, lick, tantalize, and torment her; but by doing so, pressure was building inside his own loins. Grayson didn't know how long he would be able to keep this up, but he was determined she would break first. He slid his hands down her body, past her abdomen until he came to her damp center.

"Spread your legs," he ordered. As she did so, he gave her other breast equal attention with his fevered tongue. He needed to know if she was wet and ready.

Her legs were now open, and he stroked the lips of

her sex with his fingertips. "I've been thinking about touching you, tasting you," he murmured as he slid a finger between the velvet slickness of her folds and found her sensitive nub.

Bree moaned. Then her moans became cries and keens as his thumb circled her clitoris with expert pressure. His slid a second finger inside her slick wetness, and she arched off the bed. He could feel tension building as she struggled to hold on to control, but he was relentless in his pursuit of her pleasure.

His thumb whirled and swirled around her clitoris. When he stroked a particularly sensitive spot, Bree erupted, bucking against him and coming apart. "Grayson!" she screamed.

"That's it, baby, come for me," Grayson moaned as he left her lips and added his tongue to her moist center. When he licked her inside and out, he felt her rippling around his fingers and tongue.

"Grayson, please. I need you."

"What do you need?" he asked lazily as he slid her closer to his mouth, her buttocks in his hand as he spread her shaking legs wider and gave her one long lick.

"I need you inside me."

Finally, finally, Bree had surrendered to him, giving him all of herself.

~

BREE DIDN'T THINK it was possible to have two orgasms in a row, but she had and she and Grayson hadn't even gone all the way yet. Grayson was worshipping and pleasuring her as no other man had. She dug her fingers into his shoulders, pulling him upward, and he climbed on top of her.

She opened her legs for him again, eager to have him inside her, but he wasn't going to give her what she wanted just yet. Instead, Grayson kissed her deeply and she tasted herself on his lips. It was heady knowing how intimate she was being with him. Not only had it been a long time since she'd been with a man, it had been even longer since she'd had an orgasm without stimulation from a device.

Grayson was ringing every ounce of deep-seated pleasure out of her. He shifted long enough to reach for his nightstand drawer and pull out a condom. Bree was thankful that he was thinking about protection when all she'd wanted was to have him inside her, filling her.

Then he was back, suckling hard at her pulse point on her neck. It would leave a mark, letting everyone know she'd been taken, but Bree didn't care.

"Grayson, stop tormenting me, tormenting us."

He shifted, taking his weight on his elbows. His body still covered hers from shoulder to thigh. Using his knee, he pushed her thighs wider, stretching her for him before plunging inside. Bree arched off the bed to meet him, but then he withdrew, then plunged in again, this time deeper until he filled her to the hilt.

Bree brought his head down to hers and kissed him with passion and utter abandon; she shuddered at the heavenly sensation of having Grayson buried inside her. Her walls expanded to make room for him, and it felt as if Grayson were made for her and vice versa. It was just the two of them together in this moment in time.

He grabbed her buttocks, tilting her hips to the right angle as they moved together quietly, their sighs of pleasure audible. The sensations he was evoking were almost too much. Bree didn't know she could feel so much at one time. Her feet pressed into the bed, and she dug her fingers into his shoulders as her orgasm stuck her with full force.

"Bree!" Grayson's voice was tight as he ground out her name just as his body tensed and he emptied into his condom.

Bree was still shuddering as she lay in his arms. The need to be taken by him had been strong. She'd had no control over her desire. Grayson knew she'd had walls up, and he had toppled every one of them.

Bree had not known desire like this was possible, that she could literally ache to have him inside her. When Grayson turned on his side and looked tenderly down at her, Bree knew she was falling for this incredible man.

11

Bree awoke the next morning feeling deliciously sore between her thighs and a little out of sorts. When she'd come to help find Cameron yesterday, going to bed with Grayson had been the furthest thing from her mind. She'd just been trying to help. Instead, she'd discovered nirvana in Grayson's arms. Bree was stunned by the depth of passion she'd shared with him.

And the power of that passion scared her.

Despite her best efforts, Grayson had snuck into her heart. She'd been trying her best to push the attraction down between them, thinking if she ignored it, it would go away. Instead, it had been red hot, and they'd very nearly gone up in flames.

Bree recalled making love with Grayson a few hours ago. How she'd straddled him, riding him slowly, then more determinedly. She remembered the way his hands had wrapped around her buttocks and how he had thrust upward as their thighs and bellies slapped. And later how he'd flipped her over onto her back so he could drive into her with hard and deliberate strokes. And the sounds she'd made as he'd delivered yet another mind-numbing orgasm.

Now in the morning light, Bree wasn't sure of what to do. She'd always prided herself for standing up and looking someone in the eye, but all she wanted to do at this moment was run.

Run as fast as she could.

Quietly, she slipped out of bed and gathered her clothes strewn across the floor and headed into the en suite bathroom. With any luck, she would be gone before Grayson woke up. She'd make a clean getaway and give herself time to process everything that had happened between them and her feelings.

GRAYSON REACHED FOR BREE, but found himself touching empty bedsheets. He shot up with a frown. The imprint of where she'd lain was still there, but it was cold. He glanced around the room and saw that her clothes were gone.

Had she really run out on him like a thief in the night?

Then he heard the water running. He glanced at the door. *She's still here.*

Throwing back the covers, Grayson rose naked from the bed and without any warning, he burst through the bathroom door. Bree was standing in her bra and panties, brushing her teeth. She must have found one of his spare toothbrushes in the drawer underneath the sink.

"I'm sorry," she said, spitting out her toothpaste into the sink. "I kind of borrowed it."

"It's yours if you promise to stay." He stared at her boldly and with no apologies. He'd loved having her in his bed. He'd known it would be good between them, but it had been nothing short of spectacular.

A look of unease crossed her face. "I should go." She reached for her clothing on the bathroom countertop, but Grayson was closer and grabbed them before she could.

"Grayson, give me my clothes."

"No, because you're running away. And I don't like it."

"I have to go to work."

"So do I, but that's not why you're trying to make a fast getaway. You're scared about what happened last night and you're running, just as you have been from the moment we met."

Her eyes flashed fire. "That's not true."

"You know it is."

She glared at him and then tried to jump higher to get her clothes, which he held just out of her reach.

"Grayson!" she said exasperatedly.

"Don't act like it's not true. But I'm not going to let you run away from us, from this." He motioned back and forth between them, then tossed her clothes aside and reached for her. Circling his arms around her, he pulled her toward him and then he kissed her. Bree tried unsuccessfully to push him away, but that only brought her lower half into exquisite contact with his morning erection. Their hips and thighs collided, and desire shot through Grayson as if he'd been injected intravenously with lust.

"Oh!" Bree gasped when she felt him.

Grayson rubbed shamelessly against her mound.

"Don't," Bree said.

Her pleas were useless because Grayson was already unclasping her bra with one hand while the other nudged down her panties. When she was as naked as he was, Grayson lowered her to his rug. Then he slid down her body to hook her legs around his neck so his mouth could go to her secret place. He found she was warm and moist. He swept the tip of his tongue lightly across her clitoris and felt her shudder.

Bree was not going to leave him until they were both good and ready, until they'd sated each other's desires and he wasn't nearly sated enough. He slowly entered her with his tongue and began moving in rapid circular movements. She began groping the rug wildly as he added one digit and then another along with his tongue until she was crying out with need.

"Grayson. Oh God, please—"

He felt the rush of her honeyed sweetness against his mouth as her release came and she began to shudder above him. He continued to finger her until she convulsed around him again.

Grayson reached for the box of condoms he kept in the drawer and sheathed himself, but instead of driving into her as he wanted to, he lifted her into a seated position to face him. He wanted her to look at him as he joined his body with hers. He wanted her to see what she was doing to him, to them, and that there would be no running away.

BREE WAS weak with need as Grayson grabbed her hips and surged inside her.

"Oh God!" She closed her eyes, arching her back at the intense connection of their bodies.

"Look at me!" Grayson ordered.

"Grayson." She opened her eyes and stared into his, amazed that he had aroused her yet again. Grayson devoured her mouth with greedy, hungry kisses and drew her tightly to him. She struggled to breathe as every sensation came to the surface.

"See how good it is between us," he groaned as he thrust inside her ever so slowly. An incredible sense of fullness overcame Bree, and she gave herself up to it.

Grayson withdrew almost to the tip and when she whimpered, he thrust in again and pounded into her. Her hips bucked off the floor, but he didn't stop. His thumb reached between her thighs to press against her clit, and Bree thought she would break apart.

"Promise me you won't run away again." When she didn't speak—couldn't because she was lost in ecstasy —Grayson's hands slipped behind her neck and he lightly tugged her hair. He forced her to meet his gaze. "Promise me." He picked up the pace, delivering one elongated thrust after another. "Promise me."

"I-I-I promise," Bree cried as her entire body tightened around him.

She heard a low guttural groan escape from Grayson as his release shuddered through her and a wave of euphoria took over.

Afterward, they ended up in his rainfall shower with Grayson washing every part of her body with care and concern. Bree knew she would be sore after all their physical activity, but there was no denying she was overcome. The way he'd taken her on the floor and then again in the shower had left little doubt that their night together wasn't a one-night stand for Grayson. He was determined to show her that one night would never be enough.

And that's what she was afraid of.

~

THEY DRESSED QUIETLY. Grayson donned gray slacks and a crisp white shirt while Bree was stuck with her outfit from the night before. Next time, he would be sure she had some clothes here so she wouldn't have to feel embarrassed on a walk of shame to her car.

The thought surprised him. He not only wanted Bree, but he wanted to spend more time with her outside of Wells Oil. This had nothing to do with taking revenge against Duke Hart. Grayson was developing real feelings for Bree.

"Can I interest you in some breakfast?" he asked.

She shook her head. "No. I-I need to get home and change my clothes before heading into the office."

He saw her glance around for her purse. "It's probably still downstairs," Grayson said. "I'll walk you out."

They walked toward the door, but Grayson grasped her hand, holding it in his as they descended the stairs. When they arrived to the foyer, he found Sonya had placed Bree's purse on the hall table. He smiled. She'd known he'd had company.

"Well, I'll uh, see you at the office," Bree said, reaching for her purse. She tried rushing for the door, but Grayson clutched her forearm.

"Bree, you promised," he reminded her and swept his lips across hers.

She nodded. Then without a word, she rushed from the mansion.

Grayson stared at the door. What the hell had happened last night?

Clap, clap, clap.

Grayson turned and found his mother behind him with a begrudging smile.

"Mother?"

"Well, if I hadn't seen it for myself, last night and now this morning, I wouldn't have believed it, but you're more ruthless and calculating than your father ever was."

"Pardon?"

"You've played that girl perfectly. I saw her just now." Julia pointed to the door. "She had stars in her eyes. I admire your killer spirit, son."

Fury seethed within him. Why? He had courted Bree because she was Duke's daughter, but that wasn't why he'd bedded her. Hell, he'd made love to her because it just felt right. It had been beautiful and exquisite, and now his mother was tainting it with her words and reminding Grayson that his motives where Bree was concerned had been far from good. After all, he had hired her in his attempts to take revenge on her father.

"I don't want to talk about this with you, Mother," he replied. "My love life is none of your concern."

"Like hell it isn't. You're dating the devil's daughter," Julia spat. "You can strike him at the knees with a death blow by bedding his daughter as well as ruin his company. He deserves it for what he did to your father."

"Not now, Mother," Grayson roared. He grabbed his keys off the hall table and rushed out of the house.

The last thing he wanted to hear was that he was using Bree. It would only make him feel like even more of a heel.

~

AFTER GOING to her apartment to change, Bree decided to work from home for the day. Per her contract, she could make her own schedule and hours, and she was exercising that option. She couldn't go in and face Grayson, not after everything they'd done. She'd done. After everything they'd shared. She'd never been so uninhibited with a man in her entire life, but somehow Grayson had brought out that side of her.

She knew it was a coward's way out and that she'd promised Grayson she wouldn't run. And she wouldn't. She just needed breathing room to sort through her feelings. He was so relentless in his pursuit of her that she couldn't think straight whenever he was around.

DUKE WAS SURPRISED to see Bree when she stopped by the ranch in the middle of the day. He was in the stables tending to the horses when she arrived wearing her favorite pair of Wranglers, a plaid shirt, and some weathered cowboy boots.

"Baby girl, what brings you by on a workday? Did you get tired of that new job already? You know there's always a place for you at Hart Enterprises."

Bree smiled. "Thank you, Daddy. I wanted some fresh air and a ride. I thought I'd stopped by and see Coco." She walked toward her mare's stall. Bree had wrestled with going into work but just didn't have the guts to do it. She'd called in to say she was a little under the weather and would work from home.

"You usually ride when you have something on your mind," he surmised, eyeing her suspiciously. "Care to tell your old man about it?"

She shook her head. "No, I can handle it." Or at least that's what she told herself.

He shrugged. "If that's the way you want it. How about I ride with you?"

"I'd like that." And she would. They hadn't ridden together in a long time because they'd been at odds.

They rode in silence and eventually returned to the ranch two hours later.

"It was good to see you, Bree. I miss you and so do your sisters. It's kind of quiet around here without you," Duke said as they unsaddled and cooled down their horses. "London and Jada hardly hear from you."

"I've been working really hard," Bree said, brushing down her mare as she avoided looking at her father. She didn't need a guilt-trip. She knew she'd been lax in keeping in contact.

"Does this new job mean you don't have time for your family?"

And just like that the peace that had coexisted between them for much of the afternoon disappeared. "It has nothing to do with the job, Daddy."

"So it's me." Looking at her sternly, he added, "I'm the reason why you stay away. You just can't get over me choosing Caleb to run Hart Enterprises, and you're punishing everyone else for my mistakes."

Bree glanced up at her father and found distress all over his face. "I'm not trying to punish you, Daddy, or anyone else in the family for that matter," she said hotly. "I had to do this for myself." She pounded her chest with her fist. "I had to prove to myself that I could be my own woman without your help. You have to trust me that I can do it and you won't lose me in the process."

"So why does it feel like I've already lost you?"

"Oh, Daddy." Bree dropped her brush and rushed toward her father. He quickly embraced her, hugging her tightly to his broad chest. "You haven't lost me."

Duke pulled away slightly and kissed her forehead. "I love you, Bree. Nothing will ever change that, no matter where you are or who you work with."

"I know, Daddy."

"Good. Join me for dinner?"

"I'm sorry, I can't." They'd had a good ride and managed not to get into an argument. Bree would rather leave the good feelings as they were. "Maybe another time?"

"Alright." Duke nodded. "If that's what you want."

"Thank you," Bree said and left before Duke could talk her into staying. The ride had done her good. She couldn't hide from Grayson anymore than she could hide from her father. They were both a part of her life, and she would have to face the relationships head on. She would have to talk to Grayson to find out exactly what it was he wanted from her and vice versa.

She hadn't been looking for romance, but now that it was here, Bree might be curious to see where it went.

~

GRAYSON FUMED as he drove to Bree's apartment. He'd thought after he'd walked her to her car earlier that morning that he would see her in the office later that day, maybe have lunch together. When he'd found her office empty, anger had roiled in his gut.

Her assistant had informed him that Bree would be working from home for the day. It was her right, but that didn't mean he wasn't fit to be tied. Lucky for her, his entire workday had been filled with meetings.

But now the day was over, and he was free and clear to confront Bree Hart about her running away from the blazing hot inferno they'd shared last night. No way was he going to allow her to chicken out. One evening together was not enough for him.

Just then, his cellphone rang and the name

"Arash" popped up on the screen. Grayson smiled. "Arash, what's up, man?"

"I am heading to the airport soon, and I thought you might like to join me for dinner before I leave for my overnight flight."

"I don't know." Grayson was nearly to Bree's apartment.

"Do you have somewhere else important to be?"

"Not exactly, but I would like to put a certain curly haired female across my knee and give her the spanking she so richly deserves."

"Ha-ha-ha." Arash's bellow was clearly discernible through the phone. "Well, then it appears I caught you just in time. Join me for dinner at Wolfgang Puck's? It'll do you some good before you run the poor girl away."

Grayson sighed. Perhaps Arash was right. Maybe he should let cooler heads prevail. "Fine. I'll see you in twenty."

He was there in fifteen minutes and found Arash already seated in a booth. Grayson nodded at Arash's ever-present security detail as he slid in the booth across from his friend.

"I'm glad you could make it," Arash said with a wide grin.

"Don't be smart," Grayson replied, "like you know something I don't."

"Oh, but I do." Arash laughed richly. "I know you've got it bad for that girl and that it puts a crimp in your perfectly laid plans."

"Am I really that bad?" Grayson asked, picking up a nearby knife and peering at his reflection. "Do I have *whipped* written across my forehead?"

"Nothing quite so crass," Arash responded, "but it was evident to me during dinner with Ms. Hart that you were smitten with her. And if I'm not mistaken, it was not one-sided. Was I wrong in my assessment?"

Grayson shook his head. "No, you're not. In fact, last night—"

Arash held up his hand. "No need to go any further. Your relationship went to the next level."

"It did."

"And? I would imagine you would be enjoying the lovely lady tonight instead of wanting to put her over your knee."

Grayson chuckled that Arash had remembered his turn of phrase. "You would think, but instead of enjoying each other, she's run for the hills, and I haven't seen or heard from her at all today."

"That's disconcerting."

"My point exactly!" Grayson said, pointing his index finger at Arash. "It's why I was headed to her apartment."

"To what?" Arash inquired. "Browbeat her back into your bed?"

Grayson glared at him. "Of course not. I would have used other methods." *Like seduction*, Grayson thought. He was sure it wouldn't take much. Once the match was struck, they'd burn the sheets as they'd done the night before.

"But of course."

The waiter came to the table with a bottle of Malbec and poured them each a glass. He left the bottle on the table.

Grayson was thankful that Arash knew his drink of choice and had already taken care of ordering it. "Salut, my friend," Arash said as he held up his glass.

"Salut." Once Grayson had taken a drink, he looked across the table at his dear friend. "So, do you have any advice for me?"

"I do."

"Care to share?"

"If you insist," Arash said and placed his glass back on the table. "I would suggest that you back off. Allow Bree to come to you. She's obviously a bit overwhelmed after you spent the evening together. Give her some time to process it, and when she's ready, she'll come."

"Are you of all people telling me to be patient? You've never been patient a day in your life, Arash. If there is something you want, you go after it. Same as me. It's why we get along so well, because we're so much alike. It's not in my nature to back off."

"Well then, you're in for a bumpy ride, Grayson. Not to mention you've complicated things by getting involved with Bree. What about your mission to bring down Duke Hart? How do you think Bree will feel when she finds out what you're planning, *been* planning to do to destroy her father?"

Grayson hadn't thought that far ahead. All he knew was that somehow Bree how gotten into his blood, and he couldn't focus without her entering his mind. He had to exorcise her and the only way he knew how to do that was to drown in her until he got enough. In the meantime, he wouldn't stop his quest to get justice for his father.

"The only thing I can say, Arash, is that Bree and I will burn up long before it gets to that point. It's just lust. Admittedly, it's the best sex I've ever had, but that's all it is, and after I get my fill, I'll move on."

"And you think it's going to be that easy?"

"Of course," Grayson responded, but even though he said the words, he wasn't sure he believed them. Bree was a special woman. She'd shown him last night that she *cared*, and he'd never thought he'd find a woman who wouldn't run skittish after discovering he was responsible for Cameron.

But Bree wasn't scared in the least by his brother. If anything, she was fearful of Grayson and the passion they'd shared. He would just have to convince her that they shared something worth exploring.

12

The following morning, back at work in the office, Bree was preoccupied. Instead of focusing on the reports on the monitor in front of her, she glanced down at her cellphone. There'd been several texts and missed calls from Grayson yesterday, but surprisingly that had been earlier during the day and afternoon. They'd stopped last night. Once again, he'd have to chase after her. She hadn't been playing hard to get, but she was still coming to terms about the night they'd spent together and what it all meant.

Was it just a one-nighter? Or was it supposed to be something more? Did he want it to be more? *Do I?* It was all just so confusing. She hadn't gone to Grayson's mansion with the intention of ending up in his bed. Just thinking about it made Bree remember how it had felt when he'd kissed her deeply, the touch of his hands on her breasts, the fill of him inside her.

Ring, ring, ring.

She glanced down at her cellphone and saw that Addison was calling. "Hey, girl," Bree said when she answered.

"Hello, stranger," Addison replied. "How've you been?"

"Real good. Just been busy with my new place and new job and all. How are you? How's the baby?"

"The baby and I are fine. In fact, we're hungry and we'd like to take you out for lunch if you're free."

Bree used her mouse to scroll to her calendar on her computer screen. "I'm free. Where shall I meet you?"

An hour later, Bree saw Addison walking toward the entrance of the bistro Addison had chosen. Her cousin-in-law's stomach had certainly grown since Bree had last seen her, but she'd never looked more radiant.

"Addy, you're looking well." After a quick hug and kiss, they sat down.

Addison shrugged. "You're being kind because I look like a beached whale, but thank you. I'll take any compliments that I can get." She rubbed her swollen belly. "It's just that I can't stop eating." She reached for the menu stuck in the napkin holder.

Bree smiled at Addison and let the moment pass. She'd gotten up early and gone for a morning run on the treadmill in the gym that came with her apartment. She'd hoped the exercise would clear her mind, but it hadn't. Grayson was still first and foremost on it, just like he'd been when she'd drifted off to sleep the previous evening. As she sat in front of Addison, she was reliving images of him sucking on her breasts and remembering her cries of pleasure.

"Bree," Addison called out to her, interrupting her lascivious thoughts. "Are you okay? You look like you were a thousand miles away."

Bree gave a half-hearted smile. "I'm fine. Just a little preoccupied I suppose." She began reading the selections on the lunch menu.

"With work or your *boss*?"

Bree's head immediately popped up. "Excuse me?"

"If I'm not mistaken, you were attracted to the man *before* you accepted the job offer. I can only imagine that's increased now that you're spending time with him. I would think that his effect hasn't lessened and has probably gotten stronger. Am I wrong?" Addison motioned to the waitress to come to their table.

How did Addison know? Was she a mind reader? Was it that obvious that she was in a quagmire with Grayson? "Wow! I didn't realize I was so easy to read."

"You wear your heart on your sleeve, Bree. And you say what you feel and so yes, I suppose it makes you easier to read than most. But you haven't answered my question."

A waitress came and took their drink and lunch orders. "You're not wrong. It has only strengthened."

Addison peered across the table, assessing Bree. "Do you want to talk about it?"

Bree nodded. She'd wanted to talk about it with someone. Normally, she would call Jada or even London, but she'd been avoiding most of her family because she wasn't sure if they were on her side or Duke's. So Addison's timing was perfect.

"We slept together." Bree dropped the bomb and left the words dangling in the air.

The waitress came back with the water for the table, and Addison immediately grabbed hers off her tray and gulped the entire thing before placing the empty glass down. "I'll just get you a new one," the waitress said and scuttled away.

"Alright," Addison said once she'd taken a breath. "You wanna take it from the top?"

Bree smiled. "There's not much to say. We've been circling each other for a while now and last night, it culminated with us having sex."

"Well, did you enjoy it, because from the way you're acting, I can't quite tell."

"Yeah, I did. Perhaps a little too much." Bree leaned across the table and whispered. "I've never been that, that uninhibited before."

Addison smiled. "Sometimes it just takes the right man. I mean with Caleb and I, he was the one, you know?"

"I thought I knew great sex," Bree commented, leaning back in her chair, "but this was different."

"How so?"

"I don't know. I can't put my finger on it, but it scared me enough to avoid him the last twenty-four hours."

"Wait, isn't it usually the other way around, with men avoiding us?" Or so Addison had heard from her best friend, single gal Collette.

"Sure is," Bree said, chuckling. "And he's not too pleased with me." She had the texts to prove it. She'd half-expected him to show up at her place last night. So when that hadn't happened, it had been somewhat of a shocker. He usually came on so hard.

"Perhaps you should talk to him so you can figure things out rather than hide."

"Figure what out? If it was a one-night stand? If we're to carry on an affair?"

Addison shrugged. "It's whatever you want, Bree. That's if you even know what you want. Do you?"

That was the million-dollar question. She didn't know what she wanted. On the one hand, she wanted to spend another night of bliss in Grayson's arms, but on the other hand, a relationship between them would complicate her work life when it inevitably ended. And she was just getting started at Wells Oil. She didn't want an affair with Grayson to derail the progress she'd made in striking out on her own away from Duke.

"Honestly? I'm not sure what I want, Addison."

The waitress returned with their lunch entrees, and they began digging in while they pondered Bree's comment. A part of Bree wanted to throw caution to the wind and dive in headlong with Grayson with no thought for tomorrow. It would be great to be the fearless Bree she'd been at seventeen before Duke had stifled her independence.

But that girl was gone. And in her place was a woman with ambition. She didn't want that woman to fade away either. So how did she bridge the gap with returning to the girl she'd once been while retaining her drive?

"I think you're making the right decision to avoid him," Addison said as she stopped eating long enough to resume the conversation. "Until you figure out what you want, you might do more harm than good."

"Thanks, Addison."

"But can I give you a piece of advice?"

"Sure."

"I would figure it out soon, because if Grayson is the alpha male you've indicated he is, he will come after you."

Bree nodded. She was certain that it was only a matter of time before her luck ran out and she'd have to face the man.

~

"This is great, Levi," Grayson said as he read through the paper he'd just delivered. "How did you get your hands on Hart Enterprises's offer?"

"I have my ways."

Grayson grinned. This was the closest he'd come to finally giving Duke Hart some of the payback he so richly deserved. He was looking forward to the day he'd stare Duke in the face and tell him everything he'd done to ensure his downfall. Then Grayson would tell him who he was and see if he recognized that Grayson was the son of the man he'd swindled out of land that was rightfully his all those years ago.

"Really good work," Grayson said, closing his folder.

"Sure thing, boss. Would you like me to draft a counteroffer up?"

Grayson nodded.

"I've also found that the contract HE has with their oil tanker company is coming up for renewal."

"And?" Grayson asked.

"It's with Brooke Jenkins."

"The guy who offered me a favor if I agreed to not take his precious yacht during a high-stakes poker match about a year ago?"

"The very same." Levi had been with Grayson during that game. He'd watched Grayson clean house on several influential businessmen in Dallas. Grayson had walked away with an expensive car and a rare painting; but the favor Brooke had offered had been unusual, and Grayson had felt it could be useful in the future.

Grayson had never taken him up on that favor, but now the time had come to do so.

"Set up a meeting with him."

"I'm on it."

After Levi left, Grayson leaned back in his chair and pondered the situation before him. This unexpected gift was the best part of his day, but he hoped it was going to get better.

Last night, he'd taken Arash's advice and rather than go to Bree's apartment and confront her, he'd played it cool. If she wanted him, she'd have to come for him. He was done with chasing her, or at least he was for now. He knew how good it had been between them, and so did she.

It was why she was running scared. She was going to have to choose to face it. He suspected he knew her answer. He would just have to be patient until she came around to the same conclusion.

BREE DIDN'T REALIZE she was walking toward Grayson's office later that afternoon until she was standing outside of it. It was after five p.m., and Rosalie had already left for the day. This would give them some privacy, but not too much as several executives were still working late.

Addison had been right: Grayson may have given her a reprieve, but it wouldn't be for long. He would make another play for her. Wouldn't it be better if *she* cleared the air between them? She'd decided that the night they'd shared, although memorable and the best she'd ever had, should remain just that, one night. She couldn't afford to get involved with him and muddy the professional waters any further.

Raising her arm, she knocked.

"Come in." His deep masculine voice echoed through the set of oak doors.

Taking a deep breath, Bree opened one of the doors. Grayson glanced up, and his eyes registered surprise to see her standing in his doorway.

"Are you going to stand there, or are you coming

in?" he asked as if bored by her indecision. She answered him by slamming the door behind her.

When she faced him, he was smiling. He'd gotten to her, and he knew it. "Bree."

"Grayson." She walked toward the massive glass desk he sat behind. He looked very formidable, and she knew he'd chosen it to intimidate people. But he hadn't been like that with her when it was just the two of them. He'd been soft and tender when she needed it, and fierce and frenzied when she wanted it.

"Yes?" He stared at her intently, and Bree was flattered *and* disturbed. He looked at her as though she were the most interesting thing in the universe.

She glanced up at the question in his tone. "I'm sorry for not returning your texts or calls yesterday."

His eyes narrowed. "Is that really what you came to tell me?" He rose from his seat and reached behind him for his suit jacket. She watched him swing his arms into both sides and admired how it fit him to a tee. "Because if so, you could have sent me an email."

He moved away from the desk, but instead of coming toward her as she'd thought, he was heading for his doors.

"Wait!" Bree shouted.

Grayson spun around. "For what? I won't play these games with you anymore, Bree." Grayson's dark eyes were squarely focused on hers, and the intensity in them scared her. "If you want to act like what we shared in my bed was a fluke, that's your deal, but you and I know otherwise."

"Which is?"

Bree regretted the question almost immediately because Grayson reached her in nearly two steps and grasped her arms in his large hands. Then his gaze peered down to her lips, and Bree could feel her insides quivering at his searing look. "So you need me to remind you how good it was between us? How I had you crying out my name when I was buried deep inside you? Or how about when you came all over my face, and I lapped up your juices?"

Bree colored immediately at his brazen words and at the memories they evoked. He was right. She had pleaded with him to take her. She moistened her lips with her tongue, and Grayson's eyes followed her actions.

"Or how about I show you?" he said, pulling her roughly into his arms. His lips raided hers in a passionate kiss that took her breath away. She had no choice but to give herself over to it and wind her arms around his neck to keep from falling.

Then he was moving his mouth from hers to rain a path of feather-light kisses on her face, her throat, and back to her lips while his hands freely roamed her body. Her breasts screamed for his touch, and he didn't disappoint. He sought them out, molding and kneading them until her nipples turned into hard peaks. Soon she felt his hands on her backside as he kneaded and squeezed her cheeks. She made room for him so he could settle himself between her thighs.

She loved the sensation of Grayson's hands, and she began rubbing against him. His erection grew bigger, thicker in his slacks, and Bree heard him mutter an oath as he walked her backward toward a couch.

"We shouldn't," Bree began, but Grayson silenced her.

"But we will," he said. "You want this as much as I do, Bree. You're on fire like I am and the sooner you admit it, the easier it'll be on the both of us."

It was true. Bree was hot and wet and desperate for him to fill her and answer the terrible ache she'd felt since she'd left him yesterday morning. She'd tried to ignore it, silence it, push down her feelings, but they kept bubbling up to the surface. Now she was forced to confront them.

"Yes, dammit," Bree whispered. "I want you! Are you happy now?"

A self-satisfying smirk came across Grayson's face as he looked down at her. "No, not yet," he murmured, "but I will be once I'm buried inside you."

"Oh!" He cut off her sigh with a kiss and by parting her lips with his tongue. He took her mouth as if she belonged to him. He began kissing her slowly, coaxing a response from her.

Then he deftly undressed her, not roughly, but expertly as he touched and caressed her naked flesh. Eventually, she was lying on the couch completely naked and quietly crying out his name. But he didn't take her. Not quickly at first as she would have liked.

Instead, he locked his doors and undressed himself. Then he rolled on a condom, joined her naked on the couch, and entwined their bodies. He seemed to know exactly where to touch her, kiss her, and taste her to make her feel so much. Bree didn't know if she could handle the deep need that was so overwhelming, but she knew she couldn't deny it or him any longer.

Grayson's cunning fingers ran a course. First he paid homage to her breasts before traveling tantalizingly south to reach between her thighs. When he discovered that she was wet and hungry for him, he stayed there, dragging a response from her with his fingers. Then he lowered his lips to her and caused havoc with his swirling tongue as he excited every nerve in her body, so much so that she began pleading with him to take her.

He thrust hard, entering her damp heat with a wildness he hadn't had before. It was as if he too was lost in sensation. He grasped her hips, and Bree sighed in pleasure as he hit just the right spot that no other man had ever seemed to find. But this afternoon, Grayson was finding it time and time again.

"Grayson!" Her insides clenched as she was overcome with pleasure.

"Yes, baby," he crooned as she arched to meet his thrust. "Take me," she said. He plunged in again. This time deeper and harder until he filled her completely.

Bree could feel Grayson as he sank far inside her, circling his hips. He leaned his forehead against hers as he gyrated. Bree didn't think it was possible, but she could feel pressure building inside her again. He took her higher and higher until eventually they both came together in a blaze of glory.

Afterward, they lay in each other's arms, and Bree tried to catch her breath as Grayson reached for a throw blanket lying on the back of the couch. He threw it across them. What had just happened? She'd come into Grayson's office to tell him they shouldn't see each other, that it would get too complicated because of their working relationship. Instead, she'd ended up naked on his couch with Grayson giving her another mind-spinning orgasm!

~

GRAYSON WIPED Bree's dampened curls away from her face to peer at her. "Are you okay?" he asked.

He'd been thrilled to see her when she'd walked into his office, but then she'd maddeningly been about to brush aside the amazing night they'd shared together and he'd seen stars. He hadn't meant to dominate or seduce her into his way of thinking. He'd wanted her to come to him, but she'd been about to tell him there was no chance for them.

And he couldn't, *wouldn't* accept that.

"I'm, I'm fine," Bree said, and he could see she was shell-shocked. Same as he was.

Grayson hadn't thought it possible that it would be better than before, but Bree was fast becoming an addiction he couldn't live without.

"I know you didn't come here with this in mind," he started.

Bree's voice was a whisper, but he heard her say, "No, I didn't."

Rising, he leaned his forehead on hers. "You were going to tell me you didn't want to see me other than in the professional capacity?"

When he lifted his head, her eyes were large as they looked up at him. "How did you know?"

He shrugged. "You've been hiding from me for the better part of two days. The handwriting was on the wall."

Bree sat upright, clutching the blanket to her chest. "I guess my plan got blown to hell."

"What are you so afraid of, Bree?"

If he had to answer, it would be the intensity of every time they were together. It was as if he'd come home, but that couldn't be. Bree couldn't be the woman, *that* woman. The *one*. She couldn't, because her father symbolized everything Grayson hated.

It was just lust, a physiological thing.

It would burn out. It *had* to burn out. Grayson's stomach twisted in knots at the thought.

Bree bunched her knees to her chest in a defensive position that Grayson automatically hated. "This is messy, Grayson," Bree said. "You know that. How can this," she said, pointing with her index finger between then, "work? You've hired me to do a job for you that I happen to enjoy, and I don't want this to confuse that relationship. Hell, you gave me a seat on your board. That means something to me, and I—"

Her voice cracked, and he scooted closer to her and wrapped his arms around her despite her protests. "It's okay, Bree. No matter what happens between us, your job isn't in jeopardy. We have a contract."

"Contracts can be broken."

He lifted her chin to look up at him. "Then you have my word that there will always be a job for you here, no matter what happens between us."

"There isn't an 'us.'"

"I beg to differ," Grayson responded hotly. "Hasn't this afternoon shown you just how strong the connection between us is? It's undeniable." Grayson's heart fluttered when he uttered those words. *Damn*, he admitted to himself, *this is more than lust*. "I want you to stop fighting it, Bree. Give into it. Give into me. Because if not, I'm going to wear you down until you do."

"Why?" Bree asked. Her large brown eyes spoke to his soul, and his heart turned over in his chest.

"Because I burn for you."

"Grayson."

He reached behind her, grasped her neck, and pulled her toward his waiting lips, brushing them softly across hers. "Give into me." He kissed her again, this time softer and more tenderly than he had before. "Give into me," he repeated.

He leaned back on the couch and made love to her for the second time that afternoon.

13

"Well, if it isn't my long-lost sister," Jada said when Bree called her the next day.

Bree knew she was in the doghouse, and it was time she got her groveling over with. "I'm sorry, Jada."

"For what exactly? For keeping me and London at arm's length? Or the entire family? I just want to be sure what you're groveling for."

"All of it," Bree said. "All I can say in my defense is that I needed to strike out on my own."

"Without our help?"

Bree heard the hurt in Jada's voice. They'd always been close, but she had needed this time apart. "I know this may be hard for you to realize, but I've felt like Daddy's puppet for a while now," Bree began.

"You have?"

"Our father has always been a force to be reckoned with, you know that. And it just seemed liked he had a say in all aspects of my life, from my love life to my professional life. And living under the same roof only seemed to make it worse."

"Why didn't you ever say anything?"

"Because," she said, and the word lingered. She picked up, "Maybe I enabled him, because deep down

I thought we were kindred spirits and that I was the son he never had. So when he gave Hart Enterprises to Caleb, it's like something in me died. And it died a little bit each day. Instead of talking about it, I internalized it. I forced down the hurt, until one day, I didn't even recognize myself anymore. It was then I knew I had to get out or be swallowed up whole."

"Bree, I never realized you felt that way."

"I've been good at hiding it, but no more. I used to be fearless, Jada. And somewhere along the way, I'd forgotten that girl. And I wanted her back, and I think she's slowly starting to come back to life."

"At Wells Oil?"

"Yes."

"With Grayson Wells?"

Bree thought about yesterday when she and Grayson had made love in his office. They'd christened his couch, not once or twice, but three times because he'd leaned her over the side and taken her from behind. Her breasts had filled one of his hands as the lower half of his body had pounded into hers while his free hand had stroked her clitoris until she'd broken apart in his arms. Bree still blushed at the memory of how incredible their lovemaking had been.

"Bree?"

She realized Jada was still speaking to her. "What?"

"I asked you about Grayson Wells and you became silent. What the hell is going on in Dallas?" Jada wondered aloud. "I think it's time I came for a visit."

"Jada, that's not necessary."

"I know it's not," Jada responded smartly, "but I have to come anyway for the Crystal Charity Ball. We go every year."

"Oh yes, of course." Bree didn't exactly relish getting dressed up. She'd much rather be in her jeans with a tub of Ben and Jerry's in front of the television. Or curled up in Grayson's bed.

"You haven't forgotten, have you? It's a Hart family tradition."

"Of course I haven't forgotten."

"So I'll see you in about five days?" Jada asked.

"Yes, I'll be here."

"Will you stay overnight at the ranch so we can go together as a family?"

Bree rolled her eyes. "You realize this is emotional blackmail."

"I'll use whatever methods I can to make sure I bridge the gap between you and the family."

"It's not that bad," Bree said. "I stopped by and went out riding with Daddy."

"For a couple of hours without even staying for dinner."

"What the hell? Is he reporting back to you about his thankless daughter?"

"No, he just misses you, Bree, as we all do," Jada said.

"Well, I'll see you soon." Bree quickly ended the call. She didn't appreciate the guilt-trip. She was entitled to live her life.

Her phone rang again. She picked it up and began speaking without bothering to see who was calling. "Listen, Jada. Enough is enough. I told you I'll be there for the family, and I will be."

~

GRAYSON SMILED from the other end of the line. So Bree had a beef with another member of the Hart family? He hadn't realized that her leaving HE would have such a ripple effect, but he didn't mind it at all. It's what Duke Hart so richly deserved after mistreating his father. "It's not Jada," he said, interrupting her tirade.

"Grayson, oh I'm sorry. I thought you were my sister calling again to give me grief."

"I'm calling because I want to see you again."

Silence.

Grayson sighed. He'd hoped that their frantic coupling yesterday had shown progress, though he sensed she was embarrassed by her uncharacteristic passionate behavior. He liked that he brought out her sensual side and that she wanted him, *whenever, wherever.*

He wasn't going to run away from his feelings. He decided to tackle them head on, which is why he'd called her this Saturday morning. "I haven't taken you out on a proper date," Grayson said, "and I'd like to rectify that."

It had occurred to him that he'd never really asked Bree out on a real date other than to dinner at his mansion.

"A date?"

He heard the smile in her voice, and he was pleased.

"So, what do you say?"

"I'd love to," she answered without hesitation.

Finally, they were making progress. "Great. I'll pick you in two hours, at eleven a.m."

"Eleven? That's kind of early for a date. Where are we going?"

"Leave that up to me. Just be ready when I pick you up and bring an overnight bag." He didn't intend on spending the night alone.

~

BREE WAS EXCITED about the day ahead and the romance it promised. She wanted to be sexy, yet casual, so she put on an orange maxi skirt, white tank top, a jean jacket, and her favorite weathered cowboy boots. She added some dangling earrings and a necklace for a touch of sass along with some perfume at her earlobes and wrists.

She couldn't wait to find out what Grayson was cooking up his sleeve. He was right when he'd said they hadn't been on a real date, and now they were going to a mystery destination that required her to bring an overnight bag. She'd packed a couple of outfit changes, which included a dress and some lingerie she'd bought on an excursion with Jada a few months ago. Would she wear the sexy teddy tonight for Grayson?

Butterflies flapped around in Bree's stomach. This was a new step for them. She wasn't sure what it meant. Were they dating? Exclusive? Friends with benefits? She was driving herself crazy wondering what Grayson's true motives were. She knew hers: She was developing feelings for him. Strong feelings that bordered on love, but she wasn't ready to label them as such. Instead, she would live in the moment and enjoy what he had to offer as she'd done in his office.

She'd never imagined she could be that carefree when it came to sex, but it had only taken the right person to bring out her sexuality. Grayson was that man. She was craving him. His lips. His hands. His mouth. His . . .

The bell sounded, and Bree rushed toward the door. Grayson was leaning against the doorway in jeans and a V-neck sweater. He looked equal parts sophistication and sex appeal. "Good morning, beautiful."

Bree couldn't resist returning the grin with one of her own. "Good morning."

"Is that your bag?" Grayson's head inclined toward her carry-on suitcase sitting near the door.

"Yes, it is."

"Good." He leaned in, picked up the suitcase, and reached for her hand. "Ready to go?"

As much as she'd ever be. "Yes."

Bree was elated that it was just the two of them when they arrived at the valet area of her building. Grayson would be driving her in style in his Porsche convertible, one of his many cars. After putting her bag in the trunk, he opened her door, and she sunk into the car's luxe interior.

Grayson slid in beside her and revved up the engine.

They drove in silence for several minutes before Bree ventured to ask about their destination. "Care to fill me in now on where we're going?"

"Can't you just wait and see?"

"No, I want to know now."

He chuckled. "You know you sound like a little kid who wants to see their toys *before* Christmas."

"That was me." Bree laughed. "I was always energetic and lively and into anything and everything. Drove my mother crazy. Meanwhile, my sister Jada would play quietly with her dolls."

Grayson glanced at her sideways. "I can see that about you."

"I was very much a tomboy," Bree volunteered. "I wanted to climb trees like the boys, go hunting with my dad. I wanted to do everything I saw my cousins Noah and Caleb doing."

"Did you see them a lot?"

Bree nodded. "We would always take road trips to Phoenix to see my Aunt Madelyn and Uncle Isaac. We would sing songs and camp out. Those were some of the best times of my childhood." She remembered fondly the moments when it had been Duke, her mother, and Jada, and occasionally London if her grandparents permitted. "I loved going to my Aunt Madelyn's dude ranch, Golden Oaks, because there was always something fun to do. They catered to their guests. We could go skeet shooting, hay riding, or on an airboat."

"But not here at home?"

Bree nodded. "The Hart ranch has always been a working cattle ranch first and foremost. The oil came after. So we didn't have the same activities like Golden Oaks."

"But your family was together. That's the most important thing."

"We were for a little while," Bree said wistfully. She could recall overhearing Duke and her mother arguing about his infidelity with Trent's mother. The rift had caused the end to the happy family life Bree had always known.

Grayson glanced at her. "I'm sorry if I hit a nerve. I didn't mean to bring up a bad time for you."

Bree shrugged. "You didn't. Divorces happen every day, and I'm not the only child to experience it."

"But that doesn't mean your experiences don't count. You're entitled to those feelings."

"Thank you." She wanted to say more but saw they were heading into the airport. She turned to Grayson. "You didn't mention anything about a plane ride."

He smiled mischievously. "I know, but it's not a long flight. We'll be at our destination in less than an hour." At her frown, he added, "Trust me, you'll like my surprise."

Soon they were exiting the Porsche and climbing the stairs to Grayson's private jet. It was spacious, carpeted, and easily sat six on the soft leather sofas with cup holders. While Grayson spoke with the pilot, Bree made herself comfortable. She found a small fridge in the rear of the cabin. It was stocked with supplies. She pulled out two Evians for her and Grayson before taking a seat.

When Grayson joined her, she handed him a bottle. "Hope you don't mind. I familiarized myself."

"Not at all." Instead of sitting beside her, he sat across from her, his gaze pinned to her face. "I'm glad you did."

Bree unscrewed the cap of the Evian and drank liberally. Suddenly, she felt very thirsty given the hungry look Grayson was shooting her. Immediately, she began thinking about becoming a member of the Mile High Club. She glanced behind him at the tiny restroom on board and blushed. Her eyes flew to Grayson's, and he smirked. She wondered if he knew what she'd been thinking.

She reminded herself that she knew very little about the man. This trip would give her the chance to delve deeper, so she picked up where their conversation in the car had left off. "So," she started tentatively, "I've told you what my childhood was like. What was yours like?"

Grayson stiffened, sitting upright in his seat. He hadn't been expecting this line of questioning. He'd hoped once they'd left the car that anymore trips down memory lane were done. He didn't want a repeat of how upset Bree had become earlier at the memory of her parents' divorce. He didn't relish going down that rabbit hole, but he also didn't want her to think he was withholding information. And if he knew Bree, it would be just another reason for her to pull away from him. He didn't want that.

He'd rather focus on her. She was beautiful. And today was no exception. Her clingy tank top dipped low enough to show the swell of her enticing breasts that easily filled his palms. And he'd like nothing better than to lift her maxi skirt and make her straddle him so his fingers could wander underneath and find paradise. Instead, he had to talk about the past. A past that was filled with minefields. He would share as much as he could without giving away too much information in case Duke had spoken of his father, Elijah Williams.

"It wasn't easy," Grayson started. He had to choose his words carefully. He couldn't give away too much just in case Duke had shared his history with his daughter.

Bree was silent as she waited for him to expound upon his childhood.

"It's been my mother, Cameron, Sonya, and me for quite some time," Grayson offered. "My mother was a single parent raising me and Cameron, which as you can imagine wasn't easy. Back then, many people didn't understand special-needs children. They just wanted to put a label on him or lock him away."

"I can only imagine." Warmth filled Bree's words, and Grayson knew she somehow understood.

"Kids picked on him, made fun of him," Grayson continued. "I stood up for him, of course, and got in a lot of fights in the process until eventually the principal told my mother that Cameron was too much to handle and would need to be schooled at home or in a special facility. That's when she hired Sonya. Sonya's been a godsend. She's been in Cameron's life since he was seven years old. She was a second mother to him when my mother wasn't able to be around, which was often back then."

"I can see how much she cares for him," Bree said. "She was devastated when he went missing. It's why I had to try and help."

"You don't know how much I appreciated that." Of course he'd tried to show her in every way imaginable when they'd made love that night. There was no place he hadn't kissed, touched, licked.

"What about your father?" Bree asked. "Where was he in all this?"

Grayson shrugged. "He was in the picture until I was twelve, but he had a gambling problem and ran off when the bills began to pile up. He left my mother all alone to fend off the creditors."

Grayson couldn't contain the bitterness that came through his recollection. He both hated the man and wanted revenge for him against the man who stole what should have been his. Perhaps if Elijah Williams had had the land and money due him, he wouldn't have abandoned their family, gambled, and drunk himself to death.

"That's terrible, Grayson." Bree sat forward in her seat. "How did your mother survive?"

"Working herself to death day and night. She was a teacher during the day and cleaned hotels at night. She took whatever extra shifts she could just so she could keep a roof over our heads. She couldn't even pay Sonya. Sonya was an older single woman who'd left an abusive marriage. She didn't have much, so when my mother offered her room and board, she was grateful for it."

"Sounds like you guys needed each other."

Grayson nodded. "Sonya was a lifesaver for us and vice versa. I'm sorry I don't have any fun road trip stories or singing Christmas carols in front of the fireplace memories. Life was hard, and we struggled sometimes to make ends meet and put food on the table."

"But here you are now. How'd you do it?"

"I had a knack for numbers and apparently my father's knack for gambling, except unlike him, I know when to quit."

Bree was silent as she sat back and observed Grayson. He wondered what she was thinking or what she made of him. Did she get that he was an all-around hustler and gambler? If she did, would she want to run in the opposite direction? Well, he wasn't going to let her. He liked her too much. He liked her more than he bargained for, and she'd certainly complicated his revenge plot against her father. What was he going to do?

14

A car and driver were waiting for them when their jet arrived at the Austin airport. The driver placed their overnight bags in the trunk while Bree and Grayson settled into the backseat for parts unknown.

It wasn't until they were riding on the freeway that Grayson finally shared their destination. "I guess I can tell you where we're going."

"Please," Bree said, antsy in her seat. "I'm dying with anticipation."

Grayson playfully tapped her nose with his index finger. "I don't know if you know, but the Texas Hill countryside has some great wineries. So I thought we'd go on a wine tasting expedition, thus the driver." He inclined his head toward the driver's seat.

"Grayson! That sounds wonderful. Even though I lived in Austin, I was about my studies back then. I had no idea they had wineries."

"Not many people do," Grayson replied. "But I won shares in a vineyard during a poker match, so I thought we'd check out a few along the way."

Bree reached for his hand. "I love it. Thank you."

She leaned over and was about to kiss him on the cheek, but Grayson turned his head and her lips landed squarely on his.

Then it was Grayson taking charge, turning to face her and wrapping his arm around her middle to pull her closer. His lips grazed hers and ignited a fire. Bree felt her breasts tingle in awareness, and her nipples turned into bullets. Heat began to unfurl low in the apex of her thighs when Grayson's tongue flicked over her lips, seeking entry into her mouth. She gave in to him as the feverish rise of passion began to take over her as it always did whenever she was near him.

She surrendered her mouth eagerly, excitement escalating through her as he kissed her with everything he had. He invaded her mouth, taking and possessing her, and Bree lost herself. She was completely and utterly consumed by this man and her response to him. It was real and powerful.

Bree slid her hands lower between his thighs and felt the hard ridge of his erection in his jeans. She wanted him now.

If the car hadn't come to a stop, she would have slid on top of his lap and begged him to take her. It was Grayson who tore his mouth from her lips and pressed his forehead to hers. "Damn, Bree," he uttered harshly. "You can't kiss me like that and expect me to stop."

She smiled knowingly. "You kissed me back."

"Yeah, I did, but I need time to savor you properly. That's going to take more than a few minutes. It's going to take hours or longer."

Bree pulled away and stared down into his dark eyes. They were cloudy and hooded. She believed Grayson would make good on every word of what he'd said, but not now. They had just arrived at the winery.

The driver came around to open their door and Bree exited first, giving Grayson time to collect himself before joining her.

"I thought this place should be our first stop," Grayson said, "as they have a great trattoria, and I figured we'd work up an appetite."

"Great minds think alike," Bree responded, "because I'm starting to get a bit hungry."

Bree enjoyed the Old World experience at the first vineyard. Nestled under a canopy of oaks, the vineyard was reminiscent of the hills of Italy. Bree had visited there for two weeks one summer with Jada. Duke hadn't wanted them to, but Jada had sweet-talked him into letting them go.

While Bree walked around the grounds, Grayson took care of the arrangements. He came back several minutes later to give her the rundown. "We're going to go on the tram for a short ride first so you can see their working vineyards and state-of-the-art production complex. Then we'll sample some wines directly and finish off with lunch. How's that sound?"

"Absolutely wonderful."

They boarded the tram along with several other guests for a scenic ride through the vines. They stopped first at the crush pad before heading to the tank room to see how the wine was made.

"This is where it all happens!" the guide told them.

Next, they visited the winery's barrel room and cellar, and the guide let them taste and contrast the flavors and aromas of each wine aging directly from three oak barrels.

When the tour was over, the owner of the winery, Tom Stone, came over and shook hands with Grayson. "I'm glad you were finally able to come here, Grayson," the older blond gentleman said.

"I thought it was time," Grayson said. "Tom, I'd like you to meet my girlfriend, Bree Hart." He placed his palm on the small of her back and pressed her forward. "Bree, this is Tom Stone."

Bree forced herself to keep her mouth closed and move forward to shake Tom's hand. Had Grayson just called her his *girlfriend*? Surely, she had misheard him. Did he mean it? Or did he not know what else to call her under the circumstances?

"Pleasure to meet you, Bree." Tom offered her his hand.

Bree shook it. "Thank you for having us. You've a lovely vineyard."

"Thank you. We sure do love and take a pride in our family-run establishment."

"It shows," Grayson said, circling one arm around Bree's waist.

"I've set up a private tasting for you as requested," Tom said, "so please follow me to one of our Tuscan Meets Modern tasting rooms." He led them to a private room where a table for two had been set up along with selections of the vineyard's wine and various meats and cheeses.

"I'd like you to meet Manuel, your sommelier. He will go over the different wines with you. Please enjoy."

"Thank you," Bree and Grayson said almost in unison.

The sommelier walked them through the selections and they sipped wine and ate cheese. Bree liked the fruity wines while Grayson preferred the full-bodied, earthier ones. Eventually, the sommelier left them alone with a bottle of their favorite selection while he had a waiter bring their lunch over.

"I can't believe you arranged all this," Bree said, looking across the table.

"It was high time we had a proper date."

"And is this what you always do, whisk women away for daytrips?" Bree asked, sipping on her wine.

"Not every woman." Grayson was staring at her across the table. "Just you."

Bree swallowed and licked the droplet of wine that had escaped to her lips. Grayson caught the action, and his gaze darkened. She knew that look. He wanted to kiss her. And she was sure he would have if the waiter hadn't arrived at their table with several large platters filled with pasta.

"This looks delicious," Bree said as she glanced down.

"These are our most popular dishes that Tom wanted you to try," the waiter said. "It's linguine and clams in a white wine sauce and our famous ziti Pomodoro."

Grayson took over and began serving, giving Bree spoonfuls of each dish. "Enough." Bree halted him with her hand when her plate began overflowing.

"You need to eat," Grayson said. "Otherwise you won't make it to the second winery."

Bree did as she was told, but several times when she glanced up, she caught Grayson staring at her boldly. His desire for her was so evident that Bree's stomach somersaulted in anticipation of what was to come later that night.

While they sipped on wine and sampled the different pastas, Bree mentioned the upcoming charity event. "Have you ever heard of the Crystal Charity Ball?"

Grayson glanced up over his meal. "Yeah, it's some pretty big society event they have every year, right?"

Bree nodded. "My father's a big sponsor, and the entire family goes every year. It's been sort of a tradition."

"Oh yeah?"

Bree fidgeted nervously in her seat. She wanted to ask Grayson to come as her date. It would be a big deal because he would be meeting her entire family in one fell swoop. Was it too much? Should she wait for another time?

"Bree?"

Despite her nervous stomach, she asked the question. "Would you like to come?"

"As your date?" The smile Grayson gave her was genuine, and Bree released a long sigh of relief. He wasn't going to make this difficult for her.

She nodded. "Yes. But only if you don't have any plans."

"When is it?"

"Next Saturday. My sister Jada is flying in. And because it's my mother's favorite charity, she'll be in attendance as well."

"So I'll get a chance to meet your entire family?" Grayson inquired.

"Are you up to that?"

He reached out and grasped her hand. "I'm absolutely ready, and I'd love to attend with you."

Bree was giddy with excitement, but a bit nervous. He'd just called her his girlfriend today, and now he'd be meeting her entire family. This was huge.

"Relax." He squeezed her hand. "Everything will be fine."

Once they'd finished lunch, they returned to the limo and the driver took them to yet another winery. And this time, Grayson and Bree walked through the vines and ate grapes right off them.

By the end of the day, Bree was slightly intoxicated and dozed against Grayson's chest as they made their way in the limo to God knows where. She was sure they were staying someplace locally, but for once she didn't care. Grayson would make sure they were taken care of in style.

When she awoke, he was stroking her cheek. "We're here, babe."

"Here?" Bree wiped the sleep from her eyes and glanced out the car window. "Where's here?"

"The Driskill Hotel. Ever heard of it?"

"No." But Bree soon discovered that Grayson had thought of every detail. When you looked in the dictionary, the word "opulent" would be used to describe this hotel built in 1886. The inside was breathtaking with its magnificent columns, marble floors, and stained-glass dome.

Grayson had gone a step further and arranged for them to have the Renaissance bridal suite. Bree stood immobile in the same place after the porter had dropped off their bags in their room. She'd been exposed to the finer things in life, but not like this. The palette of the suite was nothing short of regal with sumptuous gold fabrics, hardwood floors, and a tremendously large king-sized bed.

She glanced at Grayson, but he wasn't fazed and was looking at his phone. "Is everything okay?" she asked when his brow furrowed.

He glanced in her direction. "Yes, I'm fine. Just checking in on Cameron and my mother. Sonya says Mother had a bad day. Sometimes the chemo takes a toll on her."

"If we need to go—" Bree began, but Grayson cut her off.

"No, we're fine." He slid his phone back in his

pocket. "This night is for us and no one else. Come." He held his hand out to her. "I want you to see the bathroom."

Bree was ill-prepared for the stunning marble-clad bathroom with a rain shower and his-and-her rain dual vanities with crystal water faucets. But the main attraction was the oversized whirlpool tub. It was filled with bubbles and rose petals, and a bucket of champagne was chilling alongside it.

Bree turned to face Grayson. "When did you do all this?"

"I reserved the hotel a couple of days ago. I ran the bath while you were sleeping in the limo."

"How long was I out?"

"Not long." He smiled as he walked toward her. "But I thought you might need to soak after a tiring day."

Grayson slipped the jean jacket off her shoulders and let it fall to the floor. And before she could protest, he was sliding her maxi skirt to the floor as well. When she felt his hands at the hem of her tank top, she lifted her arms so he could toss it over his shoulder until she was standing in nothing but her bra and panties. The raw desire in his eyes shook Bree to the core.

His eyes darkened, and he reached behind her to unclasp her bra so it fell in a heap with the rest of her clothes. Then he hooked his fingers in the waistband of her bikini panties and slid them down her legs, lowering himself to his knees as she stepped out of them. Then he tipped Bree backward until her backside touched the marble tub.

"Spread your legs," Grayson ordered.

Bree did as she was instructed, somewhat stunned

and definitely excited that Grayson had stripped her naked. Then all she could do was feel. Her head flew back as Grayson's fingers and thumb grazed at the apex of her womanhood. Her belly tightened as he slid one finger inside her and began stroking her in and out.

"You're so wet," he murmured silkily against her thigh.

"Oh God!" A gasp wrenched from her parted lips when a second finger joined the first and he began thrusting inside her more urgently. As he did so, he watched her undulate against his searching fingers, and she nearly came apart when he placed his mouth on her womanhood and simultaneously darted his tongue in and out while his fingers mimicked the same movements, opening her up completely to his assault.

"Gr-Grayson!" she moaned and pleaded, but he just continued teasing and licking her with gentle flicks of his tongue and hard strokes with his fingers. The hard and soft motions were driving her crazy. She wanted Grayson inside her, but he was taking his time enjoying her.

Bree could feel her breath quickening and pressure building until her orgasm finally hit her with such full force that her thighs began to shake and clasp around Grayson's head.

"Easy, baby," he whispered as he moved from between her thighs. He licked his lips as if he'd just had the best meal of his life. Then he helped Bree into the water. She felt so languid, she had to force herself to remain upright. But then Grayson began to remove his clothes, one piece at a time, and she watched him eagerly as she waited for the next article of clothing to be removed. Grayson had a perfect body, beautifully toned and perfectly proportioned. He was any woman's dream come true.

And he was hers.

For how long, she didn't know. But he had called her his girlfriend. Surely that must mean something? As Grayson's briefs dropped to the floor and he put on a condom, joining her in the lavish whirlpool, Bree couldn't care less about the answer. She opened her arms to him and he swung her into his, planting her in his lap. He kissed her passionately. Bree had to suck in a deep breath when he finally relented.

He held her as his head lowered, and he took one sudsy nipple into his mouth and suckled on it hard. "Yes!" she screamed and began moving her naked bottom against his erection. Grayson was hard underneath her and she knew it had to be costing him, but he was determined that she would be thoroughly satisfied.

His hands were at the triangle of her curls yet again, sliding inside, making sure she was still wet. She was dripping for him. "Grayson, please," she murmured.

He lifted his head with a wicked grin. "Straddle me, Bree."

"Gladly," she said with a smile. She rose slightly, throwing one thigh and then the other over his and lowering herself onto his erection. Grayson slid easily inside her.

A perfect fit.

GRAYSON SLID his fingers through Bree's lush curls, and he kissed her with hungry intensity and moved her hips with the same sensuous motions as her mouth.

When he lifted his head, he said, "Have you noticed how well we fit together?"

Bree merely nodded, and he could see a myriad of emotions cross her face. Was she feeling as he was? That this woman was stripping away all his barriers, leaving him completely bare and open to her? Did she have any idea of the power she had over him?

She did, because her sweet slickness was sliding up and down as she impaled herself on him. Then she began moving over him with need and necessity, desperate to reach that plateau. She reached it first, tightening around his length. Grayson watched her face and saw it flush as her climax fluttered over her. He grasped her hips and began pounding upward, and a feral groan came from deep inside him as her spasming muscles caused his own release.

Bree fell forward, clutching his head to her breasts as she tried to catch her breath. But it was Grayson who was shattered. He was completely beguiled by this woman, and he was starting to care more for her than he ever had for any other. He hadn't intended on getting in this deep, but here he was. Today, it had felt natural calling her his girlfriend because that's what he wanted and it was the way he felt. But theirs was a course set for destruction.

He was still after her father, whom he would meet next week at the Crystal Charity Ball. He couldn't say no to the invitation. Besides, he wanted to meet the man who he held responsible for the dissolution of his family and pay him back tenfold. But if Bree ever found out the real reason he'd sought her out for a job at Wells Oil, she'd end their relationship. Grayson didn't want that. Bree was a special woman, and she'd come to mean more to him than he'd ever thought possible. Yet he didn't know how to get them out of the mess he'd made without one or both of them ending up with a broken heart.

15

Bree stared out from her apartment balcony as she waited excitedly for Jada to arrive. She couldn't stop thinking about the amazing weekend, hell, nearly a week, she'd just shared with Grayson, and she couldn't wait to tell Jada all about it.

After the amazing sex they'd had in the Driskill Hotel, the next day Grayson had arranged for them to have an en suite couples' massage. Bree had enjoyed the delicious strokes of the male masseur, but near the end of his ministrations, she'd noticed that the masseur's actions had taken a decisively less professional stance and had turned erotic.

He'd massaged her buttocks gently yet firmly before he slid up the inner parts of her legs and higher. When he reached the most feminine part of her, Bree had shot up, only to find Grayson had replaced the masseur with himself. He'd been massaging her the last ten minutes, and she hadn't even noticed.

"Lie back down," he'd said and proceeded to give her the most sensuous and erotic massage she'd ever had in her life.

Bree rolled her eyes and tried to focus on her sister's visit, but her mind drifted to another memory of Grayson, to a couple of days ago when he had arranged for them to have dinner at Reunion Tower after their return from their trip. To her delight, they had the entire restaurant to themselves to look out over Dallas. Then they'd gone back to her place, and they'd made love.

Afterward, they'd talked about their relationship. He'd called her his girlfriend again, but they'd never discussed if they were exclusive. Grayson seemed genuinely surprised by her question.

"Yes," he'd said, "at least I am. Are you?"

"Absolutely," Bree had cried, curling her arms around his neck and planting a kiss on his lips.

"Good," Grayson had stated. "I'm not seeing or sleeping with anyone else. I'm a one-woman kind of man. I have been since we met, and I would hope it's the same with you."

"It is. It is," Bree had assured him. "You're the only man I want to be with."

"Good. Because you're mine." Grayson had hugged her more tightly to his chest, and last night, he'd been especially tender in his lovemaking. Bree had cried at the sheer joy of how happy she was.

Grayson was pulling out all the stops, and Bree was powerless to resist the feelings he was evoking. And if she was honest, she didn't want to. She'd fallen in love with Grayson Wells. Even though she'd tried her best not to get involved, to keep him at arm's length, he'd slowly found his way into her heart and burrowed himself there.

She hadn't felt this way about a man since Jacob. But this was different. It was deeper. Stronger. Bree knew that if it ended, she would be devastated.

Last night, Grayson had invited her over to his

mansion to dine with him, Cameron, Sonya, and to her chagrin, his mother. At the table, he'd announced she was his girlfriend, which was met with a frown from Julia.

Bree didn't know what it was about Grayson's mother, but the woman clearly didn't like her and the feeling was mutual. Animosity came off Julia in droves whenever Bree was around, and she couldn't understand why. She'd just met the woman. Maybe his mother hated Bree for taking his time away from their family?

Just as that thought swam through her mind, from her balcony Bree spotted Jada getting out of a cab. She set aside her musings about Grayson and his family and waited to hear Jada at the door. A few minutes later, Jada knocked, and Bree was already at her door to open it with a flourish.

Jada towered over Bree in three-inch heels, which made her nearly six feet tall. Her shoulder-length dark-brown hair hung silky straight, and she wore a pair of distressed jeans and a top with the shoulders cut out. She was ever the fashionista.

"Jada!" Bree screamed and pulled her into her arms.

"Bree!" Jada returned her embrace and then pulled away. "Let me look at you. Wow! You look amazing," she said as she grabbed her suitcase and strolled inside. "What are you eating or drinking? Because you need to tell me so I can get on the same regimen. You're glowing."

Bree flushed. "Jada, that's ridiculous." She closed the door behind her. "I'm just happy is all."

Jada grinned. "Is all this happiness"—she made a circle with her index finger as she pointed to Bree—"because of boss man?"

"If you're talking about Grayson," Bree said as they entered her living room, "then yes, we are seeing each other."

"Well alright then. So in the meantime, tell me everything that's been going on with you from start to finish" Jada said, holding out her hand. Bree walked over to take it, and arm in arm they sat together on a plush microsuede sofa. "I wanna know about work, Daddy, Grayson, all of it."

"Well, that could take a long time."

Jada shrugged and pulled out a bottle of wine from her oversized purse. She held it up. "And we have all night, so let's hear it."

Two hours later, Bree was relaxed. They'd polished off Jada's wine along with the spare bottle of Pinot Noir Bree kept in the fridge. They'd kicked off their heels and were lounging on the sofa facing each other as they caught up on the goings-on in each other's lives.

Bree had learned Jada's career as a news anchor had stalled. She was stuck on the early-morning shift, and she'd broken up with a guy she'd been seeing on and off. She also learned that their older sister, London, and her husband, Chase, were considering in vitro fertilization to have a baby. Bree knew they were having trouble conceiving and that London feared it might be due to her weight. But Bree refused to believe that. Being plus-sized did not make you infertile. Apparently Chase may have been exposed to some chemicals during his tenure in Special Forces.

"I certainly hope that the specialists are able to help them," Bree said. "I know how much London wants to become a mother."

"And she will," Jada stated emphatically. "We have to believe that."

"And we will," Bree asserted.

"So now that we've talked about me and London, and hell even Mama, you wanna finally tell me how you've gotten yourself involved with your new boss?"

Bree bunched her shoulders. "Call it fate or kismet or whatever, but we met when Caleb and I scouted out the Johnson property."

"Old man Johnson's ranch?"

"One and the same."

"I thought Jack said he'd never sell, let alone to Daddy."

"Well, he passed away and his kids seem to have no problem with selling off his land."

Jada shook her head in disbelief. "That's a shame. He must be turning over in his grave."

"Probably. Anyway, we met that day and there was a spark between us, but it was only for a few minutes so I dismissed it."

"What changed?"

"I ran into him at a symposium that I was speaking at, and we had lunch. That's when he offered me a position at Wells Oil." Bree held up her hand when Jada started to interrupt. "Wait a sec, okay? I know you have a beef with me for leaving HE, but you know I've been unhappy for some time."

"Ever since Daddy appointed Caleb president."

"Yes. You know I love Caleb, but he's only been at HE for a few years. I've been working there for a decade, but Daddy doesn't think I, a woman, can handle the oil business."

"You can handle anything you put your mind to," Jada said. "But did you have to leave to work for a competitor? It's tearing Daddy up inside, not to mention causing a rift in the family."

"So this is my fault?" Bree's voice rose. "I didn't start this, Jada. Daddy did."

Jada scooted closer to Bree on the sofa and patted her knee. "It's not about who started what, or who did what to whom. It's about getting you both talking and seeing eye to eye. I don't like seeing you or Daddy this way. What can I do to help the situation?"

"For starters, you can accept that I made the right decision for myself. It's a choice that has given me a lot more say and power in running a company. At Wells Oil, not only am I head of the geology department, but I have a seat on the board and shares in the company. At HE, Daddy holds all the shares and wields his power like he's king or something."

"Don't you think that's a bit over the top?"

Bree shook her head. "No, Jada. But how would you know? You're not here. You're living your life in San Francisco."

"That's not fair."

"Listen, I don't begrudge you your happiness. Don't you want the same for me?"

"With Grayson Wells?"

"Yes," Bree stated. "We grew closer when I began working at Wells Oil. I really like him, Jada. And more than that, I respect him. If you can see how he cares for his autistic brother and his mother, who's suffering from cancer, you'd see what a wonderful man he is. And one night, our relationship went to the next level."

Jada stared at her incredulously. "You're in love with him, aren't you?"

Bree didn't look away from her sister's questioning eyes. "I am."

"And how does he feel about you?"

"I'm not sure yet. I just recognized these feelings

myself and have been trying to process them. How can I expect him to be able to verbalize them?"

"Fair enough. But eventually you have to find out how he feels about you."

"Agreed."

"Well I for one can't wait to meet this man, because he must be awful special to convince you to leave the Hart fold."

"He is, Jada. He is."

"WHAT ARE YOU DOING, GRAYSON?" Julia asked when she entered the sun room the following morning. It was Friday, and Grayson was enjoying a cup of coffee and the newspaper. He wasn't in the mood for yet another interrogation.

Last night, Bree had called him somewhat intoxicated to remind him she'd be staying at her family's ranch this evening because of the charity ball tomorrow—as if he could forget. Grayson knew Saturday would be the day of reckoning. He would be coming face to face with Duke Hart, the man who'd spurred him into a future Grayson hadn't thought possible. But with revenge fueling him, it was all the adrenaline he could ever need.

"Good morning to you too, Mother."

"Don't dismiss me, Grayson. You announced the other evening at dinner that that Hart girl is your *girlfriend* for Christ's sake. How can you be with *her* given everything her father did to this family?"

"I know what I'm doing, Mother."

"Do you?" She folded her arms across her chest. "Because it looks to me like that girl has you under some sort of spell and led around by your pants. We hardly see you around here, and when we do, you're preoccupied and your head is in the clouds."

Grayson sighed and put down his newspaper. "I'm here now, Mother. What more do you want?"

"I want you to *do* what you promised." She took a seat beside him and reached for his hand. "You promised me that you'd pay back Duke Hart for all he stole from this family. That you'd get the retribution due us."

"Due us? Or due you, Mother?" Grayson asked, turning to face her.

She snorted. "This is not about me but about you losing sight of your objective. You were supposed to be ruthless. You could have been using this Hart girl to find out more about Duke, but instead you're off gallivanting to wineries and fancy hotels. Sonya told me about Austin."

Fury burned within Grayson. He had to bite his tongue rather than tell his mother a thing or two. He didn't need her to remind him that he was getting soft on the subject of Duke Hart. He had been. He hadn't even followed through with signing the Johnson deal, even though Levi had ensured that the paperwork would be ready this week.

"Grayson, have you heard a word I've said?"

"Yes," Grayson said through gritted teeth. He rose to his feet under the guise of freshening his coffee, though really he was trying to get away from his mother's incessant nagging. "I heard you alright." He turned back to face her. "And I haven't forgotten. Duke will soon find out what it's like to lose. I promise you."

He watched her shoulders sag as if their confrontation had taken so much out of her. Grayson knew that battling cancer was taking a toll on her poor, ravaged body. He should be doing more, spending more time with her, because who knew if she would beat this disease.

He walked over to his mother and bent his knees until he could see her eyes. "I promise you, Mother, I will make Duke pay."

16

R ight after his conversation with his mother, Grayson had gotten cleaned up and made his way to the office. On the drive, he'd summoned Levi to meet him there. His mother was right. It was time he took steps to start the demise of Duke Hart's precious company. The first step was to steal Jack Johnson's property right out from under Duke's nose.

"Hey, boss," Levi said, strolling into Grayson's office. "What can I do for you?"

Rosalie was already sitting in front of Grayson's desk.

"I'm ready to execute this contract," Grayson replied. "I just need you and Rosalie to witness it." He reached for a fountain pen that he kept on his desk. He'd inherited it from his father. How fitting that it would be used to help destroy Duke.

Grayson signed the legal document and handed it to Levi. "Signed, sealed, and delivered."

Levi grinned. "You know this is going to get Caleb and Duke Hart's ire. And if you're successful today meeting with Brooke Jenkins and blocking them from moving their oil, this could be a devastating blow." On

Grayson's drive to the office, he'd told Levi about his plans to contact Brooke.

"I know," Grayson said. He expected as much. This was a big move and would put him directly in their crosshairs. They would soon find out that he was a force to be reckoned with. But it's what he needed to finally get justice for Duke's underhanded dealings all those years ago.

Duke would be livid and would want to know who'd outfoxed him. And when the time came, Grayson would be happy to tell him. He would look him in the eye and tell him to go to hell.

"BREE! JADA!" Duke was overjoyed to see his daughters for dinner that night at the ranch. He squeezed them into one large group hug as they entered the family home.

"It's good to see you too, Daddy," Jada said and Bree concurred as they sat their bags down in the foyer.

Bree didn't have any problems coming home to the ranch. She loved the place. What she wasn't looking forward to was getting into an argument with her father over how she chose to live her life.

"C'mon in." Duke motioned them into the living room.

Caleb and Addison were already there and seated on the couch with their daughter, Ivy, in Addison's lap.

"Jada!" Caleb rose when they entered the room. He greeted her with a hug and kiss on the cheek first before turning to Bree. Caleb stretched out his arms to her. "Bree."

"Hey, cuz." They hugged. She missed the closeness

they'd once shared and apparently so did Caleb; it took several moments for him to let her go. After he did, Bree bent down to give Addison a kiss and joined them on the couch.

"What can I get my girls to drink?" Duke asked.

Bree wasn't used to her father being so solicitous. "I'll have a whiskey."

"That's my girl," he commented.

"Just a soda water for me," Jada said.

"Coming right up."

While their father fixed their drinks at the bar in the corner, Jada turned to Addison.

"My God, Addison, you're starting to show!"

"Jada!" Bree admonished.

"It's okay, Bree," Addison replied. "I know, I feel very pregnant."

Everyone chuckled at her joke.

"I'm sorry, Addison," Jada apologized. "I just haven't seen you in several months. Come here, Ivy." She took their daughter in her arms and gave her a hug. But when Ivy started to cry, Jada immediately handed her back to her mother.

"And I blew up overnight," Addison responded, taking Ivy from her. "How are you anyway? It's been so long since you've been home."

"Ain't that the truth," Duke said, handing Jada her soda water and Bree her whiskey. "I'm just glad to have everyone here."

"How long are you staying?" Caleb asked.

Jada shrugged. "Oh, about a week or so. I wanted to spend some time with the family and catch up with Bree." She patted her sister's knee.

"Then you're making the right move," Duke said, "because the rest of us haven't seen much of my middle daughter these days." He focused his gaze directly on Bree, putting her in the spotlight.

Bree fumed in her seat. This was exactly why she'd stayed away. He was trying to make her feel guilty for not only leaving HE, but also for not spending time with the family. She'd looked out for her own best interests when she'd left the company. But admittedly, she had distanced herself from the family because she didn't know whose side they were on—hers or Duke's.

"How is your new job these days?" Duke asked. "Must be keeping you awfully busy if you can't make time for your own family."

Bree glared at him. "It's going quite well, Daddy. Thank you. It's rather refreshing to be included in the decision-making process for the company."

"Why would a geologist be included in that conversation?"

Of course, he would make the work Bree did seem inconsequential even though Hart Enterprises had depended on her keen senses for its success over the years.

"Because I have a seat on the board."

"What?" Duke was clearly stunned by her revelation. "How did you manage that?"

"I learned from the best." Bree responded with a smile. "You're the most cunning negotiator of them all, Daddy."

Bree and her father glared at one another, neither of them backing down from the standoff. Jada stepped in. "Is anyone ready for dinner?" she asked, rising to her feet. "Because I'm starved."

"I couldn't agree more." Caleb took Ivy from Addison and helped his wife to her feet.

And slowly, they all began making their way to the dining room. But Jada grasped Bree's arm before they walked in. "I thought you were going to be civil tonight."

"I am," Bree said through clenched teeth, snatching her arm away. "But you know Daddy has a way of getting under my skin."

"Don't let him."

Several minutes later, they were all seated at the dining room table and enjoying the delicious lamb with roasted potatoes and garlic green beans their cook had prepared.

Conversation throughout much of dinner was focused on Jada's job, Caleb and Addison getting ready for the baby, and even Duke's latest adventures on the ranch with some livestock. They all laughed and joked with one another, and the evening took on a much lighter mood.

Until dessert.

Caleb stepped away from the table to take a phone call, and when he returned, he wore a scowl. The mood at the table changed.

"Is everything alright, honey?" Addison inquired.

Caleb shook his head. "Let's table it for now. We agreed no more shop talk. Jada's here visiting, and we want her to have a great time."

"It's hard to have a good time, boy, if you're sitting there wearing a scowl," Duke responded sharply. "So spit it out. What's going on?"

"The Johnson deal," Caleb began. "It fell through."

"What?" Duke roared. "How can that be? Our offer was solid and more than reasonable for that land."

Caleb shrugged, and Bree could see defeat on his face. This wasn't his first big deal at Hart Enterprises, but it held the most significance because her father and old man Johnson had always had a beef. It was

Duke's great wish to have his land to expand the ranching business.

"How could this have happened, Caleb?" Duke asked again.

"I don't know, Duke, but I'll find out."

"Who did those greedy children of his sell to?"

Caleb looked down, and Bree could see he didn't want to say, but there was no way he was getting off the hook. Duke wanted answers. He wanted to know who'd foiled his long-held plans.

"Caleb, I asked you a question."

Caleb's chin lifted defiantly, and he glared at Duke. "I heard you, Duke. And I know how important this deal was to you, but what's done is done. Why does it matter who won?"

"It matters to me, goddammit!" Duke slammed his fist on the table with a thud. It startled Ivy, who began to cry.

"Daddy!" Jada implored. "Please settle down."

"I will do no such thing. I asked you for the name, Caleb. Who stole that land from up under me?"

"Grayson Wells."

Bree colored. Grayson had beat her father at his own game? She'd known he was interested. It was how they'd first met, but that had been the end of it. She hadn't heard a word about it, not even in the board meetings. Why hadn't he mentioned it before? Why was he keeping it a secret from her? He had to have known it would come up in conversation with her family.

"Wait a second." Duke spun around to face Bree. "Isn't Grayson the owner of Wells Oil, where you work?"

All eyes suddenly turned to Bree. So her father knew about Grayson. *How much does he know?*

"Yes, Daddy. Grayson Wells is the owner."

"Then maybe you could tell how us how in the hell did he find out about our deal?"

Tears filled Bree's eyes at her father's accusatory tone. Surely he didn't think she'd given Grayson confidential information. She would never do that. Plus she had no clue what Caleb would have offered Parker. She hadn't even worked at Wells Oil for even two months yet.

"What exactly are you accusing me of, Duke?" She used his first name, and she saw the ire cross his face. She only used it when she was upset with him, and he knew it.

"You know damn well, young lady. I want to know what secrets you've been telling Grayson Wells." His brown eyes were filled with disdain for her.

"Duke, stop it!" Caleb intervened. "Bree had nothing to do with this. She's been gone from HE for more than two months. She'd have no idea what I offered them."

Duke turned to glare at him. "Are you sure about that?"

"Daddy, please," Jada implored. "Please don't do this."

"Don't stop him now." Bree wiped an errant tear from her cheek. Her heart broke at the idea that Duke would think she'd betray him and their family. "He thinks I gave away family secrets to Grayson."

"Well, did you?" Duke asked.

"Screw you, Daddy! Screw you!" Bree yelled and rushed out of the dining room.

Jada was fast on her heels and met Bree at the front door.

"Bree, wait! Don't leave. Daddy's just upset right now, and he's not thinking clearly. He knows you would never do what he accused you of. When he calms down, he'll realize that."

"I don't care," Bree cried. "I won't be his punching bag, Jada. If he wants to believe the worst of me, let him! I'm going home."

"But what about me? What about tomorrow night?"

Bree turned to look at Jada. Tears were streaming down her cheeks too. Bree hated to see her baby sister in pain, but she couldn't stay here. Not now. Not after the awful things their father had said. "You can stay here or come with me," Bree said. "Choose."

Jada glanced behind her at the dining room and back again at Bree. She was clearly torn, so Bree made it easier for her and without a word, opened the door and left with her bags.

~

GRAYSON SAT in his home study with a glass of Scotch and the full decanter beside it. He'd done as he'd promised. Duke should have found out this evening that he'd successfully bid on the Johnson land. And about an hour ago at his office, he'd concluded his meeting with Brooke Jenkins.

Brooke hadn't been happy to hear from Grayson. Maybe he thought Grayson had forgotten the favor he'd owed him. He hadn't. He'd just been waiting for the most advantageous moment to use it. He had it now.

"I want you to refuse to renew the contract you have with Hart Enterprises to move their oil," Grayson had told the middle-aged white man.

"You can't ask me to do that. HE's business is very

lucrative. My board will never allow it. Plus, how would I make up that revenue?"

"I don't care," Grayson had said. "You owe me, and I'm calling in my marker. Now what's it going to be?"

Brooke had reluctantly nodded, so Grayson had thrown him a lifeline. "I have a new pipeline coming up with my friend, a sheikh, in a land rich with oil. He'll need your oil tankers to transport it."

Brooke had smiled.

"I believe this will help make up for some of your lost revenue in light of your not renewing your business with Hart Enterprises, yes? But in the interim, I want you to drag out negotiations, make Hart Enterprises think you're going to renew, and at the last moment, I want you to renege."

"Why? Why not let me tell them now so they can find another means of transport?" Brooke had inquired. "This could cripple them."

Grayson's eyes had turned cold. "Because I want them to suffer." Just as his father and their entire family had suffered because of Duke's greed. It was time the shoe was on the other foot.

Brooke had agreed, and they'd concluded their business, then Grayson had returned home to wait for the inevitable.

His eyes flickered as he returned to the present and poured himself another glass of Scotch. It would just be a matter of time before Bree put two and two together and realized what lengths he'd gone to for his vendetta against her father and the family business. By then it would be too late—too late for her or anyone to save it.

He hoped this wouldn't end his relationship with Bree, and with that thought, Grayson needed another drink to dull the pain. He poured himself yet another

Scotch. He wanted to drown his sorrows, to not feel, to no think about what was to come.

What losing her would do to him.

"Gray?"

Grayson glanced up to find Cameron standing in the doorway. "What are you doing up, buddy?" he asked, putting down his drink and rising to his feet, somewhat unsteadily.

It was late. Usually Cameron had already retired for the night.

"Couldn't sleep," Cameron replied.

"C'mon in." Grayson motioned him forward and moved away from the desk. Cameron sat across from him on two matching recliners. "Something on your mind?"

"No, not really," Cameron said. "But something's on yours." He pointed to Grayson. "Your face is all screwed up like you're in pain or something. You okay?"

Grayson smiled. How was it that Cameron could read him so easily when he was trying his best to cover up his emotions? "I'm fine, Cam."

"No, you're not." Cameron shook his head. "You're sad. Why? Is it because Bree isn't here? Whenever she's around, you're always smiling and happy and kissing."

Grayson smiled at the mention of Bree's name. "You're very perceptive," he said to his younger brother. "We try not to kiss when you're around."

"Why not? You love each other, right? I see you making goo-goo eyes at her from across the table."

Love.

That was the word Grayson was avoiding when it came to Bree. He didn't want to acknowledge that love could be the emotion he was feeling. It didn't line up with his objectives. His objective was to pay back Duke Hart for all he'd done to his father, not fall in love.

And he was doing that. His plan was coming together brilliantly. All he had to do now was stay the course and not let Bree, or love for that matter, get in the way. But how could he do that without hurting Bree?

"I like Bree," Grayson finally said.

"And I like her too," Cameron said without hesitation. "Will she come live here with us?"

"Whoa, buddy!" Grayson sat up in his chair. "Don't get ahead of yourself, Cameron. It's a little too early yet."

Cameron shrugged. "Maybe, but I wouldn't mind it is all I'm saying."

Grayson nodded. "That's good to know." Because he wouldn't mind it either. He'd like nothing better than for Bree to spend every night in his bed.

His cellphone began ringing, and Grayson rose from the chair to grab it from the desk. How fortuitous. It was Bree.

"Grayson?"

"Bree?" He heard the distress in her voice. "Are you okay?"

"Can I come over? I know it's late, but—" Her voice cracked, and Grayson didn't hesitate to respond.

"Of course. I'll see you soon."

"Is Bree coming by?" Cameron asked excitedly, rubbing his hands together.

"She is."

"Okay." Cameron stood upright. "I'll go to bed then. I know you guys want to have kissing time." Seconds later, his brother was gone from the study, leaving Grayson with a smile. Yet he was curious as to why Bree was so upset.

Has she already found out about the deal?

~

BREE ARRIVED at Grayson's within the hour. She hadn't realized she was heading to his place until she'd hopped on the expressway after leaving her father's home. He'd really hurt her with his accusations, and the only place she wanted to go was to the safety of Grayson's arms.

Although he'd bought Johnson's land, Bree was sure it had nothing to do with her. He'd been interested in the deal when they'd first met.

She pulled into the driveway of Grayson's mansion and was nearly at the door when it swung open and she saw Grayson. She rushed into his arms, and he held her tight against his hard chest.

"Baby, are you alright?" he asked as she closed the door behind her and they stood in the foyer.

"Can we go to your room?" Bree glanced up the stairs.

"Of course." Grayson clasped her hand in his and led her up the spiral staircase to his bedroom down the hall.

Once inside, he locked the door behind him, giving them complete and utter privacy. "Come." He led her over to his massive bed, and they climbed atop it with Bree snuggling against his chest. "Tell me, what's going on?"

Bree was silent. She just wanted to be held. She hadn't realized just how much she needed it, needed Grayson, until he was holding her in his embrace. A little shiver of pleasure coursed through her, especially when Grayson began caressing her arms to soothe her frayed nerves.

He didn't try to make her talk. Instead, he just held her and eventually she spoke. "My father accused me of cavorting with you to kill a business deal he'd been working on."

Grayson moved quickly so he could face her. "Why would he think that?"

Bree shrugged and fresh tears came to her eyes. "I don't know, but he basically accused me of corporate espionage. My own father." She thumped her chest with her fist and shook her head. "I still can't believe he'd think I was capable of that."

"I'm so sorry." Grayson clutched her to his chest. "I'm so sorry, Bree. I never meant any of this to happen."

Bree pulled away from him. "So you did buy the Johnson land?"

Grayson nodded. "Yes, I did. But you know I wanted it. I was there that day when you and Caleb were touring it."

"I know." She sniffed. "I just . . ." After a pause, she picked back up, "I just don't understand my father. Right when I think things can't get any worse between us, he takes it a step further and mortally wounds me."

"I'm sorry, baby," Grayson whispered, kissing her forehead. "I'm sorry if my purchasing this land has caused *you* any pain."

"It's not your fault," Bree stated. "You're entitled to go after the same land."

"I know, but . . ."

She placed her finger on his lips. "It's not your fault. And I'm truly not blaming you." At the disbelieving look on his face, she grabbed his cheeks and forced him to look at her. "My father is just a sore loser. He doesn't like being beat, but it was bound to happen sometime. He can't get everything he wants, and he's just going to have to live with that."

"You're pretty amazing, you know that?" Grayson said.

Bree couldn't decipher the emotion that crossed his face as he laid her down on the bed. Then a sexy smile crossed his lips as he came down beside her. He claimed Bree's lips in an unhurried kiss that sent shivers up her spine. He traced their outline with his tongue and then dipped between them to explore her mouth with skilled eroticism.

Bree gave herself up to the tumultuous feelings that he aroused in her. He was the person she would come to when she needed comfort. He was the man who'd swept away all the barriers she had around her emotions and discovered the sensual part of her nature as well as had stolen her heart.

When he kissed her again, she curled her arms around his neck and kissed him back with a fervor that drew a deep groan from his throat. Eventually he lifted his head to look down at her, his eyes cloudy with passion. It was a passion Bree felt, so much so that she began unbuttoning his shirt. When she had all the buttons undone, she slid his shirt down his muscular arms. Then she reached for his belt buckle, but Grayson was faster.

He lifted Bree's sweater over her head. Then they raced to see who could undress the quickest. In record time, they were naked and under the sheets.

"Make love to me," Bree pleaded.

She was on fire, and she needed Grayson to jump in her flames.

"Gladly."

He lowered his head to her breast to sweep his tongue across her nipple, and it swelled and tightened. Bree moaned and tossed her head from side to side. He paid its twin equal attention, tugging on it with his mouth, tongue, and teeth until she arched off the bed.

Then Grayson's head was moving lower to trail open-mouthed kisses down her flat stomach. He paused long enough to lave her navel with his tongue before going lower to the cluster of dark-brown curls between her thighs. He parted her legs and slid one finger and then two into her molten heat. He circled the sensitive nub of her clitoris until Bree began to whimper.

"Please." She wanted more, needed him deep inside her, filling her, stretching her completely. She trembled with the need to feel him.

She nearly cried out with happiness when he finally settled between her thighs after rolling on a condom and thrust into her. Bree bent her knees as he drew back and thrust in again. The exquisiteness of it all caused tears to blur her eyes, but she wiped the droplets away and focused on the feelings he evoked.

She wrapped her legs tightly around Grayson, pulling him deeper into her. He complied and began moving harder and faster with powerful strokes of his hips. He filled her to the hilt, driving all thought *but* him from her mind and taking her to a magical place Bree could only find *with* him.

Grayson powered into her and Bree anchored herself, raking her nails down his back for the most incredible ride of her life. Bree heard her screams and his shout through the explosion that shattered both their souls as they climaxed together.

~

GRAYSON GLANCED DOWN AT BREE. She was curled up beside him. God, he felt like a total heel. Although he hadn't directly used her, he had initially pursued her because of her connection to Duke. As a result, he'd caused a rift between Bree and her family.

But wasn't it what Duke deserved after everything he'd done to Grayson's father? Just look at what he'd done to Bree tonight. He'd decimated his own daughter all in the name of greed and the all-mighty dollar. He blamed Bree for the fact that he'd lost a deal for Christ's sake.

Duke didn't deserve Bree.

But do I?

It wasn't like he was any better. He'd used her as a salve for his own wounds. At first, she'd been reluctant, but slowly but surely, she'd opened up to him. And tonight, she'd come to him because she was hurt and angry. Because she *needed* him. And when they'd come together, they'd made love. It wasn't just sex spurred by a wild attraction for each other. Grayson had felt it too.

But where did they go from here?

It would be just a matter of time before Duke knew why Grayson had done all this. Soon he would know Grayson was the son of Elijah Williams, Duke's one-time friend and the man he'd swindled all those years ago.

And then what?

When all was said and done, Duke would know he'd gotten the better of him. *Where does that leave me and Bree?*

Would she even want to be with him after she discovered his real motives for hiring her?

Those thoughts made up Grayson's nightmares as he finally drifted off to sleep.

17

"You're home," Jada said when Bree made it back to her apartment the next morning. Jada was sitting on the couch in her pajamas holding a mug of coffee.

"Yes, I'm back," Bree said to Jada as she closed her front door, "though I'm surprised to see you." She had believed her baby sister would still be at the ranch.

Jada rose to her feet. "I couldn't stay there. I had to come and see you. But you didn't come back here last night. Are you okay?"

Bree swept past her sister and into her bedroom.

"Were you at Grayson's?"

Bree turned back and stared incredulously at Jada.

"Of course you were," Jada answered her own question. "I realize you have strong feelings for the man."

"I love him," Bree responded.

Jada sighed. "I know that. I'm just scared for you."

"What the hell, Jada? You've been back for all of five seconds. How dare you judge me or my relationship with Grayson."

"I'm sorry, Bree." Jada rushed to Bree's side. "I

didn't mean to imply that Grayson's feelings toward you aren't genuine. I just want you to be happy."

"Do you?"

Jada's eyes filled with tears. "Of course. How could you doubt that?"

"I don't know, Jada." Bree shrugged. "Maybe because you didn't come with me when I left the ranch last night. You didn't have my back."

"I have always had your back," Jada said fiercely. "And I never for a second believed Daddy's accusations, but I was trying to calm the waters and get everyone to see reason. It's why I came here immediately yesterday after you left the ranch. But you were gone, and your phone was off. I couldn't reach you."

Bree had forgotten her charger, so her phone had been dead. "Alright, I suppose you're right," she conceded.

Bree sat down on her bed in defeat. It was so tiring being angry with her family, especially Jada. Being less than two years apart in age, they'd always been thick as thieves. Jada was her confidante and vice versa.

"You seem okay," Jada said, sitting beside her. "I presume Grayson has a lot to do with your improved mood?"

Bree glanced at Jada. "He does."

"I want to meet him."

"He's supposed to take me to the Crystal Charity Ball tonight."

"Are you sure that's best, given how Daddy feels about him?"

"No," Bree said. "But that's business, and Duke's just going to have to deal with it. Or we don't have to sit at the family table, as I doubt very much he wants to see either of us."

"You know that's not true, Bree. Daddy will want to see you. Grayson, I can't speak for, but I'll speak to Daddy and make sure he knows he has to be on his best behavior tonight. Otherwise you won't come."

"I don't know." Bree didn't want another epic battle royale on her hands like they'd had yesterday.

"Please," Jada implored. "It's why I came."

Bree had never been able to say no to her baby sister, and today was no different. "Alright."

BREE STARED BACK at her reflection in the mirror many hours later that evening. She could hardly believe the magic Jada and her team of hair and makeup artists had performed. Jada had found her the most elegant champagne-colored strapless satin gown with a sweetheart ruffled neckline. Her unruly curls had been tamed into a flattering updo, and her makeup was so flawless it looked like she barely had any on.

"Love it!" Jada said as she came up behind her to look in the cheval mirror. "I outdid myself."

Bree turned around. "You did, but I have to say the dress you're wearing is killer."

"Thank you." Jada grinned and pranced around the room in her form-fitting black spaghetti-strap dress with a fierce slide slit. With her slender model-like figure, Jada easily pulled it off along with her signature sleek, straight hairdo.

The doorbell chimed signaling Grayson's arrival, and Bree's heart sped up. She wanted this first meeting with her sister and family to go off without a hitch. "C'mon, diva," she said, looping her arm in Jada's. "Let's go."

BREE DIDN'T ANSWER her door. Instead, another woman who appeared to be the makeup stylist let Grayson in. And just as he was about to inquire about Bree's whereabouts, she sauntered out of the bedroom with another slender female. This other woman was taller than Bree by several inches and equally beautiful, but Grayson only had eyes for Bree.

She looked like a golden goddess in the champagne dress with the sweetheart neckline that gave him a tantalizing view of her breasts as she approached him.

"Grayson, I'd like you to meet my sister, Jada."

He forced his eyes to return to Bree's face rather than her décolletage and look at her sister. He offered her a smile. "Jada, it's great to meet you."

"You as well." Jada leaned in to give him a quick, yet unexpected hug. "I've heard a lot about you."

He patted her back, then pulled away. "I hope all good things." He glanced in Bree's direction and winked at her.

"Nothing but the best," Jada responded, though for some reason she couldn't put her finger on, she felt uneasy about Grayson.

"Well, if you ladies are ready to go," Grayson said, offering them each one of his arms, "our chariot awaits downstairs."

Bree and Jada both took an arm, and he led them out of the apartment.

Once they were in the elevator, Grayson whispered in Bree's ear, "You look ravishing."

Bree glanced up at him through mascara-coated lashes. "So do you," she murmured.

"Later, when I have you all to myself, I'm going to do wicked things to you."

Bree's entire face flushed, and her sister looked over at her. "Enough you two, or I'm going to regret my decision to ride with you versus driving in with Daddy."

Perhaps it was a good thing they had Jada as a chaperone tonight. Otherwise, it would have been very hard for Grayson not to take Bree in the limo on their way to the charity gala.

The drive to the ball was relatively short, but there was a long line of cars and limos once they made it to the main street. It took nearly a half-hour, but eventually they disembarked from the vehicle with Grayson lending a hand to both Jada and Bree.

Grayson couldn't wait to see the look on Duke's face when he realized *he* was bringing both his daughters to the annual charity event. The man would probably have a coronary right on the spot. Not that Grayson wanted that. He wanted Duke to suffer, to feel the same sort of despair for years that Grayson and his family had had to endure when his father walked out on them.

Grayson saw several people he knew. He stopped to introduce Bree and Jada to them. He saw Jada's brow rise when he introduced Bree as his girlfriend. Even though she was being cordial to him, Jada gave off an air of mistrust. She didn't trust him or like him with Bree. And she was right not to, but he wasn't letting Bree go. At least not yet.

Not until she asked him to.

"Would you ladies care for some champagne?" Grayson asked when they finally had a quiet moment.

"Love some," they said in unison.

"I'm on it."

Grayson left them in search of cordials. Once he found the bar, he ordered them champagne and himself a Scotch.

"Does she know you plan on ruining her family?" a familiar voice said from Grayson's side.

He turned to find Brooke Jenkins standing next to him in a tuxedo. Brooke was frowning as he looked in Bree's direction. "Quite frankly, that's none of your business," Grayson shot back.

Brooke shrugged. "It's not my problem. I've paid you back the favor I owed you, so I am no longer in your debt."

Grayson's eyes narrowed. "No, you're not."

"Good. Otherwise, my people will be speaking with yours about transporting Wells Oil." Seconds later, he was gone.

Grayson glanced over at Bree, and his heart turned over. He was being incredibly selfish wanting to keep Bree. He should let her go so she could be with someone better. Someone worthy of her, instead of a liar, gambler, and a con artist like him.

Just then, Grayson watched Duke Hart, his nephew Caleb, Caleb's wife, Addison, and a stunning older woman who must be Bree's mother, Abigail, join Bree and Jada in a circle. A low growl escaped Grayson's lips. He didn't want Duke around his woman, but he was her family after all.

"Here you are, sir." The attendant handed Grayson two champagne flutes and his Scotch.

Once they were in hand, Grayson made a beeline for the circle. When he arrived, he stood back for a second, assessing Duke Hart. At six foot five, Duke was taller than him by a couple of inches. He was a big man who, in his heyday, could have flattened Grayson

... but not now. Their battle would be nothing short of David and Goliath proportions.

~

"DADDY, Mama, I'd like you to meet Grayson Wells," Bree stated when she saw Grayson standing slightly off to the side from their semicircle. She was happy when she'd seen his bald head behind them. He handed her and Jada their flutes and retained his Scotch.

Bree had been prepared to make small talk with her father. And, of course, he'd arrived in good spirits because her mother was there. His mood inspired him to make amends, and he tried to pull Bree into a hug, but she flatly refused. Embarrassed, he stepped backward.

The lines had been drawn.

Suddenly, Duke turned around to face Grayson, and Bree could see the two men assessing each other like gladiators in battle.

Grayson broke the standoff by offering his hand. "Mr. Hart, it's a pleasure to meet you."

"Wish I could say the same, Wells."

"Daddy, you promised," Jada hissed.

"Settle down, girl," Duke told her. "This is a night for charity. We grown folks know how to behave. Isn't that right, Wells?"

Bree knew her father was purposely calling Grayson by his last name to rile him up. She'd seen him do it with lots of men. It was a tactic he used to undermine them.

"That's right," Grayson said, sipping his drink.

"Yes, it is," Abigail said from Duke's side. She came forward to Grayson. Bree had to admit her mother looked stunning in a silk sheath dress with her dark-brown hair piled high on her head. "Grayson," Abigail said as she held out her hand. Grayson swept his mouth across it.

"A pleasure, Ms. Hart."

Abigail beamed, but Duke didn't when Grayson walked over to Bree and with his eyes not leaving her father's, circled his arm around her waist. He'd just made it clear that their relationship wasn't just business. It was personal.

First hit. Grayson.

Duke's eyes darkened at the action, but he didn't say anything.

"Caleb Hart," Caleb introduced himself.

Grayson handed Bree his drink to shake Caleb's hand. His other hand didn't leave Bree's side. "I'm Grayson. Nice to meet you. And who's this?"

Caleb motioned Addison forward. "My wife, Addison."

"Addison, you're looking lovely," Grayson said.

"Thank you." Addison beamed.

"It looks like the doors are opening," Duke finally spoke. "Shall we?"

"After you," Grayson said.

"No, after you," Duke ordered.

Bree was just happy that her mother was in attendance because she knew Duke would behave himself with her around. Abigail didn't join their family gatherings often, but this charity was near and dear to her heart, so she always came to this.

Grayson touched her arm and led her into the ballroom.

Bree sat ramrod straight in her Chiavari chair as she watched the verbal repartee between her father and Grayson now that the entire family was seated at

the table. There was no avoiding the undisguised hos-
tility in her father's eyes, but Grayson? He was definitely on edge. They were so in tune with each other's
bodies that she sensed an underlying rage even
though he was trying his best to hide it. Bree didn't
understand why he would have a beef with her father.
But there was something there that she couldn't quite
put her finger on.

While they ate their salads, her father wasted no
time grilling Grayson. "So, Wells, tell us a little bit
about yourself. You've had my daughter so holed up,
none of us have been able to talk to her. So we're *eager*
to get to know you."

Grayson feigned a smile and used his napkin to
wipe the sides of his mouth before placing it in his lap.
"What would you like to know?"

"For starters, how you amassed the kind of wealth
it would take to start an oil business at such a young
age."

"It's simple, really. I made the right connections
and of course, a lot of luck was involved."

"That's quite vague," Duke commented, regarding
him warily.

"I won my first oil well when I was twenty-five,"
Grayson offered.

"You *won* it?" Even Caleb was intrigued by his answer and joined the conversation.

Grayson turned to look at Caleb. "That's right. I've
always been quite good at poker. And well, I made
friends with Sheikh Arash bin Rashid Al Kadar and
attended a few high-stakes games with him. And the
rest, as they say, is history."

"That is awfully lucky," Duke responded. "And
damn stupid on the part of the man who gambled
away his oil well."

"My sentiments exactly," Grayson said. "He was careless with something very precious, but I don't make those same mistakes." He turned to Bree, giving her a warm smile.

Bree felt it in the pit of her stomach and slowly her unease since the evening began started to fade a bit. All Grayson had to do was look at her with his penetrating gaze and she melted.

Duke remained silent for most of the dinner and ball events, but many times throughout the course of the evening, Bree felt his eyes on her and Grayson. He was watching them. Or should she say watching *him*. Jada, Caleb, and Addison covered for Duke's lack of conversation with funny stories and anecdotes; but Bree knew her father was seething and plotting his next move. When she'd gone to the ladies' room, she'd overheard him questioning Caleb about his investigation of Grayson. She wasn't surprised that Duke wanted to know about the man dating his daughter—the man who had stolen Jack Johnson's land right out from under him.

But what does he hope to find? Bree wondered.

When Grayson departed to bid on several items for the charity's silent auction, Jada scooted next to Bree. "If looks could kill, both Daddy and Grayson would be dead."

Bree chuckled. "You're not lying. You can cut the tension at the table with a knife."

Jada rolled her eyes. "Don't talk about knives, otherwise Daddy might get ideas."

"Jada, you're incorrigible!"

Jada shrugged.

Once the program was over, the host opened the floor up to dancing and Grayson rose to his feet, offering Bree his hand. "Join me on the dance floor?"

Bree placed her hand in his. "Love to." She was happy to get away from the prying eyes.

On the floor, Grayson pulled her into his arms and placed his hands at the small of her back. His touch made Bree forget about everyone in the room but him. She felt like a giddy schoolgirl.

She loved the feel of his body pressed against hers, loved feeling his heat emanating through his tuxedo.

"Hmmm," he moaned as he leaned in closer to whisper in her ear. "I've been waiting all night to have you in my arms."

Bree glanced up at him. "Is that so?"

Grayson pressed Bree closer so she could feel the hard ridge of his erection. "Yes, and I can't wait to get you home so I can show you just how much."

He lowered his head and brushed his lips across hers, softly and gently. When he lifted his head, Bree whimpered in protest.

"Later," he murmured.

The song ended, and they left the dance floor and came back to the table. Duke was scowling. He didn't want Bree with Grayson. Bree prayed for inner strength to get through the evening. Luckily, her mother wanted to dance and that seemed to improve Duke's mood. Bree watched her parents cut the rug and wondered what life would have been like if they had remained married. It was clear that they still cared a great deal about one another.

When they returned to the table and the winners of the silent auction were announced, Addison spoke up, stating she was ready to retire for the evening.

"If you don't mind, everyone, we're going to cut out," Caleb said. "Addison's a bit tired."

"That's understandable," Bree said and gave her

cousin-in-law a hug and a kiss. "Get some rest, and we'll talk soon."

"You can count on it," Addison whispered so only Bree could hear.

After they left, Grayson spoke up. "I think Addison was right on the money. Are you ready to get going, darling?" he asked, turning to Bree.

Bree glanced at Jada.

"It's okay." Jada patted her hand. "I'll hitch a ride with Daddy."

"But all your stuff is at my place," Bree murmured.

Jada shook her head. "I'll get it tomorrow. You go on and enjoy your evening. It looks like Grayson is anxious to get you alone."

"Jada!" Bree blushed, and she could feel her cheeks burning. She refused to glance at Duke because she knew how he felt. "Alright, call me in the morning."

"Will do."

"Mr. Hart," Grayson said as he walked over to Duke, who had risen upon his approach and held out his hand. "It was great to meet you, sir."

At first, Bree thought Duke wasn't going to shake Grayson's hand, but after some hesitation, he shook it firmly and then planted another hand on Duke's shoulder. "Wells, you hurt my daughter and I'll break every bone in your body."

"Daddy!" Bree shot to her feet. She'd heard every word. "Please don't make a scene."

Duke released his hold on Grayson and raised his hand in the air innocently. "No scene. I was just letting Wells know that you have family who cares about your well-being and that we'll have our eyes on him. Isn't that right, Wells?" He dared Grayson to say otherwise.

Grayson plastered a smile across his face and through clenched teeth said, "Of course. Good evening." It was there again, that look he'd given Duke as if there was more going on beneath the surface, but just as quickly it was gone. It left Bree to wonder if perhaps her father was on to something.

"Ms. Hart. Jada." Grayson bowed his head to both women and offered his hand to Bree, and she took it.

As Bree left with Grayson and her family behind in the ballroom, she wondered, *Is Grayson hiding something from me? And if so, what is it?*

18

"**P**enny for your thoughts," Grayson said once they were alone in the limousine on the way back to her place. Bree hadn't packed an overnight bag to stay at Grayson's. Plus, it was time they spent the evening at her apartment. This way at least, she wouldn't be subjected to Grayson's mother's evil glares in the morning when she found Bree had stayed the night.

"It's nothing," Bree stated.

"I doubt that," Grayson said. "I know tonight wasn't easy for you with your father and me being at odds."

"No, it wasn't, but that's not what has me puzzled."

A cloud passed Grayson's face. "What does?"

"It's your interactions with him," Bree said. "I expected my father to be on guard. After all, you just outfoxed him out of land he's wanted for decades. But there's something more."

"Like what?"

Bree shrugged. "I don't know, Grayson. Why don't you tell me. Is there something more going on between you and my father?"

"Why would you think that? It was just business. Nothing more, Bree."

But even as he said the words, Bree wasn't entirely sure she believed him. It all sounded very above board and straight-forward, but her gut told her it was something more and she'd always relied on it. That's how Hart Enterprises had become so successful after all—on her prediction skills.

"Come here." Grayson pulled her across the backseat and into the security of his arms. Bree felt him removing the pins from her hair until her curls fell to her shoulders. "Don't let your father's doubts about me ruin what we have. We've been good together, haven't we?" He lifted her head so she could look into his eyes.

Bree nodded. She wanted to believe that what she and Grayson shared was real, but doubt had begun to creep in.

Grayson must have sensed it because he lowered his head and

fit his mouth over hers, kissing her slowly. She relaxed and kissed him back. When he parted her lips and went deeper, sliding his warm tongue inside her mouth, Bree wanted him to never stop. She loved the feel of the stubble on his cheek from his perpetual five o'clock shadow. She loved the taste of him. There was no one else but Grayson, and in that instant everything *felt real, felt right.*

Bree allowed herself to give into the moment despite her reservations. She'd never expected to find Grayson, never thought he could fall in love again, but she had with him. And she didn't want to let go of the dream and the promise of what they could be just because of some peculiar expressions.

Reluctantly, when the limo stopped, Grayson levered himself off her and pulled Bree into the seated position. They were breathing rapidly, and she could swear he had to hear her heart thumping. "We should go inside before the driver opens the door and finds we've given him a show."

Bree chuckled. "That sounds like a good idea."

GRAYSON DIDN'T LIKE the reprieve. He wished the limo hadn't stopped and that he could not only continue kissing Bree, but make love to her. The need to possess her was one reason, but the other wasn't altruistic. He needed to distract her.

Somehow Bree had sensed his hatred of her father during the charity gala. He had tried his best to hide his emotions and thought he'd succeeded, but clearly Bree had seen the cracks in his carefully crafted façade. The more time they spent together, the easier she could read him and sense his mood.

And she'd sensed something was amiss tonight.

Grayson knew it was just a matter of time before his machinations blew up in his face, before he lost Bree for good—though he'd do everything he could to not let that happen. But for tonight, for one more night, he wanted to block out the world like it didn't exist and make it about the two of them, not about the drama lurking around the corner.

When they made it into Bree's apartment, they didn't bother turning on the lights. Instead, Grayson began toeing off his shoes while Bree kicked off her shoes. Then she spun around and jumped into his arms, kissing him frantically as if she too knew this might be their last coupling.

Grayson clutched Bree's bottom as she wrapped

her legs around his waist and he carried her to the bedroom. He placed her gently against the bed, facing the headboard so he could unzip her dress. It fell to her knees, and Grayson glimpsed her strapless bra, garter, and thong.

He swore under his breath. Thank God he hadn't seen her like this earlier, otherwise he'd have rushed her upstairs into one of the hotel rooms and had his way with her. Bree turned around and helped relieve him of all his clothes until he was standing in his boxers. Then Bree sat down on the bed and Grayson joined her, and they fell backward in a mass of limbs. They were eager to feel skin on skin and dispensed with their undergarments just as quickly until they were both naked.

"You're so beautiful, so perfect," Grayson murmured as his hands trailed down her body. He could drink in the sight of her all day: her lovely bones, her flat stomach, full hips, her plump, delicious breasts. He wanted to feel them on his tongue. He closed a hand around a firm mound, and Bree trembled when his tongue flicked across the tight nub of her nipple. A throaty gasp escaped her lips.

"You taste so good." He bent his head to savor her more fully. Bree grabbed the back of his neck to hold him there. He paid homage to her breasts, licking, tasting, and nibbling one and then the other. He loved her responsiveness as he explored her voluptuous terrain.

Bree began moving beneath him, rubbing her wet mound against his erection. Grayson wasn't sure he would be able to take his time if she continued teasing him. He needn't have worried because Bree was taking control, curling her fingers around his shaft.

Grayson sucked in a deep breath as her fingers

tightened around him, and she began fisting him up and down. "Jesus, Bree, you're killing me," he groaned. He grabbed her hands and placed them over her head. As he kissed her, he shifted positions so he could nudge his erection between her moist folds.

"Yes, Grayson, yes," Bree encouraged him as he took his time entering her, inch by delicious inch. When she began moving to take him in deeper, Grayson held her hips and slowly went deeper into her slickness, then he withdrew.

"Oh God, Grayson."

Bree was trembling with need as was he, but Grayson was determined to take his time, make it last. He repeated the process and this time he went even deeper and it was he who groaned as Bree's greedy inner muscles clenched around his shaft.

Grayson watched her face. She was flushed, and her skin was moist, but her eyes were open. She was watching him too, taking in every moment as if she too was trying to memorize it. He thrust into her again and again, and Bree wrapped her legs around his spine, taking him in every time. Her eyes widened when her climax hit, and she jerked, spurring Grayson to thrust into her again before he felt a spirit-lifting release take over him.

They didn't stop at one lovemaking session. It continued throughout the night with Bree on top, riding him into the abyss. And at one point, Grayson had Bree facedown on the mattress, her behind up in the air for him to enjoy. And boy did he. He pounded into her until she was pleading with him to take her. And then finally, her legs over his shoulders, he'd brought them both home to ecstasy until eventually they'd passed out from sheer exhaustion and utter bliss.

~

THE NEXT DAY after she awoke, Bree felt sated and a bit sore between her thighs. Last night with Grayson had been *the* most epic night of sex they'd ever had. She'd lost count of the times they'd made love or brought each other to climax orally. She remembered a particularly great moment when she'd had his length in her mouth and she'd tasted all of him.

The memory made her smile, and she turned to Grayson, but he was gone.

Bree sat upright. There was a note on the bed.

Didn't want to wake you up, but had to leave for some family business. Thank you for an amazing night. Will call later.

Grayson

Bree was disappointed. She'd anticipated they'd have a morning quickie before getting up to make breakfast. A glance at the clock told her just how late it was. It was nearly noon. No wonder he'd left—he probably had a commitment to Cameron today.

Grayson had worn her out so thoroughly, she'd missed the entire morning. She donned her robe and slippers and headed to the kitchen to make coffee when the front door opened.

It was Jada.

"I would say good afternoon," Jada said, closing the door, but then glancing at Bree's outfit, she added, "but perhaps I should say good morning. Are you just getting up?"

Bree colored. "Don't judge me," she said as she set about making coffee in her Keurig. After dropping in a pod, she found a mug in the cupboard and placed it under the machine.

"Looks like someone had a long night." Jada snickered.

Bree spun around and with a wicked grin, asked, "Jealous?"

"Hell yeah!" Jada snickered. "I can't remember the last time I've had good sex, you know the kind that makes your toes curl and your eyes go back in your sockets."

Bree laughed uncontrollably. Her sister was a hot mess. "Jada, what am I going to do with you?"

"Well, you won't have to wait to find out. I'm headed back to San Francisco later today."

"So soon?"

"I know. I have to cut my trip short. I got a call from the station, and they need me to fill in for a coworker tomorrow. There's been an emergency."

Bree opened the fridge to remove some creamer. "I just kind of got used to the idea of having you here." She added a touch to her mug now that the coffee had finished brewing.

"I'm glad I made the trip and could meet the infamous Grayson Wells. That one is definitely a keeper." Though Jada didn't particularly care for Grayson, she'd seen the genuine affection he and Bree shared and that meant the world to her. She'd come to the conclusion that he was right for Bree.

"You think so?"

Jada frowned. "Are you doubting him, Bree? What changed? I thought you said you loved him."

"I do," Bree said. "It's just that . . . I dunno. I can't put my finger on it, but last night there was definitely something going on between Duke and Grayson."

"You mean the fact that Daddy could spit nails?"

Bree shook her head. "No. There's something more. In fact, I'm sure of it. I've spent time with

Grayson. I know him. I mean as well as you can know someone after barely two months, but I feel like he has an agenda where our father is concerned."

"Hmmm, like what?"

"I don't know," Bree said. "But you can be damn sure I'm going to figure it out."

~

"Arash, I'm so glad you picked up," Grayson said when he called his best friend long distance.

"You're lucky I did," Arash replied groggily. "Do you have any idea what time it is?"

Grayson glanced down at his Rolex. It was five p.m. in the United States, which meant it was two a.m. in Kadar. "I'm sorry, Arash."

"Because it's you, I picked up," Arash responded. "So what's going on?"

"I made a mistake."

"Mistake? Don't speak in riddles, Grayson. It's the middle of the night for me. Speak plainly."

"Right." Grayson took a deep breath. "I made a mistake getting involved with Bree."

"How so? Has something happened? Did she find out about your vendetta against her father?"

"No, but I suspect she will. Last night, I met Duke in person for the first time."

"And how'd that go?"

"He hates me, and the feeling is mutual."

"And Bree picked up on that?"

"How'd you guess?" Grayson said.

"Because if she's really into you as I thought she was when we first met, she's in sync with you and is starting to know when you're hiding something from her."

"What do I do?"

"Come clean with Bree. Tell her everything. About your father. The role Duke played. Your quest for revenge against the man you believe wronged him."

"And what then? What if she leaves me?"

Arash chuckled. "Honestly? It would be what you so richly deserved for not having told her the truth in the first place. But given that you've fallen for the woman, I would say hope for the best."

"Fallen for her. I didn't say that."

"You didn't have to. You wouldn't be calling me in the middle of the night if you didn't care a great deal about Bree and value your relationship. You're running scared that you'll lose her."

"I can't lose her." Grayson's feelings for Bree had grown exponentially. He knew that without a doubt he needed, no *wanted* Bree in his life, and he would do everything in his power to ensure that. But how did he go about it?

"Well then, you know what you must do."

"You make it sound so easy."

"It is. If you care for the woman, you'll be honest and up front with her and let her decide."

19

Bree dropped off Jada at the airport then headed to the Hart ranch. She needed to speak with her father and hash out their differences once and for all. But when she arrived, Caleb was already there with her father in his study. They were discussing Grayson.

"I don't trust the man," Duke said. "Did you see how he was handling Bree? As if she was his possession. I don't like it."

"You can't stop her from seeing him, Duke."

"Don't you think I know that. But there's something sneaky about Wells. I can feel it deep in my bones. He has an agenda, Caleb. I'm sure of it. The Johnson land was only one part of it. I knew I should have listened to my instinct and investigated the company and the man Bree worked for, but Abigail made me promise to let Bree make her own mistakes."

"Do you think he's after you?" Caleb asked.

"Me? Hart Enterprises? Or both of us?" asked Duke. "Whichever it is, we need to find out. He's been ahead of the eight ball on us for some time, but it's time we played defense and get caught up. We need to find out what his plan is."

"Here's what the preliminary investigation has shown."

Bree heard the rustle of papers and figured Caleb was handing Duke some sort of file on Grayson. What did it contain?

"So you're telling me this kid just materialized out of the clear-blue sky seven years ago as a millionaire? Who is his family? Where did he go to school? There has to be more than this." She heard Duke slam his fist on the table.

"I know," Caleb concurred. "Something's not right, but our investigator is on it. He'll unearth whatever secrets Grayson is trying to hide."

"And what of Bree? Are we to let your cousin continue seeing him?"

"She's a grown woman. You have to let her make her own mistakes, Duke. This isn't like when she was seventeen and you intervened on her behalf. I'm cautioning you to take a step back or you could lose Bree."

Duke sighed. "I know that. That bastard has me over a barrel. If I push too hard, I'll alienate my daughter even more than I already have and push her further into his sneaky arms."

"Bree is a smart woman. She'll figure it out if she hasn't already. Trust her to make the right decision."

"Alright," Duke conceded. "I'll stand down for now."

Bree turned away and leaned against the wall. None of this was making any sense. *There is no record of Grayson other than the last seven years? Dad is right. How can that be?* There had to be records—school, medical, or something. Grayson was purposely hiding his past, and Bree was curious why. And what did it have to do with her father?

Deciding that now wasn't the best time to confront

Duke, Bree quietly tiptoed down the hall and out of the house.

~

ON THIS TOUGH Monday afternoon in his office, Grayson replaced the receiver in the hook. It was done. Brooke Jenkins had told Caleb Hart that he would no longer transport Hart Enterprises's oil. It would be a devastating blow and one that Grayson doubted Duke Hart could recover from.

He was finally getting his revenge. So why did it feel so hollow? He'd done what he'd set out to do. He was giving Duke Hart a taste of his own medicine. Although he hadn't delivered the knockout punch as he would have liked, Grayson had definitely given him a strong upper cut.

But what should he do now? Should he continue his quest and pounce on Hart Enterprises now that they were vulnerable? Would demolishing Duke's life's work finally give him the satisfaction he sought? Grayson wasn't so sure.

And because of that, he'd avoided Bree for the first time in their relationship. He hadn't called her as he'd promised in the note he left her yesterday morning. And today, he'd remained busy, choosing to have meetings out of the office for fear he'd run into her.

He was in the office now only because he'd left a file there that he needed for an early morning offsite meeting tomorrow. He'd already called down to his driver to pull the car around when he'd gotten the call from Brooke.

It should be making him feel good to settle an old score, but Grayson suspected he'd never feel good again. Or be as happy as he'd been the last couple of months with Bree. She'd been the breath of fresh air he'd needed after years of being in a drought for affection.

Julia had never been a doting mother, at least not to him, and if he was honest, not to Cameron either. Losing his father had killed any love that she might have had in her heart, leaving him and his brother with a shell of a woman. It was Sonya who'd been the guiding light in their lives. Julia had merely done what was required of her. She'd put food on the table and kept a roof over their heads.

And now he'd fulfilled the promise he'd made her long ago when he was twelve years old and had found her sobbing in her bedroom. "I promise you, Mother, I'll get the man who double-crossed Daddy if it's the last thing I do."

He hadn't known then that he would have to choose vengeance over the woman he'd fallen head over heels for. But as sure as the air Grayson breathed into his lungs, he knew that the choice would probably be made for him. As much as he struggled with how he could keep Bree throughout these wretched machinations, he finally gave up on the idea that that was possible. Now he knew he would have to push her away. He'd have to get her to hate him because that was preferable to breaking her heart.

~

BREE STARED at her phone in her hand. Grayson hadn't called since yesterday. He hadn't called her since the wonderful night of lovemaking they'd shared when Bree had felt as if they were truly joined as one. One heart. One soul.

She'd called him several times and texted him

Sunday and again this morning before work, but he hadn't deigned to respond to any of her attempts at contact. At first she gave him the benefit of the doubt. Returning home yesterday, he could have had his hands full with Cameron and tending to Julia. But then when he hadn't called in the evening, she'd been crestfallen. *Is he angry with me because I questioned him about his motives involving Daddy?* She had a right to ask the questions. He was her father after all.

But the longer she didn't hear from Grayson, the more Bree began to worry. And then he hadn't shown up at work, and that was worrisome too. Duke and Caleb were already investigating Grayson's past. And if she was honest, Bree was curious to hear what they'd dug up. Maybe then it would shed light on the entire situation and help her understand why Grayson was pushing her away.

She was feeling down in the dumps at her desk when her sister London called her cellphone. "London, it's so good to hear from you," Bree said. "How are you? How's Chase? How's Shay's?" Shay's was the soul-food restaurant London owned in New Orleans's French Quarter.

London laughed. "We're all doing well. I was calling to check in on you. Jada told me what went down between your boyfriend and Daddy. Has everything calmed down?"

Bree snorted. "Far from it. In fact, I don't know what's going on." She filled London in on the last couple of days—the charity event, Caleb's investigation into Grayson, and Grayson's behavior toward Bree.

"Definitely sounds suspicious," London said. "And you haven't been able to talk to Grayson to clear the air?"

"No. I get the distinct impression he's avoiding me." Bree didn't like it. Now she knew how he felt when she'd avoided him after the first time they made love. She supposed turnabout was fair play in his book.

"What are you going to do?"

"Well, I'm certainly not going to take this lying down. I'm going to confront him."

"And what if you don't like what he has to say?"

Bree hadn't thought about that, at least not fully. She just knew she had to see Grayson. Look him in the eye and find out the truth. One way or another. "I guess I'll deal with it when the time comes."

"If you need me, sis, I'm here. I can always fly in for a couple of days and spend some quality with you. Chase can manage things here."

"You would do that?"

"Of course," London replied. "Remember when you called me out on being a better sister last year? Well now, it's time I put my money where my mouth is."

"I appreciate that, London, and I just might call you up on it."

~

"YOU'RE BEHIND THIS!" Duke roared when he stormed into Grayson's office barely an hour and a half after Grayson's call with Brooke. Grayson had taken another urgent call after Brooke's and hadn't been able to escape Wells Oil.

"Mr. Wells, I'm so sorry. I couldn't stop him," a flustered Rosalie said from the doorway. "Would you like me to call security?"

Grayson shook his head. The day of reckoning was

here, and it was time he put a stone in his sling and fling it right at Goliath's head. "No, Rosalie, that's not necessary. I've got this."

She glanced back and forth at both men, but eventually closed the door.

"Duke, what can I do for you?" Grayson asked from behind his desk.

"You can forget the feigned sincerity," Duke said with a snort. "I know who you really are."

"Do you?" If he did, Caleb Hart had made some fast work of investigating him. He'd heard that some inquiries had been made, but Grayson hadn't anticipated the truth would be revealed quite so quickly.

"Yes I do. And I know you're behind Jenkins refusing to transport our oil."

Grayson's eye twitched, the only giveaway of his surprise. The old bastard had given him his word. He supposed he shouldn't be startled. The old guard of Dallas oilmen stuck together, and he was just the new kid on the block.

"So?"

"I know you called in a favor he owed you because you wanted to get back at me." Duke pounded his chest.

"And you know why," Grayson said quietly.

"Yes, I do," Duke said. "But it doesn't matter now because you've put yourself and Wells Oil in the line of fire, and you can best believe that I won't go down without a fight. I'll go down with both arms swinging before I ever let a snot-nose punk like you take me out."

Grayson stood up. "You mean the snot-nose son of a bitch," he yelled, "because that's who you're talking to."

"Ah." Duke took several steps backward and regarded him. "Now the real Grayson has come out to play. The man who swindled rich men out of oil fields and millions of dollars. You're nothing but a two-bit con artist, just like your father."

Grayson lunged for Duke and had him up against the door before the older man could react. "Don't you dare talk about my father! You've no right."

"I have every right," Duke responded and with little to no effort, shoved Grayson and took several steps away from him. "Elijah was my best friend. We grew up together. We were thick as thieves. If you found one of us, you were sure to find the other."

"If he was such a good friend to you, how did my father end up with nothing, broke and alone, while you, the great Duke Hart, flourished on the land? Land that was equally his."

"Because your father sold it to me!" Duke yelled.

"You're lying."

"I'm not. Elijah was up to his eyeballs in debt to some loan shark. I'd tried to get him out of the gambling habit, but he wouldn't listen to me, to your mother, to anyone. He was too far gone. And I blame myself for that. I was too busy chasing skirts and whoring around to pay him much mind. Don't you think I blame myself for what happened to your father?"

"Don't you dare try to make me feel sorry for you, Duke," Grayson hissed. "My father ended up with nothing, while you thrived and built a ranch and an oil empire off what should have been his."

"And you blame me for that, right?" Duke's eyes blazed fury. "You blame me for your father losing everything and you and your mother ending up with nothing, poor and living hand to mouth."

"Yes, damn you!" Grayson yelled. "You're the reason for all of it."

Duke shook his head. "No, son. Who you're angry at is your father. He's the one who had a gambling debt. He's the one who didn't realize what a prime piece of real estate the Hart ranch was. But I did. I'd always had dreams of owning my own ranch after the Hart family was foreclosed upon in Tucson. It was my sister, Madelyn, and her husband, Isaac, who bought it again one day. But I, I was determined to have my piece of the pie and live the American dream. I went for mine."

"At my father's expense."

"It's not my fault Elijah was a gambler and a drunk."

"If you were his friend as you claim, you should have looked out for him, looked out for his family."

Duke nodded. "You're right. And I failed in that regard. But Elijah moved out of Dallas, and I couldn't locate him or your family for that matter. Did I try hard enough? Maybe not, and I'll have to live with my mistakes. But you—"

"Me what?"

"You came after me with both guns loaded, spoiling for a fight. And you've succeeded. I'm here now. You've got one."

"Yeah, you do," Grayson said. "And now you know what it feels like to be on the bottom for once, like my father was."

Duke threw his head back and laughed, and that only infuriated Grayson more. "You're laughing? Really? You can laugh knowing what you did to my father and our family?"

Duke shook his head. "I'm not laughing at you, son, only that you think you've outfoxed me."

"Excuse me?"

"Do you honestly think I don't have another deal lined up to transport my oil? I've been in this business much longer than you, and there's nothing a deal in a back room with a handshake over some whiskey can't fix."

Grayson fumed. "What the hell is that supposed to mean?"

"Hart Enterprises already had another oil tanker deal lined up, and now we're cashing in on it. I sealed the deal less than thirty minutes ago."

"That can't be. Jenkins is the biggest tanking company in town other than Walker Trucking. And everyone knows Addison's father hates you."

"But not the only," Duke responded. "And as for the Johnson land, I'll give you that one. That really sticks in my craw given that bastard refused to sell to me for years even though I could have made it more prosperous than he ever did. But no worries. I hope you enjoy that land and the fruits of your labor."

"I'll do that. And you want to know why?"

"No, but I'm sure you want to tell me. You've had this sitting on your chest for decades. It must be eating you alive. So go ahead, hit me with it."

"That's right," Grayson said, feeding into the morbid conversation he and Duke were having. Because finally, finally he was getting to say his peace even though he could see that his carefully calculated plans were going up in smoke. "I have made it my mission in life to destroy you, Duke, and everything you love. You may have gotten off easy this time around, but I won't stop coming after you." Adrenaline coursed through Grayson, and he continued jabbing at Duke. "I won't stop coming after you until you feel the pain that you caused me and my entire family."

"And what of my daughter Bree?" Duke asked. "Where does she fit in all your grand schemes?"

In the heat of the moment, Grayson didn't hesitate to respond and stated, "Bree is a casualty of war."

"And is that where we are now?" Duke inquired. "At war?"

"Damn straight."

"Well then," Duke said, "let the best man win." He turned on his heel and swung open the door.

Bree was standing on the other side—she couldn't stand not seeing Grayson anymore and had stopped by to see if he'd finally arrived at work. Tears were streaming down her stained scarlet cheeks, and her eyes stared back at Grayson in wide disbelief as if she couldn't have heard what she just did. But he knew she had. She'd heard everything. She was shattered. Her eyes...

He was a wretched human being because the look of pure and utter pain on her beautiful face was so great that Grayson thought he might vomit.

"So I was a pawn in your chess game?" Bree wailed as humiliation turned to raw fury.

"Bree. You, you don't understand." Grayson was flustered and couldn't get his words out. He hadn't expected Bree to be on the other side of that door. "You have no idea what your father," he said, pointing to Duke, "has done."

"Oh I heard you loud and clear," Bree said, throwing the words at him like stones. "I think the entire executive staff heard you. And I get the gist. My father took your father's land, and it left you and your family penniless. And now you've come to exact revenge against my father."

Bree shook her head as if she couldn't believe the words that were coming out of her own mouth. "Well congratulations, Grayson, on a job well done. You've done what you set out to do. And now you can go to hell because I never want to see you again."

Bree raced down the corridor and out of Grayson's view. He had to go to her. Explain somehow. He rushed toward the door, but Duke held up one large hand. "I swear to God, Wells, if you go near my daughter, I won't be responsible for what I might do to you."

Seconds later, Duke was rushing down the corridor to get to Bree, leaving Grayson standing alone in his doorway. Several of his staff members were openly staring at him, so Grayson closed his double doors. He heaved against them, sliding down until he hit the floor.

For the first time in years, he cried.

20

"London will be on her way tomorrow," Addison said as she sat beside Bree later that evening.

Bree was on the sofa, crying. Addison and Caleb lived in Fort Worth, not far from Dallas, and Bree hadn't known where else to go. She certainly couldn't go to her apartment because that's the first place Grayson would look. And she couldn't bear to look at her father after hearing all of Grayson's accusations. So she'd come here where she knew she would be safe and could talk through all that she'd heard.

"Thank you," Bree responded, "but you didn't have to call her."

"I called Jada too, but of course she just got back to work and couldn't leave again, so London was the next best thing."

Bree nodded and reached for a tissue from the box Addison had placed by her side and blew her nose. "Omigod, Addison. I feel like such a fool for believing Grayson, for thinking that he cared about me. He was only using me to get back at Duke."

"I'm so sorry, Bree." Addison reached for her and pulled her into a hug. "I'm so sorry this has happened to you. I know how much you cared for Grayson."

"Cared?" Bree let out a long sigh as a raw, almost primitive grief took over her. Head bowed, she slumped and a sob escaped from low in her throat. It was several minutes before she could look up and say, "I love him, Addison. And now, I realize it was all a lie, built on lies."

"Drink this." Addison handed her a cup. "It's a hot toddy, and it's going to make you feel a lot better."

Bree wasn't sure there was enough liquor in the world to make her feel better about herself or her relationship with Grayson, if she could even call it that. "He said I was a casualty of war." She remembered everything he'd said to Duke.

"That's horrible, Bree. Did he really say that?"

Bree nodded. "I'm struggling to see if there was anything real between us. Or maybe I just made up my mind that we meant more to each other than being sexually compatible, because all I was to him was a weapon of destruction against my father."

Bree glanced upward and continued. "Daddy warned me, but I just dove straight in. I didn't even check Grayson out enough to make sure he was on the up and up. I just saw an opportunity to escape Duke's iron fist, and I took it. Now look at where it's landed me."

A round of fresh tears overtook her, and Bree began sobbing uncontrollably. The pain in her heart was almost too much to bear, and she didn't think she could face it. She clung to Addison and her round belly as she wondered if life would ever be the same.

∼

WHEN HE FINALLY MADE IT to the mansion that evening, Grayson was decimated. After putting back on his mask, he'd settled the troops and eventually they'd returned to work, though some of his staff were still looking at him and whispering. Did they know he'd utterly destroyed Bree?

In one fell swoop, he'd single-handedly killed any feeling she had for him. Grayson doubted he'd ever forget her pained expression when he'd admitted that she'd been a pawn in his chess game to outwit and outlast Duke Hart. But she'd become so much more— a beacon of light in his otherwise dreary quest for vengeance.

She'd lit up his life and Cameron's life with her vivaciousness. He'd been completely and utterly bewitched since he'd seen her in that ditch. Every time he'd thought about ending it between them, he'd be sucked back into her silken web. A web he knew he'd never get tired of. And making love to Bree was—is— the best sex he'd ever had in his life. Of that, he was certain. No other woman would or could ever compare to her. She was so responsive to his touch, to his kisses, but she was equally giving in the bedroom. She ensured he was satisfied every time. He made love with Bree and only Bree.

Closing the door behind him, Grayson made his way to the living room's wet bar. He was making himself a drink in the dark when he noticed he wasn't alone.

"Mother?"

"Grayson."

He headed for the nearest lamp and flicked it on. His mother was holding a tumbler filled with a dark liquid. "Should you be drinking that?"

Julia shrugged. "What does it matter anyway? I'm probably going to die soon. This cancer is aggressive,

Grayson. So why shouldn't I enjoy a good Scotch when the mood strikes."

The fight was all gone out of him to argue. If a drink was what she wanted, so be it. "Why not indeed." Grayson sank in the chair opposite her and threw his drink back in one fell swoop.

"You're home early," Julia commented. "No plans with the Hart girl?"

Grayson lifted his head slightly. "There won't be any plans with Bree now or in the future."

"Really, and why is that?"

"Because I did it, Mother. I did as I promised, and I went after Duke. I ruined two prosperous deals for him."

"Bully for you!" She raised her glass.

Grayson snorted. "Too bad, the old coot outfoxed me and made a comeback on one of them."

"You did your best, and that's all I can ask," Julia said. "So does this mean the Hart girl is now out of the picture?"

Grayson raged from his seat. "And you would like that, wouldn't you, Mother? For me to end up alone and bitter just like you?"

She was silent and sipped her drink, so Grayson continued, "Do you even realize how cold and unfeeling you've become?"

"If I am, it's because of your father."

"So losing Dad did this to you?" he asked incredulously. "Well guess what, Mother? Dad left twenty years ago. How long are you going to continue to hold on to past hurts and anger—until it kills you or the both of us?"

"That's a horrible thing to say."

"Well, it's the truth." Grayson sat his glass on the

cocktail table in front of him with a thud. "I fulfilled my promise, Mother. I made it my life's work to get revenge on Duke Hart for all the perceived wrongs he's done to this family. But guess what. The joke is on me because Duke is doing just fine. He gets to go home to a loving family, while I am left with an evil old woman for a mother and to look after Cameron and Sonya, all alone with no one to love me. Is this what you've always wanted for me, Mother?" Grayson lowered his head and clasped it in his hands as the weight of the day hit him.

Bree was gone. He'd lost her because he couldn't let go of the past and move on with his life.

"Of course not," Julia responded. When she spoke, Grayson realized she'd moved from the couch and was crouching in front of him. "I've always wanted nothing but the best for you, even when I couldn't give it to you myself, Grayson. I love you."

She pulled him into her arms, and Grayson held on tightly as he cried yet again for the love he'd lost. He now knew without a shadow of a doubt what his true feelings for Bree were, but because of his vengeance, he'd lost her, the one and only woman he'd ever loved.

~

"London, I'm so happy to have you here," Bree said as her big sister made her a breakfast of pancakes, eggs, and ham two days later. "Even if it is for a short visit," she added. Since London had arrived the previous night, Bree had been crying on her shoulder on and off.

"I'm sorry I can't stay longer, but I can only leave Shay's for a few days," London said. "But I felt like you needed your big sis."

Bree stared at London. Since they had different mothers, London had gleaming chestnut hair and a curvy figure while Bree and Jada ran more slender thanks to Abigail's petite frame. At nearly six feet tall, London was conscious of her plus-sized figure, but Bree wished she had London's curves. And she was wearing the hell out of a black jumpsuit. Back in the day, London would never wear anything so bold, but since she'd married Chase last year, her confidence had grown by leaps and bounds.

"I wish you would have been here sooner. Maybe you could have talked some sense into me so that I wouldn't have fallen for a con artist like Grayson Wells."

"Baby girl," London said, turning around from the frying pan, "sometimes these things happen. You remember my marriage to Shawn. Brother man knew how to talk the talk and walk the walk that had my head spinning, but in the end it was all smoke and mirrors. I realized that too late, and he cheated on me. Sometimes, we get caught up. But it's okay to make mistakes."

"But you sure rebounded with Chase."

A smile spread across London's full lips. "Oh yes, Chase is all kinds of wonderful, but marriage is hard work and it's not always easy even after you find your dream man."

"Are you talking about how hard it's been for you and Chase to get pregnant?" Bree ventured into the taboo subject as she made a fresh cup of coffee on her Keurig. She wasn't sure she should bring it up, but since the conversation was going down that path, Bree had opened the door.

"It's okay," London said. "I don't mind talking about it. Yes, Chase and I have been challenged in that department, but we're not giving up. At least not yet. And if the Lord doesn't bless us with our own child, we'll adopt. There are plenty of children in need of parents like us."

Bree smiled at London's positive outlook. "You know what, sis, you're exactly who I need."

London beamed. "Good," she said and inclined her head toward the kitchen. "Then c'mon over and get some of these flapjacks, brown sugar honey ham, and smoked gouda eggs I've cooked up."

Bree's stomach growled. It occurred to her that it was the first time in nearly forty-eight hours that she'd stopped crying. Or thought about what a mess she'd made of her professional as well as her love life.

Bree didn't know where she was going from here. Certainly not back to Wells Oil. That dream had flown out the window the minute she'd learned Grayson had used her as a pawn in his quest for retribution against Duke. But should she go back to Hart Enterprises? She just didn't know.

"What's going on in that head of yours?" London asked when they sat down to eat breakfast.

Bree shrugged. "Just figuring out where I go from here."

"Understandable. You took a hit. Now you need to lie back for a second and reassess."

Bree reached for the coffee she'd been sipping on.

"You don't have to figure it out now either. Take as much time as you need until your heart catches up with your head."

Bree laughed. "That could be a long time, London."

"Well, you're certainly not hurting for money." London glanced around the apartment. "Just look at this place."

Bree smiled. Grayson had been paying her hand-somely and so had HE. When she'd been living at the ranch, she'd put most of her salary into stocks and bonds. She had quite the nest egg saved up for a rainy day. And apparently now was that day.

"You might be on to something, London," Bree said. Maybe she should take a sabbatical and get her head together before she made any rash decisions. Look at where that had gotten her.

"Of course I am," London replied. "I'm your big sister."

ON THURSDAY EVENING, Grayson stood on the balcony staring across at the Eiffel Tower. On a whim, he de-cided to meet Arash in Paris not only to see his best friend, but to get out of Dallas. He couldn't stay there right now without seeing Bree at every corner. He imagined her at the office hunched over her monitor with her riotous curls framing her face as she read a geology report. Or at the mansion when she'd played Jenga with him, Cameron, and Sonya. Or in bed when he was buried deep inside her, and she moaned his name.

Cameron, of course, had pitched a fit when he was leaving, and Grayson had promised to come back in a few days. Cameron had also wanted to know where Bree was and why she hadn't come by in a while. Grayson didn't have the heart to tell his brother that he'd run her away. Now he needed time to clear his head and figure out his next step.

"I've made a real mess of things, haven't I?" Grayson said as he walked back inside the luxurious apartment Arash owned in Paris. It was just one of Arash's many homes in the world's popular cities.

"I believe you know the answer to that question," Arash responded.

Grayson glared at him. "You're not helping."

"That's not why you're here," Arash commented. "You're hiding because you're afraid to face Bree after everything you've done."

"Wow! Don't sugarcoat it, my friend." He glared at Arash.

"That's not in my nature. I'm giving it to you—how do you Americans say—straight up?"

Grayson laughed at Arash's attempt to use American colloquialisms. "Please don't try to speak slang. It doesn't suit you."

Arash shrugged.

"I'll go back," Grayson stated. "I have to because I have to take care of Cameron and Mother."

"And because Bree's there?"

"Bree doesn't want to see me, and I doubt she'll ever forgive me for deceiving her and having an ulterior motive to destroy her father."

"It is quite a quandary you're in, my friend."

"And how do I get myself out of it, Arash? You're my oldest and dearest friend, and I need your sage advice."

"Which you didn't take previously," Arash commented, rubbing his chin thoughtfully. "Did I or did I not tell you to come clean with Bree before this all came out?"

Grayson glared at him. "Now is not the time to tell me 'I told you so.'"

"When is it? Because I'd like to know," Arash said with a smirk.

Despite his foul mood, all Grayson could do was

laugh. There's no way he could be angry at Arash. He was right. He had told him to be honest with Bree, but Grayson had continued on a path for vengeance and now he was alone with only himself to blame. "I ask you again, how do I win her back?"

"Typically, I would say you should make grand gestures of love and affection and such, but on Bree, it would be wasted. She's one of the most down-to-earth, unpretentious women I've ever met. My best advice to you my friend is time."

"Time?"

"Give her time. Time to forgive you. And time to remember how much she loves you."

"And what if during that time she decides she doesn't want to be with me?"

"Then you'll have to move on with no regrets. But for now, tell her how you feel—that you love her as I suspect you do and that you'll wait for her until she's ready to give you a second chance."

Grayson stared at Arash for several moments. "That was pretty profound, you know?"

Arash chuckled. "They don't call me the Crown Prince for nothing."

～

WHEN HER BELL rang Friday morning, Bree was surprised to see Duke on the other side of the door. Never in a million years would she have imagined he would lower himself to leave the ranch and come to her apartment, not when he'd been steadfastly against her moving out to begin with.

"Daddy?"

"Baby girl," Duke whispered, and immediately Bree rushed into his arms. He held her securely to his chest, and she breathed in his warm masculine scent that was equal parts hay and man. When they finally pulled apart, there were tears in both their eyes.

"What are you doing here?" Bree asked.

"Since you weren't going to come to me, I had to come and check on my baby girl."

"Come in." She motioned him inside and closed the door behind her.

"Who is it?" London inquired, barreling out of the guest bedroom. "Daddy!" she squealed and raced into his arms.

Without much effort, their father lifted full-figured London off the floor. "How's my eldest?" he asked, lowering her to the hardwood.

"Living the dream, Daddy, living the dream." London glanced at Bree and again at Duke. "But I'm awfully glad to see you. I was going to try and make it over before Bree and I head to New Orleans."

"New Orleans?" Duke turned around and looked at Bree. "What's London talking about?"

Bree bunched her shoulders. "I just need a change of scenery for a while, and when London offered that I come down to the Big Easy for a long visit, I decided to take her up on it."

"Leave Dallas? It's your home." Duke looked baffled.

"Not for good," Bree responded. "I just need to get my head together, you know, clear my thoughts."

"You can do that at the ranch."

"With you hovering over my shoulder." Bree laughed. "No thank you. New Orleans will do just fine."

"This is because of me, isn't it?" His expression was grim as he watched Bree.

London coughed audibly. "Listen, you both need

to talk, so I'm going to run to the store to get some fresh ingredients for our last day here."

Bree nodded, and London quietly exited the apartment, leaving Bree and her father alone.

"Please." Bree motioned for Duke to sit, but he remained standing.

"You're running away," Duke said, "and I never taught you that. You get that from your mama. I wish she would have stayed and fought for us instead of running away."

"Don't bring Mama into the picture. This is about you, me, and Grayson, and this triangle we're in."

"A triangle I started," Duke began, "when his father signed over his share of the Hart land to me."

Bree nodded. "I heard everything you said, Daddy. I was standing outside *his*"—she couldn't even say his name—"office. And you were right. You weren't responsible for his father's drinking or gambling."

"Yeah, I know that," Duke said and began pacing her hardwood floor. "But I should have, could have done better by his family. I could have checked in on them to make sure they were getting along alright, but I didn't. I was selfish and caught in my own life of women and business."

"It happens."

"Don't let me off so easy, girl," Duke said harshly. "I know I'm the cause of your heartache. I'm the reason that boy targeted Hart Enterprises and as a result *you*. He wanted the best and brightest petroleum geologist, and he found that in you."

Bree was speechless. Duke wasn't known for doling out compliments, so when one was given, she had to take it. "Thank you, Daddy. You've never said that before."

"Said what? That I'm proud of you and your accomplishments?" Duke's voice rose slightly. "Well, I am. Always have been."

Bree smiled, and she could feel tears stinging her eyes. "Thank you. It's nice to hear you say so."

"It's the truth. You must have known, Bree," Duke said. "You were and always will be my fa-favorite child." His voice cracked slightly. "You're the most like me, which is probably why we butt heads so much."

"You ain't lying." Bree chuckled. Sometimes they were *too* much alike.

"I'm sorry for any heartache I brought to you because of *me*." He patted his chest. "I'm sorry it came back to bite you in the ass in the form of a con artist bent on revenge."

Bree shook her head. "Please, Daddy, don't."

"Don't speak ill of him? After what he did to you? After he led you on."

"I followed him knowingly and of my own volition. He didn't force me, not into his company or his bed."

Duke covered his ears. "Spare me. I don't want to hear about my daughter's love life."

Bree let out a low laugh. "And I don't want to talk about it. What's done is done, and we just have to move on from here."

"But you want to leave and go to New Orleans."

"Only for a little while. I'll be back, because you're right about one thing: Dallas is my home. And no man is going to run me out of it."

"That's my girl." Duke grabbed her arm and pulled her into his embrace. He kissed the top of her head. "You're one tough cookie."

21

Several days later, Grayson made his way to the Hart ranch on a mission. He'd listened to Arash, and this time he'd heard him. But before he could approach Bree, he had to take care of some unfinished business.

He parked his Porsche convertible in front of the Hart ranch. He was heading up the steps when a ranch hand told him Mr. Duke wasn't in the house but at the stables.

"Thanks," Grayson said. He took a deep breath and steeled himself for his meeting with Duke Hart. If ever there was a snowball's chance in hell of Grayson and Bree making a go of it one day, Grayson had to make peace with Duke.

When he reached the stables, Grayson followed the direction of Duke's voice until he found him in a stall. But Duke wasn't alone. He was knee deep with a veterinarian in what appeared to be the delivery of a calf.

Upon hearing the crackling of the hay, Duke looked up and saw Grayson. But rather than be surprised or even angry, Duke ignored him and continued helping the vet pull the calf free from his mother's womb. It looked like a nasty task and a difficult one since both men were struggling to get the calf free.

"If we don't get her out, we're going to lose her," the vet said.

Duke glanced at Grayson. "Well, don't just stand there, boy, get in here and help."

Grayson didn't relish getting his designer jeans soiled, but he'd come to Duke on his territory and if this was the only way he could talk to the man, so be it. He pushed up his sleeves and joined them.

It took a good thirty minutes, but eventually between the three men, they freed the calf, who'd been lodged in the birth canal. When Grayson rose to his feet, his shirt and jeans were completely ruined. Duke's didn't look any better, but Grayson suspected he'd never worn a pair of designer jeans a day in his life.

"C'mon to the house and get cleaned up," Duke said, wiping his hands on a clean towel a stable hand offered him. Then he shook the vet's hand. "Good work, doc. She's a beauty."

"That she is."

Several seconds later, Duke headed toward the house. He turned behind him to see if Grayson was following. "You coming or not?"

"Yes, sir," Grayson said and walked swiftly to catch up to him.

Once they made it to the family home, Duke directed him upstairs to the guest quarters and told him where he could find the shower and incidentals.

"I think Caleb has some clothes here that should fit you. I'll go get 'em and leave them here while you're in the shower."

"Thanks." Grayson didn't know why Duke was

being so nice to him, but he'd take it. After everything Grayson had tried to pull, he'd thought he'd be kicked in his ass as soon as he set foot on the ranch.

The hot shower and a change of clothes felt good. And Duke was right: He and Caleb were nearly the same size and the T-shirt and Wranglers fit him pretty well. When he was dressed, Grayson made his way downstairs and found Duke had showered and was standing up, enjoying a drink in the living room.

Apparently Duke had poured one for Grayson too. It was the middle of the day, and though Grayson didn't usually drink then, he took the glass Duke offered him.

Duke tipped his glass to Grayson and then sat down in a large wing-backed chair. "So, you wanna tell me why you deigned to set foot on my ranch? I'd think it was beneath you, Wells, since you've been so intent on destroying me and everything I love."

Grayson's words reverberated through the room, reminding Grayson of the venom he'd spewed a week ago when Duke had confronted him in his office.

"You're right. I have no right to be here," Grayson began, "given how I've treated you and your daughter."

Duke's eyes penetrated his. "But you're here nonetheless. Why?" Duke wasn't about to make this easy for him.

"I'm here because I owe you an apology."

Duke sipped his drink. "Oh that's rich."

Grayson noted the disdain in his voice and ignored it. He continued. "After hearing your side of the story, I've come to realize that bad decisions were made by both your parts, you and my father—as well as me. I accept my role in this entire debacle. I could have come to you and talked it over and tried to resolve the matter amicably."

"Hmmm, is that so?"

"Yes, it is," Grayson replied unapologetically. "I can accept the fact that my father was a gambler and a drunk who ruined our family and drove my mother into becoming a bitter old woman, bent on revenge. A revenge she fostered in me. If you'll accept that as my father's friend, you could have done better by him and his family. You could have tried to find us, check in on us, to make sure we survived."

Duke stared at him for several long moments, not saying a word. Grayson knew that if they couldn't come to terms, he'd have no hope of reconciling with Bree.

Duke took a sip of his drink and said, "I can accept that."

Grayson let out an audible sigh of relief.

"But here's the thing, son." Duke sat upright and looked Grayson dead in the eye. "I accept the role I played in not being the best friend I could have been, but you, you took things many steps further by involving my daughter in your shenanigans. That," he said, pointing his finger at Grayson, "is what I have a hard time accepting."

"Fair enough." Grayson swallowed the bile in his mouth because Duke was right. "It was never my intention to involve your family in this vendetta, but the first time I laid eyes on Bree, I lost my head. And I admit that I was bewitched. I did seek her out, but not because she was your daughter, but because she was the most beautiful woman I'd ever seen."

"My daughter is attractive," Duke concurred, "same as her mama, Abigail. It was that way for me with Abby. Once I laid eyes on her, there were no other women"—Duke looked down at the floor—"except for that one unfortunate night." His eyes narrowed as he looked at Grayson. "Anyway, all I'm saying is I can understand love at first sight, if that's what you're saying happened to you."

"It is. And if by understanding, do you mean you won't stand in my way if I try to get Bree back?" Grayson asked. "Because I love her, Mr. Hart, and I want to marry Bree if she'll have me."

Duke threw back his head and laughed. "Marry? Bree? Right now? Son, you've lost your mind. My daughter is fit to be tied."

"I know. I know it's going to take time to win her trust."

"That's putting it mildly."

"But you won't stand in my way?" Grayson pressed for an answer. He had to know what he was up against.

Duke shook his head. "I don't speak for my daughter. At least not anymore. Those days are long gone. So you'll have to ask her."

"But you won't stand in my way?" Grayson asked again.

"Not if you're who she wants."

"Thank you, Duke." Grayson rose and offered him his hand. "I don't know what the future holds, but one day, God willing, I'm going to make your daughter my wife."

The two men shook hands, and Grayson left feeling encouraged. He'd made progress with Duke, but he wasn't so sure about Bree. She had every right to be angry at him, hate him even. He could only hope that the love he suspected she felt outweighed the negative.

❧

"I CAN'T BELIEVE I'm in the Big Easy again," Bree said a few days later as she helped London wipe down tables in preparation for the dinner rush at her restaurant Shay's in the French Quarter. The last time she'd been here had been for a girls' weekend with Jada when London had been dating her husband, Chase. Funny how long ago that all seemed. It was a like a lifetime had passed rather than a year.

"Time sure does move quickly," London said. "And I especially never thought I'd see the day when you'd clean tables."

Bree laughed. "You're confusing me with Jada. I've never been against manual labor. Our baby sister, on the other hand, would hate to break a nail."

"How long do you think you're going to stay?" London asked as she handed Bree napkin holders and salt and pepper shakers for the tables.

"I don't know. Not long," Bree replied with a shrug. "You're not kicking me out already, are you? I know you and Chase are newlyweds and all."

"We would never kick you out," Chase Tanner said, coming behind Bree. She glanced behind her at her big lug of a brother-in-law. His amazingly fit physique and broad shoulders were shown off to perfection in his fitted T-shirt and jeans, and his ruggedly handsome face with a trim goatee completed the look. Bree had to admit London had lucked out. "We love having you here, don't we, babe?" He leaned over to plant a kiss on London's full lips.

"That's right." London smiled when Chase playfully smacked her bottom before he went back into the kitchen. "Stay as long as you need."

"Thanks, London."

Stay. That's exactly what Bree intended to do. She would go back to Dallas when the hurt stung a little less and she could stand to face Grayson. It was inevitable that their paths would cross again—they were in the same industry, after all—but she refused to fall apart when that happened. Right now, however, she was too weak.

If she saw him, she might make a complete and utter fool of herself and beg him to take her to bed. When it came to Grayson, she had no self-control. Given the way she felt about him, if he made one move toward her, she would lose her self-respect as well.

When she thought about how she'd behaved with Grayson, how she let him all the way in and not just physically, she grimaced. She'd let him into her heart, into her soul. She'd thought they were building on something—if not a future, a solid foundation. The times she'd stayed over at the mansion she'd seen how easily she could fit into his life, and he seemed to be making room for her. Although Julia had been frigid, Sonya and Cameron loved her and the feeling was mutual.

How could I have gotten it so horribly wrong? Clearly, she'd seen only what she wanted to see—a fantasy that wasn't built on reality. The entire time Grayson had been wheeling and dealing, scheming to get back at Duke for the perceived wrongs against his father. In the process, he'd shattered her trust and faith in everything they'd shared.

Looking back, Bree would never know if he'd meant any of the things he'd said or things he'd done. Was any moment of their time together real? Or had he created this relationship for his own sadistic purposes?

No, she needed to stay in New Orleans for a few weeks if not months, until she could trust herself enough to go back to Dallas.

~

SHE WAS GONE. Grayson stared inside Bree's empty apartment and knew she was nowhere near. He could feel it. Whenever Bree was around, there was a certain energy and vitality in the space she occupied. From the looks of her place, she'd been gone for several days.

Had he missed his chance? Had he stayed away too long and lost the woman he loved? Fate couldn't be that cruel. He couldn't find the one woman he was meant to love, meant to be with, only to have her taken away because he couldn't let go of the past.

Grayson sat down on her couch and shook his head in despair. He'd royally screwed up their relationship. Was there even the slightest chance that he would ever get Bree back? That she would forgive him and give him a second chance to prove he was a man worthy of her love?

He knew she loved him.

And I love her.

He'd known it for weeks, but he'd been afraid to voice it because they were on borrowed time because of his lies, his deception. Instead, he'd shown her his love with his actions, with his body. He'd shown her that he loved her mind, body, and soul.

And somehow, someway, someday, he would get Bree back.

22

Three months later.

"You know you didn't have to come out here yourself," Caleb told Bree as she took dirt samples while knee deep in a ditch of mud. "You have staff that can handle dirty tasks like this for you. And now that you're a member of the board, this is beneath you."

Since returning from New Orleans a few days ago, Bree had rejoined the fold at Hart Enterprises, and to her utter delight, Duke had given equal shares to her, Jada, London, and even her wayward brother Trent, along with seats on the board.

"You forget yourself, Caleb Hart," Bree said with a smile. "This is actually the part of the job that I like. Feeling the wind in my hair, the dirt under my feet. It's how I get a sense of the land."

"It's a great piece of property," Caleb said. "I can't believe Grayson sold it to Duke."

At the sound of Grayson's name, Bree's back stiffened as she placed the test tubes in her duffel to take back to her lab for sampling. Even though it had been over three months since she'd last seen him, Bree's stomach still took a nosedive every time she heard

Grayson's name. She wondered if she'd always feel this way. Or if in time, the pain would lessen.

"I suppose he feels guilty," Bree said, not turning around, "for all his underhanded dealings. Maybe it was his way of making peace with the family. But it doesn't matter. Grayson is a non-factor."

"I hope that isn't true," a deep masculine voice said from behind her, "because I haven't forgotten about you, Bree. Not by a long shot."

Bree glanced up and saw Grayson smiling down at her. She hadn't seen him in months, but he looked nearly the same—bald with a perpetual five o'clock shadow. But his jeans and T-shirt gave away that he'd lost some weight. And dark circles rung his penetrating eyes. Had he been as miserable as she'd been all these months?

Well, good. He deserves it.

"What are you doing here?" Bree said, hating that once again she was meeting him in less than preferred circumstances. Her jeans and T-shirt were plastered in mud and grime, but she didn't care. She was long past caring what Grayson thought about her. He'd shown her exactly how he'd felt when he'd used her to destroy her father.

~

GRAYSON STARED AT BREE. Three long months of not seeing her, smelling her, having her lips on his had devastated him. She looked different. Skinnier. Her once lush behind was more slender, but she was still beautiful. He couldn't believe she was back and he could finally see her. Hear her voice.

He'd thought about going to New Orleans dozens

of times once he'd discovered her whereabouts from Levi and forcing her to talk to him. He'd started dozens of texts and emails in which he begged her to give him a chance so he could explain and hold her. But how could he explain what he had done? And he doubted his alpha male personality would be greeted with anything other than contempt because she'd been so hurt by his actions. He'd hoped that eventually she would want to rail at him, call him names, say anything, but in three months, his phone had been silent.

Radio silent.

So he'd taken Arash's advice and waited. Waited for her to come back... he hoped to him.

But it hadn't been easy. He couldn't eat. He couldn't sleep. He would have stayed in his study with a bottle of Scotch and drowned himself in his sorrows if it hadn't been for Cameron. His little brother needed him. And his mother's condition had worsened until she'd finally passed away a month ago. Her death had been hard on all of them, especially Cameron, but Grayson and Sonya were there for him, comforting him. Cameron had asked about Bree and when she was coming to see him, but Grayson had changed the topic.

He'd wanted to call Bree then, but Grayson didn't feel he had the right to. So he'd grieved alone, putting one foot in front of the other, the last for Cameron's sake, until finally the hurt began to ache a little less.

And then a glimmer of hope appeared. Levi had heard rumors that Bree was returning to Hart Enterprises, and thus Dallas. Grayson would get a chance to plead his case and beg for her forgiveness. He wasn't going to waste it. Not now.

But she was staring back at him. Her eyes were cold and indifferent, and the candle of hope had almost gone out. But he wouldn't let it.

Bree meant everything to him. She was the center of his world.

~

GRAYSON OFFERED Bree his hand as he'd done the first time they'd met and just like then, Bree ignored it and climbed out of the ditch herself. When she did, she glanced around. "Where's he going?" She saw Caleb heading back to his truck.

"He left so we could have time alone."

Bree snorted. "For what? I have nothing to say to you, Grayson." She started walking away, but he grabbed her elbow.

"Well that's too bad, because I have an awful lot to say to you and I've been waiting months to say it."

"I don't care!" Bree tried to leave, but Grayson had a grip on her and he wasn't budging.

"I don't believe that, Bree Hart," Grayson responded softly. "I believe you care *too* much, which is why you left Dallas and ran away."

Bree snatched her arm away and this time she won out. "I didn't run." Her eyes flashed with anger at his audacity. "I left because you hurt me."

"Partly, but you were scared too."

"Scared?"

"Of how you felt about me," Grayson said, "because you'd fallen in love with me."

"Love! You wouldn't know the first thing about love unless it bit you in the ass," Bree responded hotly.

Grayson's laugh was scornful.

"Don't you dare laugh at me." Bree pointed her finger at him. "Nothing about this is funny."

Grayson's face tightened. "You're right, Bree. Nothing about this entire situation is funny. And I need you to hear me when I say this: I'm sorry."

"Excuse me?"

"I'm sorry," Grayson repeated the sentiment. "I'm sorry for lying to you. I'm sorry for manipulating you into working for me. I'm sorry for going behind your back and plotting revenge against your father and your family business. I'm sorry for all of it."

"That's a helluva lot of sorries."

Grayson nodded. "I know that, but I can't say it enough because I mean it, Bree. I'm sorry for hurting you and for throwing your love back in your face."

"I never said I loved you."

"You didn't have to, sweetheart," Grayson said, and he reached out to stroke her cheek.

"Don't," Bree said, but she didn't step away. It was like she was a boat, and even though there was a strong current she was battling against, he was slowly tugging her back to shore.

His shore.

Grayson came closer toward her until they were only inches away. "I know you love me," Grayson murmured. "I saw it, felt it when we were together, because I felt it too."

"What are you saying?"

"I think I fell in love with you, Bree, the day I saw you in that ditch," Grayson admitted. "I didn't know what the emotion was back then. I just thought I was enamored or bewitched by you and once we had sex, it would *poof*"—he snapped his fingers—"all go away. But it didn't. It only deepened and became stronger.

So strong that I didn't want to let you go. But the longer I continued the lies, the deeper and harder I fell."

Grayson tipped her chin upward so his dark eyes could stare into hers. "I love you, Bree." He wrapped his arms around her.

She shook her head as tears spilled down her cheeks. "No, no." She stepped backward and out of his embrace. "I can't do this. I left so I could get over you, not have you draw me back in."

Grayson smiled. "And how's that been working out for you, sweetheart? Because it certainly hasn't worked for me. I love you as much now as I did back then. Maybe even more so, because I realize what I lost when you walked out of my life. And I want you back, Bree."

"We can't go back." Bree shook her head as she glared at Grayson with burning, reproachful eyes. "There's no going back. *You broke us. You broke me.* My trust and my faith in you are gone!"

"Please." Grayson reached out and grasped her hands. He faced a lightless future without Bree in it. "Tell me how to go forward then. I'll do *anything*. I just want another chance with you, Bree. A future. Please, baby, I can't lose you. You're the only woman I dream about at night, and you're the only woman I want to wake up to in the morning."

Bree's heart warred with her head as the torment of the last few months came roaring back at her. Her head told her to let him go and move on with her life with another man she could trust, but her heart couldn't let her. "I don't know, Grayson. I honestly don't know." Her teeth began to chatter, and her entire body trembled as she fought with her emotions.

"Then I'll wait for however long it takes to win

you back," Grayson stated, squeezing her hands. "I'll wait for you because I love you, Bree, and I want to marry you. And one day if you let me, I promise I'll spend the rest of my days making it up to you. I just need you to forgive me and give me a second chance."

Bree spun around, tears blinding her eyes. She glanced over the land and its vastness. She couldn't believe Grayson was here and saying everything she so desperately wanted to hear, but she was afraid to believe him. But the alternative, letting him go, was far worse.

When Bree finally turned around, her eyes were misty with tears. She murmured, "We can start over, but there can be no more lies between us, Grayson. Not now. Not ever."

"Oh thank God." Grayson sighed loudly and rushed toward her. His hands slipped up her arms, bringing her closer to him.

"Wait." She began to push him away. "I need you to make peace with Duke."

"That's already done."

Bree relaxed slightly but raised a disbelieving brow.

"I met with Duke a few months ago when you first left. We talked about the past, and I've made my peace with what happened with my father."

"You did?"

Grayson nodded. "I knew that if I didn't find a way to bridge the gap between us, that you and I"—he pointed to Bree—"would never have a future."

Bree nodded. "That was very wise, but you should know that I can't marry you, Grayson, at least not now. You'll have to work on rebuilding my trust."

"And I will gladly wait for that day."

"As will I," Bree responded with a smile, "because if you ask me again someday, I might say yes."

Grayson pulled Bree into his arms, grabbed her cheeks, and reclaimed her lips. The surprisingly tender kiss sent shivers through Bree. It reminded her that she was his, now and forever.

Six months later

"She's beautiful," Bree said as she held London and Chase's daughter, Bella, after her christening.

London hadn't realized she was already pregnant when Bree had arrived in New Orleans nine months ago. Thank God, the in vitro fertilization had worked after all. Bree was so happy for her sister.

"Well, even though you're her aunt, we couldn't think of anyone else we'd like to be her godmother," London said with a smile.

"I promise I will watch out for her always," Bree replied, but before she could continue doting on her goddaughter, Bella was being taken out of her arms by yet another member of the Hart clan.

They'd left the church an hour ago, and the entire family had convened at the Hart ranch: Caleb and Addison with their beautiful children, Ivy and baby Ethan; Jada, who had flown in from San Francisco; Bree's Aunt Madelyn and Uncle Isaac, who'd driven from Tucson; and Caleb's sister, Rylee, and her husband, Amar, who had flown in from California with their young son. And last but not least, Bree's cousin,

Noah, and his wife, Chynna, the incredibly talented and famous pop singer, who came with their son, her entire entourage, and Chynna's twin, Kenya, her husband, Lucas, and their twin girls.

Bree had never seen the house so full and lively and with so many Harts. Even her parents were getting along well. In the last few months, they'd been spending more time together. Bree wondered if a reconciliation was in their future.

Eventually, she snuck away for a few minutes of peace and quiet on the terrace. She sensed Grayson behind her even before she felt him circling his arms around her waist. "I bet you didn't expect to have so many Harts all in one place, huh?" she asked, glancing behind her.

Grayson laughed. His deep throaty sound made Bree feel warm and tingly in her lower regions. "Actually, I enjoy that you're part of a large family. It was always just me, Cameron, Sonya, and Mother." His voice cracked, and Bree squeezed his arm. She knew how hard Julia's death had been on Grayson. "So it's nice to feel *included*," Grayson finished.

Bree turned toward Grayson and wrapped her arms around his neck. "Well you are. You're a part of this family now."

"Oh yeah?" Grayson asked with a smirk. "Care to make it official?"

"What?" Bree was perplexed, but she didn't get a chance to stay that way because Grayson pulled away from her and bent down on one knee. He opened a ring box to reveal a brilliant princess cut diamond ring cushioned inside. "Omigod!"

"Bree Hart, I know I'm not an easy man to love," Grayson said, pulling the ring out of the box, "and I've tested your love for me. But I've been incredibly honored that you've given me a second chance to prove to you the man I can be. I'm just hoping and praying that today is the someday you'll agree to be my wife. Bree, will you marry me?"

"Yes!"

Bree didn't get another word out because Grayson was slipping the ring onto her finger and circling his arms around her as he planted kisses all over her face. "I love you, Bree. And I promise I'll love you forever. You won't ever regret giving me a second chance."

"I love you, too, Grayson Wells, and I know without a doubt I'll never regret a single day with you."

-THE END-

BOOKS BY YAHRAH ST. JOHN

ABOUT THE AUTHOR

Yahrah St. John became a writer at the age of twelve when she wrote her first novella after secretly reading a Harlequin romance. Throughout her teens, she penned a total of twenty novellas. Her love of the craft continued into adulthood. She's the proud author of thirty-nine books with Harlequin Desire, Kimani Romance and Arabesque as well as her own indie works.

When she's not at home crafting one of her spicy romances with compelling heroes and feisty heroines with a dash of family drama, she is gourmet cooking or traveling the globe seeking out her next adventure. For more info: www.yahrahstjohn.com or find her on Facebook, Instagram, Twitter, Bookbub or Goodreads.